“I really had better run.”

Tom had followed Suzanne to the door and now reached over her head to hold it open, which meant he stood so close to her she could feel the heat of his body. She knew if she lifted her gaze just a little, she’d see his mouth—which she’d never looked closely at before—and even the color of his eyes. Instead, she backed away without once letting her gaze rise higher than the strong column of his throat, stumbled over the doorjamb because she wasn’t watching where her feet were going, said, “Good night” and fled, her cheeks blazing.

Grateful for the darkness once she’d left his front porch, she pressed her hands to her cheeks. What on earth was wrong with her?

But the funny thing was, Suzanne was glad she’d gone. She thought he really might have been hurt if she hadn’t. He’d seemed genuinely interested in hearing about Jack and Sophia.

And…she now knew something about him. Only a little, but it was a start.

Of what, she didn’t let herself wonder.

Dear Reader,

Big sister Suzanne is at the heart of all three books in the LOST...BUT NOT FORGOTTEN trilogy. She's closest to my heart (although I did love Gary in *Lost Cause!*), perhaps because I, too, was the child who always tried to shoulder responsibility for the happiness of everyone else in the family. I was the peacekeeper when anger fired, Miss Perky when I sensed tension brewing. To this day I have a hard time delegating any kind of responsibility, driven still on some level to make everything right all by myself.

Suzanne has a better excuse than I do. Imagine being six years old and having your parents die. All you hear is your mom's voice saying, "You're the big sister. Take care of your little sister and brother." Only, you can't. They're taken away and adopted out, seemingly forever beyond your reach. How could you help living with a powerful sense of failure?

But because Suzanne is the responsible one, as an adult she takes action, tracking down her sister and brother. In *Kids by Christmas,* she realizes she's fulfilled her lifelong goal and is disconcerted to find she still feels empty. It's time she reached for happiness for herself, not for everyone else. Suzanne being Suzanne, though, she can only keep giving. But one of the miracles of Christmas is that usually when you give a gift, you get one in return. Suzanne's just might be a real family.

Merry Christmas!

Janice Kay Johnson

KIDS BY CHRISTMAS

Janice Kay Johnson

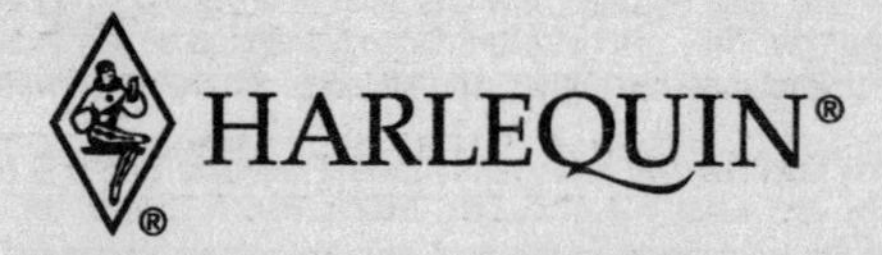

TORONTO • NEW YORK • LONDON
AMSTERDAM • PARIS • SYDNEY • HAMBURG
STOCKHOLM • ATHENS • TOKYO • MILAN • MADRID
PRAGUE • WARSAW • BUDAPEST • AUCKLAND

ISBN-13: 978-0-373-71383-7
ISBN-10: 0-373-71383-5

KIDS BY CHRISTMAS

This edition published by arrangement with Harlequin Books S.A.

www.eHarlequin.com

Printed in U.S.A.

ABOUT THE AUTHOR

The author of more than forty books, Janice Kay Johnson has written for adults, children and young adults. When not writing or researching her books, Janice quilts, grows antique roses, spends time with her two daughters, takes care of her cats and dogs (too many to itemize!) and volunteers at a no-kill cat shelter. Janice has been a finalist for the Romance Writers of America's prestigious RITA® Award four times.

Books by Janice Kay Johnson

HARLEQUIN SUPERROMANCE

854–THE WOMAN IN BLUE*
860–THE BABY AND THE BADGE*
866–A MESSAGE FOR ABBY*
889–WHOSE BABY?
913–JACK MURRAY, SHERIFF*
936–BORN IN A SMALL TOWN
(anthology with Debbie Macomber & Judith Bowen)
944–THE DAUGHTER MERGER
998–HIS PARTNER'S WIFE†
1009–THE WORD OF A CHILD†
1040–MATERNAL INSTINCT†
1092–THE GIFT OF CHRISTMAS
(anthology with Margot Early & Jan Freed)
1140–TAKING A CHANCE‡
1153–THE PERFECT MOM‡
1166–THE NEW MAN‡
1197–MOMMY SAID GOODBYE
1228–REVELATIONS
1273–WITH CHILD
1332–OPEN SECRET**
1351–LOST CAUSE**

HARLEQUIN SINGLE TITLE

WRONG TURN
"Missing Molly"

SIGNATURE SELECT SAGA

DEAD WRONG*

*Patton's Daughters
†Three Good Cops
‡Under One Roof
**Lost...But Not Forgotten

CHAPTER ONE

SHE HAD NO REASON to be depressed. None whatsoever. Especially after having spent a nice Thanksgiving yesterday with her sister, Carrie, and Carrie's family.

Suzanne Chauvin pulled into her driveway, the trunk of her car full of groceries, but didn't move even though she'd turned off the engine.

It's the gloom, she told herself. This was her least favorite time of year, with the days so short she left the house every morning in darkness and didn't go home until after dark, too. And these past few weeks had been particularly rainy, even by Pacific Northwest standards. The drizzle and gray seemed unending.

But Christmas was coming, Suzanne reminded herself, and it would be even better than Thanksgiving. This year would be special, even if she hadn't heard from the adoption agency. Special because it would be the first Christmas spent with her sister and brother since she was six years old and their family had been torn apart after their parents were killed in a car accident.

So there. She had every reason in the world to be cheerful. She'd found her younger brother and sister after years of searching, had reunited with them and liked them both, had rejoiced when in turn they'd both fallen in love. Carrie was married now, to the private investigator Suzanne had hired to find her, and Gary was planning a wedding right after Christmas.

Suzanne's business was going well, too. She'd opened a yarn shop in downtown Edmonds this past year, and despite her trepidation had been overwhelmed by support from area knitters. With Christmas shoppers in force today, her receipts had been the second highest since she'd opened.

Maybe she was just tired. She was working six days a week, plus doing the books on her one day off.

Once the agency calls me and I have a little girl or boy of my own, I'll cut back, she promised herself.

If they ever called.

Chilly now after sitting so long in the car in her own driveway, Suzanne finally sighed, grabbed her purse and keys and got out.

Forget adopting a child so that she finally had a family of her own. Her mood could have been improved by something a whole lot more modest—having an automatic garage door opener. *And* a garage that actually had room for her car to be parked inside it.

Which only required the time to hold a garage sale, and the money to buy and have someone install the opener.

For once, she didn't give a thought to her next-door neighbor, even though she usually sneaked a glance at his house to prepare herself in case he was out front. Not that Tom Stefanec was stalking her or anything like that. He just made her uncomfortable. And she preferred to avoid him when possible. But he'd be eating dinner by now, not hanging around outside on a damp night.

The little lever beside her seat no longer unlatched her trunk. Heck, she was lucky the car was still running. She went around back to manually unlock the trunk, hitched her purse over her shoulder and reached for the first bag.

"Need a hand with those groceries?"

At the voice from behind, she jerked her head up and rammed it against the trunk lid. Tears sprang into her eyes. Swearing, she let the grocery bag go and rubbed the bump she could already feel rising.

"I'm sorry," Tom said, stepping closer. His voice had roughened in contrition. "I startled you. Are you okay? I can get you some ice...."

Suzanne blinked away the tears. "No, I'll be okay. I just didn't see you."

A big, powerfully built man, he had a rough-hewn face that wasn't ugly but was far from handsome. The combination of porch light and streetlight cast shadows on his face, accenting cheekbones and a nose that looked like it had been broken at some point.

"Sorry," he said again. "I should have realized you wouldn't see me coming. I have a package for you. The UPS guy left it with me since you weren't home."

Head throbbing, she said, "Really?" A package? She wasn't expecting anything.

He handed it over, and after a glance at the return address label, Suzanne said with pleasure, "Oh, it must be my new pattern!"

"Pattern?" he asked.

"I sell knitting and crochet patterns for publication. I work out designs, mostly for kids, like sweaters with flowers or horses or whatever on the front."

He nodded, apparently satisfied by this explanation. "Congratulations on the new one. You must be really creative."

Pleased despite her headache, the drizzle that had begun anew and her weariness, Suzanne said, "Thanks."

"I'd be glad to give you a hand with those groceries."

No way she was letting him in her front door, especially since she'd been so busy over Thanksgiving weekend she hadn't done her usual thorough housecleaning.

Tom was... *Neat* didn't cover it. Obsessive-compulsive? Maybe not certifiable, but close. Suzanne was quite sure his garage floor was cleaner than her kitchen counters. His *lawn* looked better than her living-room carpet. His flower beds were tidier than her coffee table. She was afraid to see what the inside of his house was like.

"No, I'm fine, but thank you," she said, once again gathering plastic grocery bags.

He bent his head in acknowledgment and melted into the darkness. But then, barely visible, he paused.

"Any word on the adoption?"

"No." She awakened every morning thinking, *Maybe today,* and went to bed every night thinking, *Maybe tomorrow.* But she was afraid the loss of her caseworker at the adoption agency would mean delays. Rebecca Wilson had resigned to move to Santa Fe, New Mexico, and at some point in the near future marry Suzanne's brother Gary. Suzanne was very glad to welcome her into the family; she *liked* Rebecca. She just wished Rebecca had waited to quit until after she'd found a child for Suzanne to adopt.

"Oh. Well, good luck," her neighbor said courteously, at last leaving her alone.

Suzanne made two trips to carry her bags into the house. Then she made herself put away the frozen and refrigerated food before she opened the package and took out twenty copies of a pattern she'd designed last spring for a sweater that could be knit in any children's size from 2T to 6T, as well as preteen sizes. The photo on the front of the glossy booklet showed three children modeling the sweater in different colors. She'd knit all three herself. Fish leaped across the front. A toddler boy wore the sweater in aqua with a single red fish. A girl a few years older wore it in white with two fish in sea foam green, while a preteen wore the longer, slouchier version with smaller red fish on black. They'd come out really cute, and she thought the pattern would be popular. She'd order it right away to sell in her own shop, open only a few months.

This probably wasn't the world's best timing for adopting a child, not with the hours she was putting in getting the business off the ground. And especially not with money so tight. But Suzanne didn't want a baby. She'd asked for an older child, one who needed her. She would manage financially, just like other parents did.

Rebecca had hoped she'd have one by Christmas, but here it was, the twenty-fourth of November, and she hadn't heard a peep from the agency.

Quit obsessing, she ordered herself. It would happen. She'd been approved. Somewhere there was a child who would become a Chauvin who was probably, right this minute, scared and wondering what would happen to her. Or maybe him, although Suzanne thought that as a single woman she was probably better suited to raising a girl.

Darn it, she'd revel in Christmas this year whether she had a child by then or not. Being with her brother and sister would be enough.

Their parents had died when Suzanne was six, Lucien three and Linette just a baby. Suzanne had stayed with their aunt and uncle, but Lucien and Linette had been taken away to be adopted. This year, finally, Suzanne had been able to let go of the awful sense of loss she'd lived with for twenty-five years.

She'd found them. Mom had always said, "You're the big sister, Suzanne. You take care of your little brother and sister." She hadn't been able to, not then, and had suffered irrational guilt as well as loss. But just this fall, all three had finally been together again, and they would be on Christmas Day. And she and Carrie would be there to see Gary marry.

Best of all, their family now included Carrie's husband, his son and parents, and Carrie's adoptive parents. It was going to be quite a crowd at Carrie's house in Seattle. Every time she thought about it, Suzanne got tears in her eyes.

She had fulfilled that long-ago promise to herself to reunite the three of them. She'd started forging a satisfying life for herself by quitting her job and opening Knit One, Drop In, her yarn shop. Remarriage clearly wasn't in the near future—in fact, after the disaster her marriage had been, she wasn't all that interested in the possibility. But she did want children. And adopting one... Well, she thought she could once and for all lay to rest that irrational guilt. She could do for some little girl or boy what she hadn't been able to for her sister and brother. For her, that would be every bit as fulfilling as bearing her own child.

She'd jumped through every hoop the agency held up. Now, she was just waiting.

But the answering-machine light wasn't blinking, and the phone was silent. Another day closer to Christmas, and the bedroom down the hall stayed empty.

THE PHONE DID RING Monday morning just as she was going out the door. Laden with her purse, her lunch and two knitting bags, one of which held the sweater she was currently knitting for Michael, Carrie's stepson, and the other a project she intended to teach in her morning class, Suzanne hesitated with the front door open. For goodness sake, the caller was probably a telemarketer! But if Carrie or Gary was calling this early, it might be important. So, with a sigh, she closed the door, set down her lunch and one knitting bag and went back to pick up the phone on the last ring before voice mail turned on.

"Hello?"

"Hello." The voice was a woman's, and unfamiliar. "May I speak to Suzanne Chauvin?"

What was she selling—aluminum siding or cellphone service?

"Speaking," Suzanne said warily.

"Oh, I'm so glad I caught you! Rebecca Wilson passed your file to me."

She kept talking, but Suzanne didn't hear a word. Her heart was drumming too loudly. It was the adoption agency. At last.

"I'm sorry," she said into a pause. "I didn't catch your name?"

The woman's laugh was pleasant. "I don't blame you! It's Melissa Stuart. I worked with Rebecca, and she asked that I take your file rather than it going to her replacement. I gather you're to be sisters-in-law."

"Yes, that's right." Sick with anticipation, she reined in her impatience. This new caseworker might be assessing her despite Rebecca's recommendation. She couldn't be crazy and scream *Get to the point!* "Mine was the best home study Rebecca ever did. I'm pretty sure she didn't expect to fall in love that day."

Another laugh. "No, I'll bet she didn't. Well. I'm sure you're wondering why I'm calling."

Major understatement.

"Rebecca had noted that you might consider taking siblings, not just a single child. I have a brother and sister right now who need to stay together, and I was hoping to discuss them with you. Might we be able to get together?"

A brother and sister. Two children, not just one.

"I... How old are they?"

"The boy is seven and his sister ten."

Would they want to share a bedroom? Suzanne wondered. Or would they each need their own? Well, of course their own eventually—no teenage girl could share with a bratty little brother. But for now?

Wait! she ordered herself. She didn't know anything

about them. What had happened to their parents, how traumatized they were, or whether they had special needs she couldn't meet, not with the long hours she had to put in with a new business.

She was getting ahead of herself.

"When did you have in mind?" she asked.

"The sooner the better," Ms. Stuart said. "I'd be free at three this afternoon if you can get away, or…" She paused. "Let me see. Eleven tomorrow morning."

She couldn't wait until tomorrow morning. Her afternoon beginner's class ended at 2:50. If she could get someone to mind the store… Suzanne calculated quickly.

"I could make it to your office by about 3:15. Would that work?"

"Perfect! Shall I expect you, then?"

"I'll be there," she promised.

She pushed End, then stood for the longest time staring at the phone as if she had no idea what to do with it.

Not just a child, but *children.* Two of them. Children by Christmas.

She was in shock and knew it.

Two? Her preconceptions were dissolving and floating away before her eyes. Her sitting on the sofa with a little girl leaning against her as she read aloud. One small bike in the garage. Sewing and knitting lessons. Giggles. An incredible bond, with just the two of them.

A brother and sister already *had* a bond, with each other. They needed her more, in some ways, and less in others. Most boys wouldn't want to learn to knit. She'd have to juggle two sets of activities, two parent-teacher conferences, two bikes and demands for sleepovers and struggles with math or reading.

She'd be doubling the grocery bill she'd anticipated, the after-school care bill, the back-to-school shopping bill.

She didn't know whether to be excited or terrified. No, she did know. Terror was winning. What if these children didn't like her? What if one or both had big emotional problems? What if they whispered with each other and shut her out? What if, what if, what if.

"You haven't made a commitment," she said aloud.

She hadn't. She'd talk to this Melissa Stuart. Find out more about the children. Maybe she wasn't right for them.

Ashamed of the trickle of relief she felt at the idea that she would have a justifiable reason for rejecting two children who needed a home, Suzanne finally hung up the phone, grabbed her bags and left.

Was she not as committed as she'd thought? Had she been enamoured with the idea of a fairy-tale adoption and not the hard reality of older children traumatized by dysfunctional parenting, loss and rejection?

Or did anyone in her situation feel these mixed emotions? This *was* a huge step, without the phasing in you got when you had a baby in the normal way. Maybe panic was natural and normal.

Call Rebecca, she decided. She'd know.

Suzanne was ten minutes late unlocking the door of her small business, but fortunately—or unfortunately—no customers stood on the sidewalk with their noses pressed to the glass. The first hour was usually slow, even in this pre-Christmas season. In fact, she'd already decided that, once she had a child, she'd change her hours. Nine to five-thirty was too much. She could open at ten, close at five. And close two days a week instead of just one. Sunday and Monday, she thought.

Two women wandered in shortly thereafter and wandered out again without buying anything, but with copies of Suzanne's class schedule tucked in their tote bags. They might be back. They might pass on the schedules to friends or daughters who would sign up. She never knew, but she hoped each time.

After the bell tinkled and the door closed behind the two women, Suzanne grabbed the phone and dialed Gary's number in Santa Fe.

Rebecca answered on the second ring. "Suzanne! How nice to hear from you. I'd been meaning to call to find out if Melissa has been in touch."

"She called this morning." Suzanne repeated what the caseworker had said. "I have an appointment to talk to her this afternoon, but I'm petrified. And that makes me wonder if I really want to do this, and I'm ashamed of even wondering, and..."

Rebecca laughed. "Well, of course you're scared. This isn't like adopting a newborn. And, believe me, even those couples are nervous as well as thrilled. They aren't sure they'll know what to do. What if the baby won't quit crying? What if they don't feel instant love?"

Her heart lurched. "Oh, God. I didn't even think of that. What if I don't?"

"Then it will take time," Rebecca said practically. "It's kind of like an arranged marriage. Plenty of those ended up blissfully happy, but I'll bet virtually every bride and groom was scared to death when they said, 'I do.'"

"I guess that's true."

"And remember, the adoption won't be final for some time. If you're really a poor match, a better one can be made, for the kids as well as you."

"Will Melissa think poorly of me if I decide I can't take these kids?"

"No, of course not! She'll just look for the right single child for you."

Her palms were still sweaty, but Suzanne said, "Okay. I feel a little better. You know, my first reaction was to be excited, but then this wave of panic just crashed into me! I tried to tell myself it was normal, but I was ashamed of myself for even hesitating."

Rebecca soothed her for a couple more minutes, then said, "I was also meaning to call you to let you know that Gary and I are talking about getting married while we're there over Christmas. Maybe the first week in January?"

Pure delight overcame Suzanne's panic. "Really? Oh, Rebecca! That would be wonderful. Where? Have you made plans?"

The doorbell rang again as a group of four women entered. She smiled at them, then said into the phone, "I'd better call you this evening. Business is picking up."

"I'll be waiting to hear how your meeting with Melissa went."

"Oh, what a darling sweater!" one of the women cried, as Suzanne hung up the phone. They'd all stopped in front of a mannequin that wore a cropped, electric-blue and hot-pink off-the-shoulder angora sweater that Suzanne had designed as part of her planned book of styles meant to appeal to women in their twenties.

"Hi," she said, coming out from behind the counter. "Are you knitters?"

Two were, two weren't, but one of those decided on the spot to sign up for the next session of the class for beginners. All helped one of the experienced knitters choose yarn for an afghan, and they left declaring, "You have an amazing selection. I'll tell everyone I know who knits or crochets."

Feeling gratified, Suzanne squeezed in a quick call to one of her customers who was happy to fill in for a day or a few hours now and again. An older woman, she liked earning a little extra income.

"I'll be there by 2:45," Rose promised. "No need for you to hurry back."

Suzanne's afternoon class, now in its fourth week, was her largest yet, with a number of the women determined to knit a Christmas present for someone in their family. They'd started out making scarves, then had moved on to projects of their choice. One was doing baby booties and a hat for her soon-to-be-born grandson, another a simple afghan, several others sweaters. One seemed to be a natural; the sweater she was knitting for a ten-year-old was nearly done, arms and body proportional. Another was struggling with constant dropped stitches. She made jokes about the name of Suzanne's store.

"It's all your fault," she declared, laughing ruefully.

Suzanne helped her unravel and get started again, one eye

surreptitiously on the clock. Rose came in quietly before the end of the class, and at 2:50 on the dot Suzanne stood up.

"Don't feel you have to hurry out. I have an appointment, but Rose is here to help you with your projects or purchases."

She thanked Rose, an older woman who was fast becoming a friend as well as an occasional employee, took her purse from the drawer and hurried out. She'd been able to park less than a block away that morning, and she took a back route up the hill to Lynnwood.

Melissa Stuart came out to the reception area the moment Suzanne's arrival was announced. Perhaps in her early fifties, she was a plump, attractive woman who was comfortable letting gray creep into her dark, bobbed hair. She had a nice smile that immediately set Suzanne at ease.

"How nice to meet you." Melissa extended her hand. "Have you talked to Rebecca? How is she?"

They shook hands.

"Really good," Suzanne said. "She just told me she and Gary are planning a wedding right after the holidays."

"Not exactly a shock. They didn't waste any time, did they?" She turned. "Let's go on back to my office."

Following her, Suzanne agreed, "They were in love within days of meeting."

Her office was simple, decorated with children's artwork on white walls. Only one manila file folder lay atop her desk.

Sitting, Suzanne couldn't take her gaze from the folder.

Seating herself behind the desk, the caseworker said, "Let me tell you about Sophia and Jack."

The names alone made them more real. Suzanne leaned forward.

"As I told you on the phone, Jack is seven and Sophia ten. Nearly eleven. She's in fifth grade, he's in second. Sophia is very bright and did quite well in school until this past year, when she's done some acting out. Jack is good at math but is having trouble with reading. His most recent teacher isn't sure whether he has a reading disability or whether, once again, this past year has been so difficult that he can't concentrate."

"This past year?"

"Their mother died. She had MS and received poor or no health care because she didn't have insurance. She'd been raising the kids on her own, and once she could no longer work they moved between shelters and motel rooms at the kind of place that rents by the week. The past couple of years were disruptive for the children. As a result, they're very mature in some ways. After all, they had to care for her. I gather that Sophia even did the grocery shopping toward the end. In other ways, they're lost in a normal school or home situation. They've not been able to have friends the way other kids do. They had no home to invite other children to play at, no parent to pick them up at anyone else's home. They changed schools five times in the last two years."

"Oh, dear," seemed inadequate, but it was the only thing she could think of to say.

"Indeed," Ms. Stuart agreed. "Sophia had to call for an ambulance when she got home from school and found her mother dying."

"How long ago was that?"

"In early September. Unfortunately, that meant yet another change in schools when they went to a foster home. In late October, we had to move them to a second foster home."

"Their father?"

"Hasn't seen them since Jack was a baby. He's been moving regularly to avoid having to pay child support. I understand that, when told his ex-wife had died, he said, 'You don't expect me to take the kids, do you?'"

Rage for children she had yet to meet tightened Suzanne's throat. "How horrible."

"He gladly relinquished his parental rights. At least the children were quickly freed for adoption. So often they're stuck in the foster-care system for years."

Suzanne's brother had lived in a succession of foster homes for nearly two years before he'd been adopted. She nodded.

"Their foster mother says Sophia is fiercely protective of her little brother but also displaying some generalized anger. He's reverted to some behaviors typical of much younger children, including bed-wetting."

No, these children wouldn't be easy. Suzanne let go once and for all of her vision of that perfect little girl who leaned so trustingly against her and who giggled with uncomplicated joy.

"Naturally," the caseworker continued, "it's important that they stay together."

"Of course!"

At least Suzanne's sister and brother had been young,

able to forget each other and her. Only she had carried the memory of them through the years.

"I know these two may not be at all what you had in mind...."

"As I told Rebecca, I didn't have any particular ideal. Somehow, the idea of shopping for a child with a wish list strikes me as repugnant."

"Good for you." Ms. Stuart's smile was warm and approving.

"My parents died when I was six."

"I know. I have to admit, that's one reason I thought you might be just right for these particular children." She lifted a hand, hesitated with it over the file folder. "Would you like to see their pictures?"

Suddenly unable to breath, Suzanne could only nod.

Opening the file, the caseworker removed two five-by-seven school photos and laid them on the desk, facing Suzanne.

She took one look at the two faces, both so hopeful, so wary, and felt a painful squeeze in her chest she was astonished to recognize as the first symptom of falling in love.

Without a moment's hesitation, she asked, "When can I meet them?"

CHAPTER TWO

THE CASEWORKER HAD PREPARED the kids for Suzanne's visit. Younger children could be fooled into thinking the visitor was a friend of the foster mom's, or another social worker. Kids the ages of Sophia and Jack would see through the lie and feel betrayed.

Melissa had arranged for this visit only two days after their initial meeting, scheduling it right after the children got home from school. Suzanne was once again depending on Rose.

Now, parking in front of the shabby rambler and setting the emergency brake, Melissa said, "I've introduced two other sets of potential adoptive parents to Sophia and Jack. In both cases, they felt the fit wasn't right."

"Why?"

"I believe it's Sophia. She's almost eleven, and, um…" The caseworker hesitated. "Well, she's *precocious.*"

Puzzled, Suzanne said, "You did mention that she's mature beyond her years."

"Yes, but what I'm trying to tell you is that she's also ahead of most girls her age physically."

"Physically?" For a moment, Suzanne didn't get it. Then understanding dawned. "Oh. You mean, she's getting breasts."

"Yes, but it's more than that. Part of the trouble is her choice of clothing. She looks like a thirteen-year-old who's pretending she's sixteen."

"Oh," Suzanne said again. She frowned. "You mean, the two couples were okay with a ten-year-old who looked like a little girl, but not one who's essentially a teenager?"

"Exactly."

She wanted to say that was lousy, but she remembered the few parameters she'd given Rebecca originally. She'd wanted a child who would come to think of her as a mother, not a teenager who'd be gone in no time. An almost-eleven-year-old who looked older... No, Sophia definitely wasn't what Suzanne had had in mind, either.

But then, from the beginning she'd vowed to be open-minded, to take a child who needed her. It sounded like these two did.

She nodded, and the two women got out of the car, walking in silence up the driveway.

On the way over, Melissa had told her this foster mother was having health problems and had given them a deadline of the first of January to find alternative placement for Jack and Sophia.

"They've had so many disruptions already," she'd said. "I'm really hoping to find them a permanent home now, so that they don't have to adjust to yet another temporary one. I want you to feel free to take your time to get to know them, but if you decide they might be right for you, I can also accelerate the steps we usually go through."

Suzanne was so nervous, she felt light-headed by the time

Melissa rang the doorbell. What if they were unfriendly? Disinterested? Wild? What if she didn't *like* them?

How horrible it must be to be looked over like apples in the produce section, put back when buyers saw a bruise. She didn't want to do something like that, but it would also be disastrous if she took on something she couldn't handle.

Someone, she reminded herself. Not a situation. Kids.

The door opened without warning. It had to be the foster mom who smiled and pushed open the screen. "Melissa. Hi! The kids have been waiting. You must be Suzanne. Hello."

She was in her sixties or perhaps even seventies, and overweight. She moved as if she hurt.

The television in the living room was on, a well-known talk-show host grilling someone to the shrill encouragement of the audience. She turned it off and called, "Kids! Melissa is here!"

There was a moment of silence. Then one of the bedroom doors down a short hall opened and two kids came out. The boy had his head hanging, but the girl ignored the other two adults and studied Suzanne with frightening intensity as she sauntered behind her brother. Suzanne could see right away why Melissa had warned her. It was more than the breasts. It was that hip-swinging walk, the curl to her mouth, the ferocity of that stare. No, this wasn't your average ten-year-old. She might have had trouble fitting in with other girls her age even under normal circumstances.

"Sophia, Jack," Melissa said. "I'd like you to meet Ms. Chauvin."

The boy stole a quick look up at her, then ducked his head again. The girl stopped and appraised her.

"Hi," Suzanne said. "I'm glad to meet you after Melissa told me so much about you."

"Why don't you have kids of your own?" Sophia asked, with a tone of insolence. *Why are you such a loser?* she seemed to be asking.

"Sophia!" the foster mom intervened. "That wasn't very polite."

"No, it's okay. My husband and I hadn't started a family before we got divorced. Since I've always wanted to have children, I chose to adopt."

"So how come *us?*"

It was as if no one else was there, just Suzanne and this dark-haired girl with riveting blue eyes.

"Because Melissa told me about you, and I thought we might be a good fit. My parents both died when I was six years old, so I know better than most people how you feel right now."

The girl's mask slipped. "Did you get adopted?"

Suzanne shook her head. "My aunt and uncle took me in, even though I don't think they really wanted any more children. They had two of their own. But they surrendered my little brother and sister. They were adopted by other families."

Sophia cast a shocked glance at her little brother, who had finally lifted his head and was watching Suzanne and his sister with eyes that were a paler blue than hers. His hair was lighter, too, the shade of brown that might become blond after a summer in the sun.

"So you never saw them again?" the girl asked.

"Not until this year. I hired a private investigator to find them."

"Oh."

When she fell silent, Melissa smiled and moved forward. "Why don't we all sit down so you can get acquainted?"

The kids went docilely to the sofa and sat next to each other. The boy leaned against his big sister.

Jack was small for his age, Suzanne decided, and made smaller by a posture that suggested he wanted to disappear. In contrast, his sister was nearly as tall as Suzanne already, and with that disconcertingly curvaceous body, no one would have guessed that only three years separated the two children in age.

Suzanne chose the recliner facing them. Melissa spoke quietly for a moment to the foster mother, who said, "I'm going to lie down for a few minutes. You just call me when you're done."

"Tell me about your mom," Suzanne suggested.

Jack ducked his head again.

Sophia jerked her shoulders. "She was sick. She couldn't walk. Sometimes she, like, fainted or something and wouldn't wake up for a long time."

"But before that, when she felt better. Did she sew for you? Paint your fingernails?"

"She didn't sew. I guess I helped with dinner sometimes. You know. And she took us to the library." She pressed her lips together. "I remember her pushing me on a swing."

Suzanne looked at the seven-year-old. "What do you remember, Jack? Did she teach you to throw a ball, or read to you?"

"Mommy read all the time," he whispered. "She still read to me sometimes, before..." His voice died.

Before their mom *hadn't* woken up.

"This must be really scary for you." Suzanne took a deep breath. "*I'm* scared."

They both looked at her. "Why?" Sophia asked.

"Because adopting someone is a huge commitment. And the truth is, I've never been a mom. I don't remember mine as well as I wish I did. So I don't know how great I'll be at this. And I don't want to disappoint a boy or girl who trusts me."

"Does that mean you're not going to take us?" Clearly, Sophia was used to taking the lead. "Because that's okay. Other people have come and decided they weren't going to."

Hurting at her brave attempt to sound as if she didn't care, Suzanne shook her head. "No, that isn't what I'm saying. I guess I'm asking you what you're hoping for in a family. Did you really want to have a dad? Or a certain kind of mom?"

Sophia frowned. "What do you mean, a certain kind of mom?"

"Oh..." She thought. "One who laughs a lot, or is really pretty and smells good. Maybe a mom who's there every day when you get home from school, so you don't have to go to day care. Or parents who have lots of money, so you could have something you've always dreamed about."

"Like a horse, you mean?"

"Like that," she agreed.

"I don't know about a dad. 'Cause we've never had one. Right, Jack?"

He nodded.

"And my mom. Maybe she was pretty before she got sick. I don't remember."

"Do you have pictures?" Suzanne asked gently.

She nodded. "We have a box of stuff."

Suzanne waited.

"We want a dog," the ten-year-old declared. "Or a cat. We couldn't have a pet before. Because we moved a lot, to places where you couldn't have one. Do you have a dog?"

"No, but I wouldn't mind getting one. I do have a fenced backyard."

Jack looked up, his face filled with naked hope. "Do you have a house? A real house?"

"Yes, I do. It's not fancy, but it has three bedrooms. You could each have your own room if you wanted. And it has an old apple tree in the backyard that's perfect for climbing. I like to garden, so in the spring there will be daffodils and a big lilac in bloom." She could tell from their faces that they didn't care about the flowers. "The bedrooms are really plain right now, but we could decorate them the way you liked."

"I could have my very own?" Sophia spoke as if the idea was wondrous beyond imagining. And perhaps it was, for a child who'd probably shared a single hotel room with her mother and brother for nearly as long as she could remember.

"Yep. I thought you might like to share for a while, until you got used to living with me, but that would be up to you."

"Jack wets his bed."

The boy jerked as if in protest, but didn't say anything.

"We got in trouble a lot, because the hotel managers didn't like the smell."

Oh, dear. Suzanne had forgotten the bit about Jack

having regressed to some infantile behaviors. How did you help someone *not* wet the bed?

"You know what?" she said with false confidence. "He'll outgrow it, just like other kids. Who ever heard of a grown-up wetting the bed?"

"Our last foster mom spanked him when he peed in his bed."

Out of the corner of her eye, Suzanne saw Melissa's face harden.

"Do you spank?" Sophia asked.

Suzanne shook her head. "No. I don't believe in it. And besides, bed-wetting is something Jack can't help."

"He sucks his thumb, too."

"I do not!" the boy flared.

Lifting her brows, Suzanne looked at his sister. "Do *you* have any bad habits? Things you do you're not supposed to?"

She seemed interested in the idea. "I punched a boy at school. I had to go to the principal's office."

"Why did you punch him?"

"He called me a name."

She hardly blinked, that intense gaze fixed on Suzanne, who wondered if she was being tested. *What will you do when I'm bad?* she seemed to be asking.

"Did you try telling an adult what he'd said?"

Sophia shook her head. "I was mad."

"We all get mad without hitting people." To avoid a continuing debate, Suzanne asked, "What else?"

"Mostly I just get mad. I told a teacher last year he was a big fat liar."

Well, that had probably gone over well.

"What did you do when you got mad at your mom?"

For a moment, her long, dark lashes veiled her eyes. "I didn't get mad at her."

"I was mad at mine for dying. Really mad."

"I'm not." But that unnervingly direct gaze didn't meet Suzanne's.

She knew a lie when she heard one, but let it pass.

"Is there anything you want to know about me?"

They were momentarily silenced. Then Jack whispered something to his sister, who said, "Can we see your house?"

How humbling to know that they were more interested in her home than in her.

Sitting to one side, Melissa smiled. "That will be for another visit, kids. In fact, I have an appointment, so it's time for Suzanne and I to go. Jack, will you go let Mrs. Burton know we have to leave?"

He nodded, slipped off the couch and went down the hall.

"Would we still go to the same school?" Sophia asked.

Suzanne shook her head. "I live in Edmonds, so you'd have to transfer there. I know it's hard to move in the middle of the year…."

"I hate it here," she said with startling vehemence. "I want to move."

"What about Jack?"

"Kids pick on him. He doesn't like it either."

Oh, Lord! What was she getting into? Suzanne asked herself, knowing full well she'd long since made a decision. Jack and Sophia had no resemblance to her dream child, who neither wet beds nor slugged other kids, but were also far more real, more needy and interesting and full of promise.

She hoped they liked her, but would settle for them liking her house.

The foster mother reappeared and they said their goodbyes. The children stood in front of Mrs. Burton on the front porch and watched as Suzanne and Melissa went to the car and drove away.

"So, what do you think?" Melissa laughed. "Or do I have to ask?"

"Wow." Suzanne felt dazed and a little limp, now that it was over. "I think I'm even more scared than I was on the way over."

"And with good reason! Sophia is…unusual."

"She is, isn't she? But amazing, too. She's so strong! At her age, I was timid and apologetic and unwilling ever to cause trouble or draw attention to myself."

"She won't be easy to parent," Melissa warned. "You did notice her challenging you?"

"I suspected. But that's going to happen with any child, isn't it? Unless I start with a toddler."

"Yes, but most kids would wait a while. They're usually saintly for a few months. Then, at some point, they start wondering if these new parents would want them if they *weren't* so good, if they really love them. That's when the tough times start. Now, with Sophia…"

"They've already begun?"

Melissa had a hearty laugh. "Something like that."

"I like her." She thought. "Did you see her when I suggested she might be mad at her mother for dying?"

"I did. But she can't let herself, so she'll be mad at everyone else instead."

"When can I see them again?" Suzanne asked.

Melissa laughed again. "Are you sure you don't want to let first impressions settle a little?"

"But it was such a short visit. I'm not sure I can wait for days and days."

"I can ask whether Mrs. Burton could bring them over Saturday for a while."

Suzanne turned a hopeful gaze on the caseworker. "Please."

Another laugh. "I'll call her." But her expression was serious when she said, "But you have to promise not to rush into anything, either. You're right. It *is* a big commitment. The adoption won't be final for months, so you have time to back out, but I'm sure I don't have to tell you how tough that would be on the kids."

Her excitement dimmed. "I know it would. I won't make up my mind for sure until we get a chance to spend more time together."

"That's all I ask. And here we are." She signaled to turn into the parking lot in front of the adoption agency. "I'll talk to Mrs. Burton and give you a call."

"Thank you," Suzanne said fervently.

She drove back to her shop wishing she could rush home instead and prepare. What she'd actually do to prepare, she wasn't sure. Paint the bedrooms tonight? But she'd already promised to let them choose their own decor. Clean house? Well, she had to do that tomorrow anyway. With the long hours at Knit One, Drop In, Sunday was no day of rest for her. But maybe she could get started tonight. Vacuum and scrub the bathroom. She'd put out her prettiest guest towels.

Suzanne made a face in the rearview mirror. As if they'd care. The only time she could ever remember as a child even noticing someone's towels was when she'd gone to a sleepover at a classmate's house and found out her family was really rich. The bathroom fixtures were shiny gold, maybe even plated with real gold. The floor was stone with pale veins running through it—marble, she'd later realized. And the towels were half an inch thick, a deep maroon jacquard, incredibly soft and textured in a basket weave. They were nothing like the towels at Aunt Jeanne and Uncle Miles's house.

Even if Suzanne's house was a step up from the cheap hotels where Sophia and Jack were used to living, there was nothing about it to dazzle them. Certainly not her best guest towels.

But she would put them out anyway. And she'd bake something, so the house smelled homey and welcoming. She'd wash the windows in the two bedrooms, too, so they would sparkle and let in whatever sunlight was available.

At the shop she thanked Rose and resigned herself to making it through the last hour before closing. Traffic was heavy with Christmas so close. She had knit several afghans hoping to sell them as Christmas gifts, and they had gone way back in early November as had several baby sweaters. Next year, she'd try to have more items available for sale. Perhaps some of her customers would like to offer hand-knit items on consignment. But shoppers were also buying gift certificates for classes as well as yarn, knitting books and individual patterns. And more people were discovering her store, just because they were out shopping anyway.

At 4:45 p.m. Melissa called. "Mrs. Burton says she'd be glad to bring the kids over. If you're okay with them on your own, she could leave them for an hour or two while she grocery shops."

"That sounds great," Suzanne agreed. "One o'clock? Perfect!"

She waited on a couple more customers and pretended to be interested in their crochet projects, but was secretly dying to close and go home. She could hardly wait to call Carrie and tell her... But then, on a wave of disappointment, she remembered that Mark and Carrie were going out tonight. They'd gotten a babysitter for Michael and were having dinner at Le Gourmand and then going to see a play at the Intiman. And Rebecca and Gary had flown to Chicago this weekend because he had a business meeting Monday morning and they thought they could take a couple of days to themselves in advance. Rebecca hadn't found a wedding dress she liked in Santa Fe and intended to shop in Chicago while he was conducting business.

Turning the sign to Closed, Suzanne opened the till and thought, *I'll call a friend.* But it was an awful time of day to call anyone who already had a family. They'd all be making dinner or sitting down to eat by the time she got home. Frustrated, Suzanne promised herself that she'd call everyone she knew later tonight.

The trouble was, she felt like a child bursting with

news. She wanted to tell someone right now, not two hours from now.

Well, tough. She wasn't a child, and her news could hold. She'd vacuum instead.

Pulling into her driveway, she glanced as she almost always did toward her next-door neighbor's house. The light in his front window was on, and she saw the blue flicker of a television. He was probably watching the six o'clock news. Somehow she couldn't imagine him sitting in front of a rerun of *Friends* or *Full House.* No, he was definitely the news type.

He might like to know about the children who would be visiting tomorrow and might be living next door.

The thought crept in out of nowhere, startling her.

She wasn't friends with Tom Stefanec. They rarely exchanged more than a few words. She made sure they didn't.

It was probably dumb, but she'd been self-conscious around him since he'd moved in. She'd still been married, but her marriage had been disintegrating. She and Josh had seemed to yell at each other constantly, and neighbors—or one particular neighbor—had had to call the police to report domestic disturbances. Twice.

She hadn't been able to look him in the eye since.

But he had never, not once, referred in any way to Josh or those ugly fights. Tom had been really nice since he'd found out she wanted to adopt. He'd mowed her lawn the whole last month of fall so she didn't have to get her mower fixed before spring. He knew she wanted the house to look extra nice when the caseworker did a home visit. Suzanne had noticed that her lawn looked better than it ever had after a few weeks of his attention, too. She suspected he'd fertilized it with a weed and feed, which had killed some of the dandelions.

Ever since, he'd asked regularly if she'd heard from the adoption agency. She didn't know whether he was just being polite or really hoped for her sake that she had. But he did seem interested.

She'd never actually gone to his door and rung the bell before, but she could. Since he did often ask, and since the kids were coming tomorrow, it would be the civil thing to do, wouldn't it? Instead of him seeing them and her having to say, *Oh, I forgot to tell you that the caseworker did call.*

Besides… She really wanted to tell someone.

Taking a deep breath, she got out of her car, hurried into her house to deposit her purse and the day's receipts on the small table just inside and then, instead of going to the kitchen to find something for dinner, she went back out and marched across the strip of lawn that separated her driveway from her neighbor's. Her feet carried her up his walkway and onto his porch.

Her courage was already faltering by the time she rang the doorbell, but she didn't let herself chicken out. They were neighbors. She'd known him for years. It was silly to be shy.

Besides, he might have seen her coming onto the porch through the big front window. She *couldn't* flee.

The light came on and the door opened. He filled the opening, wearing a sweatshirt, jeans and slippers. Somehow he was always so much *larger* than she remembered.

"Suzanne!" he said in surprise. "Are you okay?"

Apparently he figured the only reason she'd come knocking was if she desperately needed help. And who could blame him since she'd never made the slightest overture of friendship before?

She produced a smile. "I'm fine. I just stopped by to let you know that I finally heard from the agency."

He stood back. "Come on in. Sit down and tell me about it."

She hesitated.

"Aren't you having dinner, or..."

Or what? Entertaining? She hardly ever saw anyone else at his house. She didn't know if he *did* entertain.

"Haven't even started to cook yet. I just got home and thought I'd have a beer and watch the news." He picked up the remote control and turned the television off. "None of it's good, anyway."

"I know what you mean." Feeling timid, she stepped inside.

Trying not to be too obvious, she took a swift look around. His two-story house was more imposing than her small rambler, but in all her years here she'd never even peeked in his front window.

His living room was more welcoming than she would have expected. It was dominated by the big-screen television, but that was probably a man thing. His recliner was large, too, but then it had to be, didn't it? The sofa was soft rather than spare looking, and a pair of bookcases flanking the fireplace were filled with hundreds of books, a mix of fiction and non-fiction.

"Please. Sit down." He closed the door behind her and

gestured toward the couch. "Can I get you a cup of coffee? Or a beer?"

"No, I'm fine." She did perch at one end of the couch, her thigh muscles remaining tense. "Thank you. I really didn't intend to stay. I just wanted to share my news."

For some reason, as he sat back down in the recliner she fixated on his slippers. They were perfectly ordinary, brown leather with a dark fleecy lining. But his ankles were bare, and the very sight of him in slippers somehow created a tiny shift in the universe. Tom Stefanec was so disciplined, so boot-camp sergeant with that buzz-cut hair, she'd never pictured him coming home like other people and changing immediately into old jeans, a sloppy sweatshirt and slippers.

"Were you in the military?" she blurted, then was immediately embarrassed. "I'm sorry! That's none of my…"

"That obvious?" He gave a crooked smile, either chagrined on his own behalf or amused at her discomfiture, she wasn't sure. His homely face was considerably more attractive when he smiled, a realization that startled her.

"Well, it's just…" Frantically, she searched for words. "Oh, you wear your hair so short and, um, you obviously keep in good shape, and…" She couldn't think of anything else and trailed off, embarrassed yet again that she'd admitted to noticing the powerful muscles emphasized by the well-worn jeans.

"I was an Army Ranger. Got out after I was wounded in Kuwait."

"Oh. Oh, I'm sorry. I didn't know."

He shrugged those broad shoulders. "No reason you should. So. What did you hear from the agency?"

Agency? For a moment, she was blank. Then her whole reason for coming here returned as if floodgates had opened, and she felt foolish.

"They called to ask whether I'd consider two children. A sister and brother. I met them today for the first time."

"Really? Two?"

Since he didn't sound disapproving, she said, "The boy—Jack—is seven and his sister is ten. Their mother had MS and died recently. The father has been skipping on child-care payments and was apparently happy to relinquish his parental rights."

"A real great guy."

"Isn't that awful? He didn't care at all." She marveled at the notion. How could he not love his own children?

"So, what did you think?" Tom leaned forward, his elbows on his knees, looking as if he was really interested.

"I fell in love with them," she admitted. "The caseworker tried to warn me to take it slow, but... This just feels right. *They* feel right. They need me."

He was quiet for a moment. She could feel his gaze on her face, although as always she didn't meet his eyes. In fact, she didn't know quite what color they were. Not particularly blue, like Sophia's, or a rich chocolate-brown, like George Clooney's—either she'd have noticed. So something in between. A color she'd have to study to identify.

"Is that why you're adopting?" he asked. "Because you want to feel needed?"

"I suppose that's part of it." Did he really want to know? "But also...I like kids. I want a family."

He opened his mouth, then closed it. Too polite, she diagnosed, to ask what other people had: Why didn't she just find a husband, like most women did, and have children in the normal way?

Or perhaps that wasn't what he was going to ask, because he likely knew quite well why she wasn't all that excited about finding a husband. He'd known Josh, had heard the hateful things he'd yelled at her. And the pitiful things she'd screamed back at him.

The memory had her surging to her feet. "They're coming tomorrow to see the house and so we can get better acquainted. I need to do some tidying, but I wanted to tell you in case you saw them tomorrow, and because..." She hesitated. "Because you ask. And I was excited, and wanted to tell someone."

He rose, too. "So I was handy?"

Did he sound a little hurt, or was she imagining things?

"No, because you always seemed interested. I've appreciated that."

"Oh." Apparently mollified, he nodded. "I like kids."

"You do?" The surprise she felt could be heard in her voice, and she blushed.

"What makes you think I wouldn't?"

"Oh, I didn't think that," she babbled, edging toward the door. "Just that I don't know anything about you, and you don't have kids of your own—" She slammed to a stop, both physically and verbally. Oh, God. What if he did?

As if he'd read her mind, he said, "No, I don't, but I've always figured I'd have my own someday."

She almost blurted, *Really?* but stopped herself in time. Thank goodness. She'd already tromped on her own toes until they should be black-and-blue. She didn't have to compound her tactlessness.

Grasping the doorknob, Suzanne said, "I really had better run. But if you happen to be home tomorrow when they arrive, please come and say hi."

He bent his head. "I'll do that."

He'd followed her to the door and now reached over her head to open it, which meant he stood so close to her she could feel the heat of his body. She knew, if she lifted her gaze just a little, she'd see the individual bristles on his chin, his mouth—which she'd never looked closely at before—and even the color of his eyes. Instead, she backed away without once letting her gaze rise higher than the strong column of his throat, stumbled over the doorjamb because she wasn't watching where her feet were going, said, "Good night," and fled, her cheeks blazing.

Grateful for the darkness once she'd left his front porch, she pressed her hands to her cheeks. What on earth was wrong with her? It wasn't as if she was totally lacking in social skills!

But the funny thing was, Suzanne was glad she'd gone. She thought he really might have been hurt if she hadn't. He'd seemed genuinely interested in hearing about Jack and Sophia.

And...she now knew something about him. Only a little, but it was a start.

Of what, she didn't let herself wonder.

CHAPTER THREE

TOM WAS SHAKING HIS HEAD in amazement when he shut the door behind Suzanne. He'd never thought he'd live to see the day when she actually sought him out. She was so scared of him, she jumped two feet every time he approached her. He'd always pretended he didn't notice, figuring someday she'd get over it, but that hadn't happened.

What he didn't know was whether she was afraid of all men. She had reason to be gun-shy after being married to that son of a bitch. The fights weren't even the worst of it; what had really galled Tom were the constant put-downs. Summer evenings, with the windows open, he'd heard plenty.

"You're not going out, looking like that," the guy would say, with a sneer in his voice. Or, "Can't you even have goddamn dinner on the table when I get home? You can't keep the house clean and you're a lousy cook. What did you do all day? Sit around and knit?"

Tom had been out dividing perennials the day she had greeted her husband at the door to tell him that she'd sold her first original knitting pattern to a company that published them. He still remembered how her face had shone with delight.

"Big whoop-de-do," the bastard had declared. "What's for dinner?"

That beautiful glow had gone out, as if her husband had thrown a rock and broken the bulb.

Tom had wanted to punch the SOB, and despite his special unit training, he wasn't a violent man.

When things had got too loud, he'd called 911. He'd been scared for her. He'd fought his every instinct to intervene, because he'd known that he would make things worse. Josh Easton wouldn't have liked another man telling him how he could treat his wife. And he was just the kind to take his anger out on her.

What Tom had never known was whether her husband had hit her, too. Tom had heard enough crashes during their fights to be afraid he had. Once he'd seen bruises on her face when she'd left the house. He'd told himself there could be an innocent reason for them but hadn't believed it.

Tom had never been happier than the day he'd come home to see half the household possessions piled in the driveway. A man's clothes and shoes in a jumbled pile. The TV, VCR, stereo system, recliner… Tom didn't know how she'd managed to haul the heavier stuff out, but she'd been more generous with the creep than he'd deserved.

Tom also didn't know how she had held onto the house, but was glad she had. Josh Easton was nobody Tom wanted as a next-door neighbor.

Six months after the SOB was gone, she'd marched out one Saturday morning and painted over the Easton on the mailbox. A couple of hours later, the black paint dry, she'd used a stencil and white paint to put Chauvin in its place.

When she'd finished and seen Tom in his yard, she'd said, "I'm divorced," and marched back in her house, head held higher than he'd seen it since the day he'd bought his place and moved in next to her.

He hadn't known then how to say *Good for you,* not without letting on that he'd heard and noticed more than she probably wanted him to have. Maybe someday, he'd figured, when they got friendlier. No reason they wouldn't, now that she didn't have a husband who didn't seem to like her talking to anyone else.

But Tom had realized shortly thereafter that Suzanne was still skittish around him. When he directly addressed her, she'd gaze in his direction without ever really looking at him. He had to be careful how he approached her because she startled easily. Like the other night, when she'd banged her head on the trunk of her car just at the sound of his voice.

It seemed to him she'd loosened up just a little lately. She'd seemed really glad to have her brother reappear in her life, and she apparently had a new brother-in-law, too, who had introduced himself one day while the two women had been chatting. Kincaid. Mike...no, Mark Kincaid. Tom had seen her hug him casually a couple of times.

He knew she dated once in a while, too, although none of the men ever came around for long. So she wasn't afraid of all men. Or else she hid it better around most of them than she did with Tom.

The why would likely remain a mystery to him. He didn't look like her ex, who had been sandy-haired, handsome and charming. None of which applied to Tom, who had dark brown hair, didn't know how to be charming and who had never been called *handsome,* even by his own mother.

But tonight Suzanne had actually come to his door and had even sat on his couch. She still hadn't met his eyes, but she'd talked to him. He might have even been the first to hear the kids were coming over tomorrow to scope out her house. And she'd invited him to say hi to them.

Tom had intended to run errands tomorrow, but to hell with them. He'd stick around until the kids had come, find an excuse to be out in the yard so he could meet them, maybe be out in the yard again after they left in case Suzanne wanted to talk some more. Tell him how the visit had gone.

Taking his plastic-covered dinner out of the microwave, he issued himself a warning. For God's sake, the woman was afraid of him! She wasn't likely to go from that to wanting to share his bed.

His bed? Who was he kidding? Suzanne Chauvin was a marry-or-nothing kind of woman if he'd ever seen one.

Nope, stick to admiring from afar, he told himself.

But he was still going to be out there tomorrow, both to meet the kids and because he'd decided he liked Suzanne the day she'd hauled that son of a bitch's stuff out to the driveway.

MRS. BURTON DROVE a rattle-trap of a car, even worse than Suzanne's. It gasped and coughed as she pulled into the driveway and turned off the engine.

Suzanne hurried out even before the car doors had

opened. After the foster mother laboriously cranked her window down a few inches to greet her, Suzanne smiled. "Thank you so much for bringing them. You take your time with your errands."

"I'll do that." She fixed a stern gaze on Sophia and Jack, who had come around to Suzanne's side of the car. "You two do what Ms. Chauvin asks you to do, hear?"

"Yes, Mrs. Burton," they chimed, heads swiveling as they tried to see the yard and house and street all at once.

"I'll be back around two-thirty." She rolled up her window again and backed out of the driveway.

Glad it wasn't raining today, Suzanne said, "Do you want to see the yard quick before we go in?"

"Sure," Sophia agreed.

Jack nodded. His eyes were wide and he was sticking close to his sister.

Suzanne led them toward the back gate. As she did so, Tom's garage door began to roll up.

He stepped out and glanced their way as if surprised to see them, which didn't fool Suzanne for a minute.

"Your visitors are here, eh?"

"Yes, Sophia, Jack, this is my closest neighbor, Tom Stefanec."

They both nodded shyly.

He smiled at them, once again startling Suzanne. Had he always looked so kind? How was it she'd never noticed?

"Good to meet you. Suzanne is excited about you coming."

"I've been sitting by the window for the last hour," Suzanne admitted.

"We could have come sooner," Sophia offered. "But

Mrs. Burton kept saying no, that we'd said one so it was going to be one."

"She probably didn't want to take me by surprise." Suzanne opened the side gate. "Mr. Stefanec was nice enough to mow my lawn this fall. My mower wasn't starting."

He looked over the two kids. "You two ever mowed before?"

They both stared at him, their heads shaking in unison. "We never had a yard before," Sophia told him.

"Might be a good chore for you to take on."

"Jack never had chores," Sophia said with a sniff. "*I* did everything."

"Did not!" her little brother protested, if quietly. "I helped, too!"

"Did not," she repeated under her breath.

He smouldered.

Laughing, Suzanne laid a hand on each of their shoulders. "It doesn't matter. Here, you'll both have to help, because we have the whole yard *and* house to keep up."

"Well, I'm glad I met you," Tom said again. "Suzanne, you let me know if I can help haul anything you'll need for the kids with the pickup."

Letting the kids go ahead into the backyard, she turned back. "Really? You've been so nice already about the lawn...."

"You didn't ask. I offered."

She smiled at him, thinking again what a nice face he had. "I can get mattresses delivered, but I'll probably scour thrift stores for other furniture. Just in case I buy something too big for my car, I'd really appreciate it if you'd pick it up for me."

"Glad to." He nodded toward the excited voices that came from around the house. "You'd better catch up with those two."

"Yes." She bit her lip. "Thank you."

His answering smile was friendly, his stride relaxed as he walked away.

She'd felt really comfortable with him there for a minute, as if they were old friends. Shaking her head in bemusement, Suzanne headed into the backyard.

Jack was standing under the apple tree staring up at the gnarled dark branches, bare of leaves at this season. "I could climb it."

"Do you like to climb?" Suzanne asked.

He stole a shy glance at her. "I never had a tree. But I like the monkey bars at school."

"When he was real little, he climbed on top of a dresser and freaked Mom," Sophia said. "And he used to get out of his crib. I remember that."

"In the summer, I eat out here sometimes," Suzanne said. "The patio furniture is in the garage. But we can go in that way."

The sliding door led directly into the dining area and kitchen. The kids crowded behind her, craning their necks again.

"It's not very big," she began apologetically, before seeing the expressions on their faces.

They looked as excited as if her modest house was a mansion.

"Pretty." Sophia touched the quilted runner on the table. "You even have flowers."

She'd bought the bouquet on impulse at the grocery store yesterday, a spray of showy blooms in yellow and lime-green and hot-pink. They weren't fragrant the way flowers from her own garden were, but Sophia was right. They were pretty.

"And here's the living room." Suzanne trailed behind them.

Sophia sat briefly on the sofa and bounced. "Your TV is little."

"I don't watch very often."

She received two identical, dumbfounded stares.

"Mom had it on all the time."

"But she was bedridden, wasn't she?"

"She didn't ride anything." The ten-year-old looked at her as if she were stupid.

"I mean, she was in bed most of the time. So she didn't have much else to do."

"I guess not." She lost interest. "Can we see the bedrooms?"

"You may."

She'd expected them to race down the hall. Instead they went slowly, wonderingly, Sophia touching the frames of pictures she had hung on the wall, then hesitating for a moment before turning into the first open doorway.

This bedroom was at the front of the house and was slightly the larger of the two.

"I used to store yarn in here, until I opened my own yarn shop."

"Can it be mine?" Sophia asked. She turned in a circle, taking in the bare, off-white walls, the empty closet, the scuffed wooden floor.

"You haven't seen the other one yet."

"I like this one."

"Then if everything works out, this one will be yours." Suzanne smiled at Jack. "Let's go look at the one right across the hall."

She could tell he didn't want to leave his sister, but he did follow Suzanne. "I've used this one for my guest room," she told him, "so it already has a bed in here. You'd probably want a twin size instead, so there'd be more space to play in here. And for a desk and a dresser and…"

He'd gone directly to the window and looked out. "I can see the tree. It's practically touching the glass! I like this room."

"I'm glad. If you could pick any color for the walls, what would it be?"

He turned, thin face serious. "Green is my favorite color in the whole world."

"I like green, too."

Sophia jostled past Suzanne. "This room is way cool, too!" Her eager gaze turned to Suzanne. "Can we decorate our own rooms the way we want?"

"Let's not get ahead of ourselves. We still have a lot to talk about, don't we?"

"*If* you decide to adopt us," Sophia said, "can we decorate our bedrooms the way we want?"

"Within reason," Suzanne agreed. "What's your favorite color?"

She pursed her lips. "Um, let's see. Some days purple is. And some days pink."

Pink and purple. Well, that was reassuring. Suzanne had

half expected her to say orange and black. At least in this way, she marched in step with all the other girls her age.

"You two would share the bathroom next to this room." They followed and she pushed open the door.

"My bedroom." Suzanne continued the tour, letting them wander to her dresser and look at the framed photos, stroke her coverlet and the hand-knit salmon-colored throw that lay across the foot of the bed, and rock experimentally in the maple-and-caned rocking chair that sat on a rag rug by the window. They even peeked in her bathroom.

"In the other direction," she said, "there's room to keep bikes or whatever in the garage. I keep meaning to have a garage sale so I can park the car in there, too."

"I bet we could do lots of the work," Sophia said. "We could put stickers on everything, and take money, and try to talk people into buying stuff."

"I'll need all the help I can get," Suzanne said noncommittally. She glanced at her bedside clock. Her time with the kids was expiring rapidly. "Have you had lunch?"

They nodded. Jack was getting braver, because he volunteered, "Mrs. Burton made us eat before we could come."

"Well, how about a snack? And we can talk a little."

"Do you got cookies?" Jack asked.

"No, but I made a coffee cake."

His face scrunched up. "Coffee is gross."

She laughed. "It doesn't have coffee in it. It's a kind of cake that tends to be eaten during a coffee break. This one is lemon. I promise, it's good."

They came with her, both stopping to take one last, lingering look at the bedrooms that would be theirs, before bouncing along to the kitchen.

"I like your house," Jack confided. His face was flushed, and he was increasingly animated. "Sophia does, too. Huh, Soph?"

"Of course I do, dummy!"

Unoffended, he said, "See? We both like it."

"I'm glad," Suzanne told him. "Why don't you two sit down? I'll get the cake and pour milk."

"Can we have pop?"

"I'm afraid I don't have any."

Both looked incredulous again. Sophia voiced their shock. "You mean, you don't drink pop? At all?"

Suzanne laughed, something she knew she was doing too much. But she couldn't seem to help herself. She felt giddy. "Of course I do, sometimes. I just don't always have it. Milk is better for you anyway."

Their expressions of relief were comical, but also sobering. What were they accustomed to eating? Had they stayed in hotels with kitchenettes? Sophia remembered cooking with her mother, but that might have been years ago. Had they become accustomed to nothing but prepackaged and fast food?

She sat down and cut the coffee cake. As she dished it up, she said, "I do try to eat a healthy diet. Lots of fruits and vegetables and not much junk food. If you're used to lots of potato chips and pop, you'll find it's a little different here."

They exchanged a glance. If it was in code, she couldn't break it, even though clearly they were communicating.

"What happens to us now?" Sophia asked, picking up her fork. "How long do we stay with Mrs. Burton?"

"I don't know," Suzanne admitted. "I think usually Ms. Stuart would want us to take weeks and even maybe months to get to know each other."

Despite her full mouth, Sophia said, "But Mrs. Burton says she can't keep us that long. She said only through Christmas break."

"That's what I understand, too," Suzanne agreed. "I'm hoping you can come here instead of to another foster home."

Both their faces brightened. "Really?" Sophia said. "That soon?"

"If you want to." Suzanne set down her fork. "But I don't want you two to feel rushed. Once you come, you're going to be stuck with me and my rules."

"Do you have strict rules?"

"I think they'll be pretty normal. I'll expect you to have chores here at home, and to make sure I always know where you are. We'll set a bedtime, and you'll need to do homework before you watch TV or play. Stuff like that."

"Is that all?" the ten-year-old asked suspiciously.

"No, I'm sure it's not. I don't like to be lied to, for example. I'm going to ask you to be honest. That's really important to me."

"Mr. Sanchez says I'm too honest," Sophia told her. "He says sometimes I shouldn't say what I think."

"*Not* telling somebody you think their new outfit is ugly isn't quite the same thing as lying about where you went after school, or what a teacher told you, or whether you've done your homework."

"But if I say the new outfit looks cool, that's lying."

"It's what's called a white lie," Suzanne told her. "That means you're not being honest, because being honest would hurt the other person's feelings. But instead of telling even the white lie, you can say something like, 'Wow! Did your mom take you shopping?' and the person thinks the 'wow' was a compliment."

"That's sneaky," Sophia said with apparent admiration.

"For now, I'll have you both come to my shop after school, not home. You can do your homework there, and we can come home together after I close at five."

She had to tell them about Knit One, Drop In, including an explanation of the name of the store. Sophia thought it would be way cool—her favorite words of enthusiasm—to learn to knit.

"Is there anything you want to ask me?" Suzanne concluded.

Jack scraped his plate in search of any last crumbs. "What would we call you?"

"Hm. What did you call your mother?"

"Mom," said Sophia.

"Mommy," said her little brother.

"Well, definitely not either. Because she'll always be your mother, in your hearts."

"Do you still think about your mother?" Sophia asked, sounding a little shy.

Suzanne nodded. "I wish she could meet you, for example. Be your grandmother."

"Oh." She looked down.

"I think maybe you should just call me by my name for

now. What do you think? Then, later, if you want maybe we could think of some variation on *Mom.*"

"You mean, we should call you Ms. Chauvin, like Mrs. Burton said?"

She smiled at Jack. "No, you can call me Suzanne."

Sophia's forehead crinkled. "How do you spell it?"

She spelled it for them. Sophia frowned, taking it in, while Jack kicked his heels on the chair and gazed out the sliding door.

"Will we have your last name?" Sophia asked.

"Yes, once the adoption is complete. Are you okay with that?"

"Sophia Chauvin," she tried out loud.

"That's an elegant name," Suzanne said. "I like Jack Chauvin, too."

"It's lucky Jack isn't Van. Then he'd be Van Chauvin." She cackled.

Her brother doubled over and pretended to laugh hysterically. His elbow caught the glass of milk and knocked it over, sending the milk in a river across the table.

"I'm sorry! I'm sorry!" he cried, scrambling up, something very close to fear on his face.

"He didn't mean to do it!" Sophia said, leaping to her feet. "I'll clean it up, so you don't have to do anything."

Taken aback by their reaction, Suzanne rose, too. "I know it was an accident. Everybody knocks things over sometimes. Don't worry. Here." She grabbed a roll of paper towels from the holder. "Let's sop it up with this."

Arms close to his body, Jack stood frozen by the table, his eyes saucer-wide.

Suzanne went to him. "Jack, don't look so scared! It's okay. Really." She took a chance that she wouldn't scare him more and bent to give him a quick hug.

He stood stiff in her embrace, but when she let him go she saw some of the tension leave his body. "I'm sorry," he whispered again. Then, "Can I use your bathroom?"

"Of course you can." The minute he'd left the room, she turned to his older sister. "Why was he so frightened? Mrs. Burton doesn't, uh…"

Sophia shook her head. "She gets grumpy, but that's all. It was the other foster mom, the first one we had. She yelled a lot and spanked Jack when he made mistakes."

"What an awful woman!" Suzanne said with indignation. "Did you tell the social worker who supervised you?"

"After we went to Mrs. Burton's."

Suzanne smiled at her. "Good for you."

Hands full of wads of soggy paper towels, Sophia said, "The quilt thing on the table is wet, too."

"I can throw it in the washer." Suzanne bundled it up. "Oh, shoot! I hear a car. I bet it's Mrs. Burton."

She put the table runner in the sink and went to the front window just as the kids' foster mom beeped her horn.

Jack came from the bathroom, head hanging again, somehow appearing smaller than he had when he'd been excited and happy. Suzanne ignored the burning at the back of her eyes and smiled at him and then his sister.

"Shall we go shopping next weekend? Start looking for things for your bedrooms?"

"Yeah!" Sophia said.

"If it's okay with Mrs. Burton and Ms. Stuart, we'll plan

on Saturday." She could take a whole two days off. Rose would be glad for the hours.

"Wow! Okay. Bye."

They raced out and tumbled into the back of Mrs. Burton's car. Suzanne followed and spoke briefly with their foster mother, who thought Saturday would be great.

Suzanne stood in the driveway and waved as the car backed out. She didn't want them to go, but she also realized she felt a little shaky. She'd been so nervous about what they'd think, whether they'd like her, she'd been operating on adrenaline.

The car disappeared down the street, and she sighed, giving herself a little shake.

"How'd it go?" a voice asked from so close, she jumped.

Tom, of course. He'd approached as soundlessly as always.

"Oh! You startled me." She pressed a hand to her chest.

His forehead creased. "I'm sorry. I came out my front door. I assumed you saw me."

"No, I was too busy trying to decide if the visit went well. I think it did."

"You think?"

"Well, they seemed to like the house. But Jack freaked when he accidentally knocked over his milk. Sophia told me their foster mom spanked him when he made any messes."

The lines in his face deepened. "That poor kid."

"It worried me a little." She didn't know why she was confiding in him, but the words just kept coming. "I realized how many issues they probably have. Did I tell you their mom had MS? As her health deteriorated, they moved from shelters to cheap hotels where she could rent a room by the week. Sophia did the grocery shopping. I guess the mom must have gotten a disability check or something. But it sounds really grim."

"And they watched her die slowly."

She nodded. "After their mom got really sick, Jack started wetting his bed, and Sophia... She acts as if she doesn't care, but she must. She says she hates the school she's going to and doesn't have any friends, and apparently Jack gets bullied. And I'm coward enough to think *What do I know about traumatized children? What if I foul up?*"

"You won't," he said with a certainty that surprised her. "If I've ever seen anyone meant to be a mother, it's you. Anyway, if they need counseling, you can get them that, too."

She drew a deep, ragged breath. "I can, can't I? I don't know if I'm *meant* to be a mother, but I want to be one. Wow. I really panicked. Look at me! I'm shaking." She held out her hands, which indeed had a tremor.

He smiled at her, that amazingly kind smile transforming his blunt-featured face to one that was almost handsome. "You panicked because suddenly your fantasy kids are real, with real problems."

Another deep breath, this one filling her lungs. "You're right. That is why, isn't it?" She gave a little laugh. "You aren't a parent, either. How did you get so wise?"

"Guess I was born that way." This grin was more mischievous. "So, when will you see them again?"

"Saturday. We're going shopping. We'll start with bedding and then look at paint, and I'm hoping to have time to hit a couple of thrift stores, too. They'll both need dressers and desks."

He nodded. "Let me know what I can do. Anything at all. Just ask."

She gazed at him in amazement. "Thank you. Really. Thank you."

He smiled again, and crossed their strip of lawn, disappearing a moment later into his house.

Still not having moved, Suzanne stared after him. Now she felt teary because he'd been so understanding and so nice. She'd known him for over five years, and had never known a thing about him except that he was obsessively tidy.

But today, she'd learned all kinds of things. And one, she thought in astonishment, was the color of his eyes. They were gray, with tiny flecks of green.

She'd looked into his eyes, without even realizing she'd broken years of habit.

Was it possible they could actually become *friends?*

Suzanne shook her head again in bemusement. Who'd have thought?

CHAPTER FOUR

SUZANNE WAS AT WORK on Wednesday when Melissa Stuart called again.

"Suzanne," she said without preamble, "I'm afraid we have a problem."

The tone, a little cool, was one Suzanne hadn't heard from her before. Her heart seemed to skip a beat, then gave an uncomfortable bump in her chest. "A problem?"

"I got to looking through your file and discovered that the background check was never completed. Unfortunately, when I ran one it turned up something you didn't warn us about. There were apparently two domestic-disturbance calls made to your address during the time when you were listed as owner."

Feeling a little sick, Suzanne turned her back on the one customer browsing the bins of yarn. "No charges were filed," she said, hating the way her voice shook. "My ex-husband and I were on the verge of divorce."

"Can I assume there was violence in your home?"

"No!" she protested. "No. Not the way you mean. We..." She took a breath. "He threw things. Once he punched a hole in the wall. His anger was one of the reasons for the divorce."

"I did locate your ex-husband." There was a momentary pause. "Josh Easton. He said, I quote, that maybe you both had a little trouble controlling your tempers."

The air escaped her with a whoosh. "Josh said that? Did he know why you were asking?"

Another brief pause. "Yes, I did explain."

Oh, God. This was her worst nightmare. "He was very controlling," she tried to explain. "And angry when I asked him to leave. He's trying to hurt me now by lying to you."

"Suzanne, I want to give you the benefit of the doubt. You have really outstanding character references. But I can't ignore this kind of red flag. I'm sure you understand."

Her stomach actually hurt now. She hunched slightly, one hand splayed on it. Tears burned in her eyes. "So…that's it? You won't approve an adoption? What about Sophia and Jack?"

"Can you suggest any witnesses to these fights?"

Grasping at any hope, she asked, "Aren't there police reports?"

"The reports are brief. Neither officer seemed able nor willing to assign blame. They apparently issued warnings and left."

"You could talk to them…"

"One has long since left the department. The other officer has no recollection of that particular call."

Suzanne squeezed her eyes shut. She couldn't picture either face. Only the uniform, the flashing lights atop the squad cars that had recalled for her the night her parents had died, when police had brought word.

"The neighbors," she said, in a voice just above a whisper. "You could interview them."

Behind her, a voice said, "Excuse me. I wonder if you could help me decide whether a yarn this thick would work for my project."

She swung around, covering the phone with her hand. Somewhere, she found a smile that she prayed didn't look ghastly. "Can you give me just a minute?"

"Of course," the woman said, and retreated.

Suzanne lifted the receiver again. "The neighbors on both sides were living there then. I always suspected one of them called the police." Tom. In her heart, she'd known. It had to have been him at least once. Long after the police had left the first time, she'd heard the neighbors on the other side come home and seen their lights go on. "They may have heard enough to support me."

The caseworker's voice softened a little. "I'll be glad to interview them, with your permission."

"Please do. Please." Despising the tremor in her voice that made her sound weak, Suzanne pushed on. "I'm the opposite of violent. I've always been humiliated by what happened. That's why I didn't tell you."

"I understand. Thank you for your suggestions. I'll be talking to you shortly."

Despite the fact that she wanted to go hide in the back and cry, Suzanne made herself help the customer choose a yarn that was more suitable for the pattern she'd selected. After ringing up the purchase, she sat on the stool behind the register and prayed no one else would come in until she'd pulled herself together.

She'd never even thought of those awful scenes with Josh as something that might keep her from being able to adopt a child. Her humiliation at the knowledge that neighbors had heard and even called the police had strengthened her resolution to end her marriage. Private shame, she'd been able to bear, but not public. And now, to think that Josh could kill her dream this way....

As bewildered as she was angry, Suzanne was as bereft of understanding as she'd always been where he was concerned. Didn't he remember the time when he loved her? Why was he still lashing out at her?

She stared at the phone and wished she could talk to someone. But who? Tom Stefanec? What would she say? *Gee, I don't know how much of my fights with my ex you heard, but I hope it was enough.* He had said he thought she'd be a great mother, so maybe...

Panic and hope beat their wings in her chest, tangling and tearing. He probably hadn't heard anything but raised voices and crashes. And however kind he'd been to her recently, she had a suspicion he was too honest to lie.

She could call a friend. But she'd never told any of them about the way Josh had sometimes talked to her, had made excuses when they'd commented about a put-down or his lack of interest in something that mattered to her. Even after she'd found the resolve to stand up for herself and tell him to leave, she had still never wanted to admit how badly she'd let herself be treated.

Carrie? But all Carrie knew was that her sister's marriage hadn't been good. To this day, Suzanne had managed to evade any conversation about what had really gone wrong. She didn't think she could bring herself to tell the whole bitter history, not right now.

Despair washing over her, Suzanne pictured Jack and Sophia on Sunday, imagining having their own bedrooms. How would they handle being told, *Gosh, sorry, forget those bedrooms you were dreaming about, we'll have to try to find you another adoptive family*?

Right that minute, Suzanne felt cruel at having given them hope, and worthless. Exactly, she realized, what Josh wanted her to feel.

TOM WAS SURPRISED TO GET a call that evening from a woman who introduced herself as an adoption counselor at the agency where Suzanne had been approved.

"We're following up on some information we recently received," she said, "and I'm wondering if you'd be willing to meet with me."

Keeping an eye on the steak he'd just put on the broiler, Tom shrugged, then realized she couldn't see him. "Yeah. Sure. Anything I can do to help."

They established that he wasn't available during the day. He told her he could be home by five, and she said, "Tomorrow? I hate to hold up her application any longer…."

He didn't like the way the sentence trailed off. Hadn't Suzanne told him her application already *was* approved? What was the deal?

"Tomorrow's good," he said into the silence.

He'd heard Suzanne coming home a while back, so he knew she was there. He was tempted to go over and ask why all of a sudden this social worker wanted to talk to him, but what if she didn't know? He didn't want to alarm her. Anyway, he'd never actually knocked on her door before, and after the way he'd kept popping up over the weekend, he didn't want to seem too pushy.

No, wait and hear what this is about, he counseled himself. It was probably just a formality, them finding out what the neighbors thought of her and the plan to add a couple of kids to her household.

But the next evening, he realized within minutes of the social worker's arrival that the visit was no formality. A middle-aged woman with short, graying hair, this Ms. Stuart sat on one end of his sofa and opened her notebook with the brisk panache of a detective ready to interview a suspect.

"Mr. Stefanec, I'm not sure if you're aware that the police were called to Ms. Chauvin's home twice several years back."

Three and a half years back. He didn't correct her. "I called them," he said.

Her back straightened. "Ah. Well. Ms. Chauvin gave me permission to talk to her near neighbors. I'm sure you can understand our concern about placing children in her home given a possible history of domestic violence."

"Her husband was a son of a bitch. Pardon me for my bluntness. I called 911 when I heard him make threats. I was afraid for Suzanne's safety."

She scrutinized him. "Are you friends with Ms. Chauvin?"

He shook his head. "We're neighborly. I don't know her well. I've never been in her home."

"Her ex-husband insinuated that she, too, had trouble controlling her temper."

Tom made a sound of disgust. "Yeah, that sounds like him. You've got to understand. I don't know if he ever hit her, but he belittled her constantly. I heard him yelling if she had friends over, if she wasn't home when he thought she should be, if she smiled at another man. He fought like hell to keep her under his thumb. When she stood up for herself, he lost it. I called the cops to make sure she didn't get hurt."

"And in what way did she 'stand up for herself'?"

"Not by violence. She refused to give up some friends he didn't like. He called them names."

"You heard that much?"

"It was summer. I was out back on my deck, their windows were open." He was losing patience. "Ms. Stuart, I feel like I'm violating Suzanne's privacy. She's a nice lady. In the case of her husband, she was too nice. She'll be a great mother."

Without having written a word in her notebook, his visitor closed it. "That's exactly what I was hoping to hear, Mr. Stefanec. I'm required always to err on the side of protecting the children, but in this case I had difficulty imagining Ms. Chauvin even raising her voice."

"When she did, she sounded scared," he told her. "My impression is, she's a gentle woman who was trying real hard to hold her marriage together."

The caseworker smiled and rose to her feet. "Thank you very much for your time. You've been a big help."

He stood, too. "You're welcome. I happened to be out in the yard and met Jack and Sophia the other day. They seemed like great kids."

"Yes, they are." She buttoned her coat and slipped on gloves, then after a few more words of thanks departed.

Going to the living-room window, he pulled aside the drapes and watched her walk down the driveway, hesitate at her car, then continue the few steps on the sidewalk to Suzanne's driveway and up it. He hoped like hell that meant he'd tipped the balance. He didn't like thinking how devastated Suzanne would be if she wasn't allowed to adopt.

Letting the drapes fall, he went to the kitchen to figure out something for dinner. At least a couple of nights a week, he made himself cook. Living alone shouldn't mean existing entirely on prefab meals that could be nuked in the microwave. Tonight, though, he chose a frozen chicken pot pie.

He'd just finished eating it and throwing away the container when his doorbell rang. He wasn't altogether surprised. Without realizing it, he'd been listening for footsteps on the porch.

Earlier, he'd left the porch light on, and now he opened the front door to find Suzanne shivering in jeans and shirtsleeves on his doorstep.

"You don't have a coat on." He stood back. "Come on in before you freeze."

"I didn't expect to get cold going twenty feet." She scooted past him and hugged herself while he shut the door.

"Cup of coffee?" As pinched as her face was, he was getting a bad feeling he should put a dash of whiskey in it. Maybe he *hadn't* tipped the balance.

"Oh, I shouldn't stay." She was back to avoiding his gaze. "I just came over to thank you."

His worry subsided. "Nothing to thank me for."

"Yes, there is. Whatever you told the caseworker was

enough to change her mind. I think—" her teeth worried her lower lip "—she wasn't going to let me have Jack and Sophia."

"You're still shivering. Sit," he ordered. "Some coffee will warm you up. I have it ready."

"I don't want to be a bother…."

"You're not." He went to the kitchen, leaving her standing in the middle of his living room.

When he returned a minute later with the two mugs, a sugar bowl and a carton of creamer balanced on a large platter serving as makeshift tray, Suzanne was sitting on his couch, just about exactly where she had the last time she'd been here, and just as uneasily.

In fact, she shot up at the sight of him. "Oh, you didn't have to—"

"I wanted a cup myself."

"Oh." She sat back down, barely perched on the edge. "Well, thank you."

Damn, she was beautiful. She had the kind of face that would still be beautiful when she was eighty, so perfectly were her bones sculpted. With her smooth dark hair, big brown eyes and slim, delicate body, she could have been on the big screen. Instead, she lived next door to him, fueling a few idiotic fantasies.

He added a dash of cream to his own cup and stirred. "I thought you said you'd already been approved."

"I was. But then Melissa noticed no background check had been run for some reason. So she went ahead, and the two domestic-disturbance calls popped up."

"I take it she called your ex."

Stirring her own coffee, she kept her head bent, hair screening her face. "Yes. He could have defused the whole thing and didn't. We...we had problems, but I thought—"

Tom raised his brows. "That he'd remember you with enough fondness to help you out?"

She lifted her head to expose a twisted smile. "Something like that."

"I heard his language when he came home and found his stuff in the driveway. Didn't he break your front window with a rock?"

She ducked her head again. "The thing is, we met in the sixth grade. We were high-school sweethearts. You saw the bitter end, but there were good times."

He wondered. Had there been good times only because she'd been compliant?

"Some men don't take rejection well."

She looked up at him at last, her cheeks as bright as a twelve-year-old girl's who's been experimenting with makeup. "I'm really embarrassed that you heard our fights."

Enlightenment dawned, and Tom felt particularly dull-witted. Was *that* why she shied away from him the way she did? Because she was embarrassed?

"I was raised better than to have knock-down, drag-out fights with my husband that all the neighbors can hear," she continued, her cheeks if anything getting brighter.

"Far as I could tell," Tom said, voice laconic, "the only way you could have avoided those fights was to do everything he wanted you to do."

Her hands were curled into fists. He bet her nails were drilling into her flesh.

"You heard a lot, didn't you?"

Tom's brows drew together. "Enough to know I didn't like your husband. I'm betting I wasn't the only neighbor cheering when you threw him out."

"Really?"

"Yeah. Really."

"God." She uncurled her fingers to press her hands to her hot cheeks. "Melissa wouldn't say, but… Was it you who called the police?"

He tensed, instinct telling him his answer would make or break any possibility of friendship between them. But how could he lie?

"I didn't want to see you get hurt."

"That's why you called?"

"I was afraid for you."

Her eyes closed, luxuriant lashes fanned on her cheeks. Almost inaudibly, she said, "I always thought that you, or whoever called, just wanted us to shut up."

"No." He couldn't help himself. He stood and went to the couch, sitting beside her although he didn't touch her. "I should have said something then. I'm sorry."

She let out a breath that made her body shudder and turned toward him. "That last time, he did hit me."

Tom swore.

"I lied to the policeman who came to the door. I agreed that it was just raised voices. But I made up my mind then that I couldn't live that way."

"A couple of those times, it was all I could do not to come over. But I thought it might make things worse for you."

"It would have. He got mad one time when I smiled and

waved at you. Wanted to know when we'd gotten so friendly. If you'd intervened, he would have thought it was because..." She couldn't say it.

"He was an idiot." A nice way of saying Josh Easton was a jackass. One of the world's luckiest men, too stupid to know it.

"Anyway." Her cheeks were still hot, but Suzanne Chauvin smiled at Tom. "I never thought I'd say this, but I'm glad you heard as much as you did. And I'm so grateful you spoke up for me tonight."

That smile, shy and sweet, flattened him.

"Like I said, you're welcome." He sounded so gruff, he hoped she didn't take it as unfriendly.

"You saved my life."

He shook his head. "Another agency would have seen reason and approved you."

"But I wouldn't have gotten Sophia and Jack, and I think now it has to be them. Thanks to you, it can be."

He opened his mouth to protest again, then thought, *She wants to make you a hero, let her. That could be good. Really good.*

"Are you sure you're ready?" he asked.

"Am I rushing?"

"Maybe. Maybe not. Sometimes, you just know the right thing to do."

"I think that's it." She sounded amazed. "I do know. Oh. I can hardly wait for Saturday!"

He and she were so close to each other, he saw the wonder in her eyes, the fine texture of her skin, the whorl of her ear decorated only with a gold stud. Out of left field came a sudden deep ache of envy because the glow wasn't for him. What was that about? They were neighbors, no more, no less. At least she wasn't afraid of him anymore, but Suzanne had never shown even a flicker of interest in him as a man. He'd be an idiot to ruin their increasingly friendly relationship by coming on to her.

Nope, someday Suzanne Chauvin would bring home a new husband along with the kids. She'd give Tom sunny smiles when they both happened to be out in their yards. Which beat the days when she'd skulked around avoiding him.

"Right," he said. "Let me know what I should pick up and where."

"Thank you." Suzanne held out a hand.

He looked down at it. Like the rest of her, it was fine-boned. They shook, with him thinking, *This is the first time I've ever touched her.*

She got to her feet as if energized, said, "Thanks for the coffee, too. And for mowing my lawn, and listening to me."

"What are neighbors for?"

Another smile, more thanks, and she was gone, leaving him pretty damn depressed for a man who'd just become a hero.

SATURDAY'S OUTING WAS FUN. Both kids were either on their best behavior or were basically well-mannered children. Jack got bored at Linens 'n Things once he'd picked out his own comforter, but he trailed along without complaint while Sophia agonized over the look she wanted for her own room. Then they lugged bulging bags out to the car, had lunch at the nearby Spaghetti Factory, and visited a couple of thrift stores where they were lucky enough to find one nice desk and a dresser with a mirror that Suzanne could afford. The dresser needed refinishing, but she and Sophia agreed it would be beautiful once it was glossy instead of scratched and chipped.

The clerk agreed to tag and hold both pieces of furniture until Tom could pick them up.

"I'll keep looking this week when I get a chance," Suzanne told them, back in the car. "If you'll trust me."

The desk was to be his. Jack had seemed awed enough to have his own. "Sure," he agreed without hesitation.

After a moment, Sophia nodded, too. "Can we help paint our rooms?"

"They won't be ready to move into if we wait," Suzanne warned.

"Jack is too little to help anyway."

"I'm not!" he declared, his belligerence immediately fading. "But I don't really want to paint."

Suzanne looked over her shoulder and smiled at him. "Then I'll start with your room."

He gave a triumphant glance at his sister. "Okay!"

She looked less pleased now, but said only, "Can I pick out the color?"

Rodda Paint loaned out a metal ring strung with a sample of every paint color they carried. It was a wonderful kaleidoscope, from pastel to jewel-bright and back again. Suzanne had hurried over there after closing yesterday and signed it out.

Now she said, "I have samples at home. And I made

cookies, so we can have a snack and then see how the colors look with your new comforters."

"Cool!" they declared.

Jack, it developed, didn't much care. He gave a cursory glance at Suzanne's suggestions and said, "I like that one. No, that one. Or that's okay."

She laughed. "I'll surprise you."

Sophia was pickier. Although she liked pink and purple, her tastes didn't run to unicorns and lacy pillows and girlie stuff. She'd seemed dazzled anew at being able to choose any comforter or bedspread in the store, in the end settling on one that looked exotic with a crazy-quilt of silky fabrics that might have come from Indian saris.

Now, she finally decided on a sherbet-orange color for her walls that picked up a minor note in the comforter.

"It's going to be gorgeous and sophisticated," Suzanne said, putting a sticky note on the sample so she'd remember.

"You can paint it if you want to," Sophia told her. "I don't mind."

Suzanne smiled at her. "I can hardly wait to have you here."

"I think Mrs. Burton wants to get rid of us. She's been grumpy."

"I'll talk to Ms. Stuart and see if there's a plan yet." Suzanne hadn't said anything about the close call and didn't intend to.

Both heard the horn sound outside. Sophia didn't move. "I guess that's her."

"I guess it is."

Jack had been sprawled on his stomach on the floor engrossed with crayons and paper that Suzanne had provided. He jerked and said, "I ruined my picture," with tears in his voice, and crumpled the drawing up. "I wish she wasn't here."

"At least we've started getting your rooms ready," Suzanne said, voice artificially cheerful.

"Yeah." Sounding glum, Sophia stood up. "Come on. We gotta go, or she'll get mad."

"I hate Mrs. Burton!" Her little brother stood, kicked the crayons lying scattered on the floor, and didn't seem to notice that a couple broke as they bounced off the molding.

Suzanne opened her mouth to say something, then closed it. There'd be time enough when they lived here. This transition had to be really hard for them. What were a couple of broken crayons?

She walked them out, saw that Mrs. Burton did indeed look grumpy, and thanked her effusively for bringing the children over. "I have so few days off. I really appreciate you making it possible for me to spend time with Sophia and Jack even when my timing might not be the best for you."

The foster mother's face relaxed. "Oh, it's no trouble. Next weekend?"

They agreed, in the absence of hearing anything from Melissa, on the following Saturday.

"Thank you," she said again. "Bye, kids!"

She stood in the driveway waving until the car turned the corner at the end of the block. She felt both elated at how the day had gone and let down now that Sophia and Jack were gone. She was ready to bring them home, not visit them once a week.

Make sure before you commit.

"I *am* committed," she said aloud, to nobody.

She felt unreasonably let down yet again when she went next door and found her neighbor's house silent and dark. Tom had been home after the other visits to talk to her. Today, all she could do was leave a note on his door telling him about the two pieces of furniture at the thrift store and thanking him again for offering to pick them up. She squeezed her phone number down at the bottom, hesitated, then went home.

It was silly to feel so deflated. She had plenty to do. Housecleaning tonight, so she'd be free to shop for mattresses tomorrow, buy paint and possibly even start on one of the rooms.

Maybe Carrie and Mark would want to help. Mood improving, Suzanne reached for the phone.

CHAPTER FIVE

SUZANNE HURRIED TO THE PAINT store in the morning and returned loaded with rollers, brushes, plastic liners for the roller pan, masking tape for molding and, of course, cans of paint. She'd just hauled it all in when she heard what sounded like a pickup truck in her driveway.

Sure enough, her doorbell rang and she found Tom on the porch, alarmingly burly in a sweatshirt with the sleeves shoved up and faded jeans. "I've got your furniture," he announced. "Shall I bring it in?"

She felt self-conscious all over again, after the other night. He knew so much about her, so much more than she'd ever realized, and she knew hardly anything about him.

To hide her awkwardness, Suzanne hurried into speech. "Oh, how nice of you! No, let me open the garage door and we can put both pieces in there. I'm going to paint the bedrooms before I put any furniture in them. Besides, the dresser has to be refinished. And dang it," she remembered, "I forgot to pick up the stuff to strip it."

She came out with him and heaved open the door while he let down the tailgate of his pickup.

In a lithe motion that demonstrated how well-muscled he was, Tom swung himself into the bed. He lifted the desk as if it weighed nothing and moved it to the edge of the tailgate, then jumped down and picked it up before she could offer to take an end.

"I could help...." she said, hurrying after him.

"No need." He set it down in an open space and turned to look at the tarp-covered pile in the middle. "What's this?"

Would he be peering under her sinks if she'd let him in the house? With as much dignity as possible, she said, "I've been meaning to have a garage sale."

"Mind if I take a look?" Without waiting for her assent, he lifted the tarp. "Hey, this dresser isn't in bad shape."

"I thought about refinishing it, too, but the drawers stick."

He crouched, the denim pulling taut over powerful thighs, and moved drawers in and out. "Hm. Might be fixable. Can I work on it?"

"If you want to have it..."

He flashed her a surprised glance. "No, for one of the kids' bedrooms. I just like to work with my hands. Don't have any projects right now." He shrugged.

"Are you sure?" She seemed to be saying that to him a lot lately.

He nodded toward the dresser still in his pickup. "I could strip that one, too."

"Really?" Suzanne couldn't help sounding hopeful. She hated stripping old paint and varnish and trying to get it out of cracks.

"I enjoy jobs like that. And you've got plenty on your plate if you're going to paint two rooms."

"If you mean it..."

"I'd be dumb to offer if I didn't."

She couldn't help laughing. "Then…thank you. Um. I suppose we should put it in your garage instead of mine, then. Unless you'd rather work on them here, since you garage your truck."

"My tools are over there. It's no problem." He experimentally hefted the dresser, then began to remove drawers. "Looks like oak under this paint."

"I bought it at a garage sale a long time ago. I always meant to strip it and never got around to it." Like all too many projects she initiated in a burst of enthusiasm. "I used to store yarn in it."

The drawers stacked, he went to one side of the dresser and she went to the other. They lifted in concert.

"Not too heavy for you?" he asked.

"No, it's fine."

Together they carried the dresser out of the garage and across the strip of grass to his driveway. They set it down and he went back to his pickup to use the remote control for the garage door.

"Wow." She gazed in awe at his garage. She'd seen the way he hung tools and the spotless concrete floor, but never so close up. Now she saw that the floor had actually been painted with something rubbery that could be easily cleaned—and, obviously, often was. Tools hung in spots sized just for them, not on any handy hook. The window that looked out on his backyard sparkled. His workbench could have modeled in a magazine for do-it-yourselfers. All in all, she was really glad she hadn't let him in her house, as short shrift as she'd given housework last night.

"Wow?" he asked, from right behind her.

She blushed. "Oh. It's just so…neat."

"Obsessive, you mean." He sounded wry, surprising her.

She turned to look at him. "I wouldn't be that rude. I'm just jealous because I'm so messy."

"I think it's my military background. They don't tolerate anything out of place."

A perfect opening to ask what he actually did for a living *now.*

But, no. He had already gripped the dresser and was waiting for her to take her side. They carried it to the back of his garage, by the window and the workbench, and set it down.

"I'll move my pickup."

Instead of just standing there, Suzanne fetched the drawers, two at a time. Then she helped him unload the second dresser.

He scraped some of the chipped white paint away and said knowledgeably, "Cherry."

"You can tell? I just thought it would be really pretty. We talked about just painting it again, but…"

"Painting?" He leveled her with a stare that suggested she'd just proposed holding up the Bank of America branch. "You can't paint solid cherry."

"I didn't know it was cherry. I just thought I'd wait until I'd stripped it to see how the wood looked."

He stroked the curved edge of the top. "This one is going to be a beauty. Look at what good shape that beveled mirror is in. You were lucky to find this."

Pleased, she said, "I thought so."

"This one's for the girl?"

"Sophia. Yes. Do boys bother looking into a mirror until they're at least sixteen? It would be wasted on Jack."

"You sound like you know something about boys."

"I grew up with two cousins a little older than me." Emboldened, she asked, "What about you? Do you have brothers or sisters?"

"Had a sister." He paused. "She died of leukemia when she was eight."

"Oh, Tom! I'm so sorry!"

He shrugged. "It was a long time ago. I was only ten. It was hardest on my parents."

"They didn't have any other children?"

"Just me."

Now she knew something else about him: he'd grown up an only child after a terrible tragedy that must have left an echoing silence in his home.

"I'll strip these," he said, as if they hadn't been discussing anything but old furniture, "then we can talk about finishes."

"Okay. Although I suspect you know more than I do."

A faint smile touched his mouth. "Could be."

"Thank you," she said again. "Doing this for me… It's really amazing."

"They seemed like good kids."

As they walked out of the garage, Suzanne said, "They are *so* excited about having their own bedrooms. I told you about the way they've been living, didn't I? In hotel rooms and homeless shelters?"

"I imagine they're more interested in having a mom again."

They stopped in his driveway.

"Maybe," she said uncertainly. "I suspect they're a long

ways from thinking of me like that, though. Maybe it's just permanency they're hoping for."

He nodded. "That counts with kids."

"At least I can give them that."

"You're doing a good thing."

"Thank you. How silly of me to ever be afraid…" She stopped. Oh, when would she learn not to open her big mouth without thinking first?

When she didn't finish, he nudged. "Afraid?"

"Oh, I just worried. With your yard so nice, that you wouldn't want kids next door."

A couple of furrows drew his brows together. "Afraid I was the scrooge who'd throw their baseball away if it landed in my yard?"

She tried to sound shocked. "No, of course not. I just don't want them cutting across your lawn or damaging your perennial bed when it's so gorgeous. Kids can be careless."

"Flowers grow back." He studied her, the creases that had deepened in his face making him look troubled. "I just have too much time on my hands. Have to use it somehow."

"So you garden?" she asked, puzzled.

"So I edge the lawn, or prune the hedge when it doesn't really need it."

The explanation was unbelievably sad. She'd noticed he didn't seem to have family or frequent visitors. She'd never thought of him as lonely, but he must be.

Suddenly ashamed of herself, Suzanne realized she'd never thought about Tom Stefanec in any way that didn't relate to her. About all she'd ever noticed about him was his intimidating tidiness. Forcing herself to be ruthlessly honest, she also admitted she'd been all too aware of how well-built he was. Only, she hadn't liked being aware of that.

What she hadn't done, even once, was wonder why he didn't have a family, whether he had friends, who he was.

Appalled, she wondered if she was always so self-centered.

"I'm sorry," she said awkwardly. "I didn't think."

He'd turned to regard his yard, perhaps to avoid her gaze. "I do like things neat."

There was an understatement. This fall, she'd speculated about whether he had vacuumed the leaves off his trees. Hers had still been hung with black, soggy, rotting leaves, while the branches of his were bare and his lawn spotless. But she had enough self-control not to ask.

"I wish I had more time on my hands so I could be neater. You must hate having me next door."

He turned his head to look at her, his expression unreadable. "No. I don't hate having you next door."

Her heart was suddenly doing double time for reasons she didn't understand. "Oh," she said softly, before recovering. "But I'll bet you do hate my dandelions."

"The dandelions, I could live without."

"Did you use weed and feed on my lawn fall?"

A quick grin transformed his face. "Yep."

"So we may be living without dandelions come spring?"

"No, they're persistent buggers. They'll need to be hit more than once."

Feeling reckless, she said, "Well, I won't promise, but if you're willing to spread the stuff, I'll buy some bags."

"Done." He held out a hand.

She let him engulf hers and they shook. Perhaps for a moment longer than they needed to. He looked a little embarrassed when he let her hand go. Suzanne knew her cheeks were pink again.

"I'd, um, better get to painting if I'm going to get much done." She backed away. "Thanks again, Tom."

He dipped his head. "You're welcome."

Hurrying back to her own house, Suzanne wondered how she could ever have been so dumb as to misinterpret her neighbor so badly. And after she had, he was still willing to help her. She remembered saying snide things about him to her brother when he'd visited from Santa Fe. She'd have to make a point of telling Gary how nice Tom had been.

And she'd have to think of some way to thank him beyond saying it over and over again. With Christmas so close, she'd buy him something.

No. Not buy. She'd knit him something. Would she have time? If it wasn't done for Christmas, that would be okay; she'd take him a plate of cookies or something. Not a sweater, she decided; that was a little too intimate. She'd have to study him closely to guess size, and then the whole time she was knitting she'd imagine how it would fit over his broad, powerful shoulders.... No, definitely not.

Okay, an afghan, then. She'd be more comfortable decorating his sofa than him.

Itching to dash down to the store to pick out yarn, she made herself go into the garage instead for a screwdriver to open the cans of paint.

Finish one thing before you start another.

TOM WAS SURPRISED AT HOW MUCH he enjoyed working on the two dressers. Clearly, his life hadn't been full enough, not if he was now excited to get home and scrape layers of paint off an old piece of furniture.

But he did like working with his hands. He was reminded how much he'd enjoyed shop in high school. Maybe, given a different background, he'd have gone into cabinetmaking or the like. But his father had been Army, and he'd never seriously considered any other path.

He tackled the cherry dresser and mirror first. He had a feeling the girl would care more about having something beautiful than the boy would. Besides, once he started, he found enormous pleasure in exposing the beautiful wood. As he stroked on the stripping compound with a brush, he shook his head. It ought to be a crime to paint over wood like this.

He'd started Sunday; now, on Tuesday evening, he was done but for the mirror. The old beveled mirror itself, wrapped in a blanket, now leaned against a wall. Tom was having to use some ingenuity and great care to get the last traces of old paint and varnish off the delicate, curved frame.

About eight o'clock, he was satisfied and set down the sanding block and fine sandpaper he'd been using to make the wood silky smooth. He wiped the frame with a rag, then ran his thumb over it to feel for any rough spots.

Was it too late to get Suzanne over to take a look? He'd gone ahead and bought a stain today, but wanted to be sure she didn't have a different idea before he applied it.

After hesitating, he went in the house and called her. He'd kept the note she'd left on his door that day in the drawer beneath the phone, even after adding her to his phone book.

When she answered, he said, "Suzanne, this is Tom Stefanec. I've finished stripping that cherry dresser and wondered if you'd like to take a look before I stain it."

"Already! That's amazing!"

"I've enjoyed working on it."

"I'd love to see it. Shall I come over now?"

"You bet."

He went out and opened the garage door, then waited for her. When he saw her, he grinned.

She wore old jeans and a white T-shirt, both splattered with orange paint. Orange dotted her face like freckles, too, and streaked her hair where she must have pushed it back with a careless hand.

She wrinkled her nose at him. "That bad?"

"The color is good on you," he told her.

"And may be for some time." She sighed. "I should have worn a bandanna."

"How's the room look?"

"Bright. Way brighter than I pictured." She sounded doubtful. "But I think it'll be okay once we get furniture in there. I've brought the comforter in a couple of times to make sure the effect is really as pretty as I imagined. I just hope Sophia doesn't hate it."

"Her own bedroom? I doubt it."

She looked past him, her eyes widened. "Ooh," she breathed. "It's beautiful."

Pleased, he stepped aside so she could walk around the dresser and stroke the smooth wood.

"It's fantastic!"

"Yeah, you got yourself a treasure here. You're lucky a dealer didn't see it before you did."

"Wouldn't it be pretty painted white?" she mused.

He pokered up.

Suzanne laughed, her eyes sparkling. "I just had to see your face."

Tom shook his head. For a minute there, he'd thought she wasn't such a perfect woman after all.

"I picked up a stain today, but I can exchange it if you'd like darker or lighter." He picked up the can and the flyer that showed the different colors.

She studied it, then said, "I think I would have picked this one, too."

They talked about final finishes and agreed on a semi-satin—not too shiny, but with enough sheen to make the wood glow.

He calculated. "If I put the stain on tonight, I should have it done by this weekend. Are the kids coming over?"

She nodded. "They're going to spend the night Saturday. I'm hoping to have both rooms painted by then so they can get an idea. I haven't had a chance to buy mattresses, so I'll set up the double bed I had in one of the rooms again."

"Did you say Jack wets at night? You'd better get a plastic mattress cover."

She nodded again, worry lines creasing her forehead. "Did you know kids who wet the bed at his age?"

He shook his head. "It's not surprising with everything that's happened to him, though. I wouldn't make too much of it."

She gave a funny little laugh. "I worry about everything. It's my specialty."

"Really?"

"I think maybe it was my parents' death and me knowing my aunt and uncle didn't really want me. And losing my brother and sister, of course. I just grew up trying to avoid causing even a little bit of trouble."

He had to ask. "Then why didn't you marry an easy-going man?"

Her gaze flicked away from his, and he cursed himself for raising a sensitive subject. But after a minute, her mouth twisted into a smile.

"Josh seemed big and strong and protective. And passionate about me. I was too naive to guess what a fine line there is between protective and jealous."

Tom had to concede, "Not the kind of thing you expect, I guess."

"No. Well, I'd better get back to my painting."

"And I'll get that stain on the dresser." Unable to resist, he reached out and touched the streak of orange in her dark hair. "You might want to coordinate your outfit for tomorrow, too."

She made a face at him, but didn't flinch from his hand. "Thanks. Too bad it's not Halloween."

He laughed. "I'll let you know when I'm done here. Maybe we can get the dresser moved in Saturday morning before the kids come. I can help you haul Jack's desk in, too."

"That would be great." She gave him a last, dazzling smile. "Thanks."

Alone again, he didn't move for a moment. Damn it,

he could no longer fool himself into thinking he'd be content to become friends with Suzanne. So what was he looking at here?

Option one: the ache of seeing every day what he couldn't have.

Two: She was interested, too, and they started…what?

Not a fun, casual relationship, that was for sure. He couldn't imagine Suzanne settling for less than marriage.

Which made immediate a push/pull Tom had felt his entire life.

When he sat in his empty house at night, the TV on for company, he imagined a different life. Wife, kids—people who cared, people he cared about.

But then memories would surface of his parents' chilly civility with each other, the way his father had escaped every night to the non-commissioned officers' club, his mother to whatever book she was reading, Tom to his bedroom. Family pictures, the three of them smiling at the camera, gave no clue to the ice chamber their home was behind closed doors.

What he mostly remembered was that living with other people was lonelier than living alone. He knew it wasn't always like that, but he also knew how much it hurt when it was.

He was both painfully drawn to the kind of family he'd never had, and terrified that he would be doomed to a replay of his childhood. Part of him had always assumed he'd get married some day, have kids; he *liked* kids. But when he actually met a woman he could imagine marrying, he invariably felt a chill. What if it turned out badly? What if he ended up living in hell the way his parents had because… He didn't know why they had. Him, he might stay no matter what for the sake of kids.

He'd always chickened out before he gave any woman ideas. But this time… Tom muttered a word he rarely said. This time, he was tempted as he'd never been before. And this time, he couldn't quit seeing her.

Remembering the feel of her hair under his hand, he swore again. Maybe their friendship *hadn't* just gotten complicated; maybe what it had gotten was really, really simple.

He was falling in love. Which was going to hurt like hell unless she felt the same, in which case it could *still* hurt like hell.

He just didn't know what to do about it.

Well, then, get back to work, he ordered himself.

Tom hit the button to close the garage door and carefully swept up the sawdust so he didn't inadvertently stir any up and get it stuck in the wet stain. Then, refusing to think about anything but the piece of furniture in front of him, he wiped down the mirror frame and dresser yet again and began applying the stain, gratified by the way it brought out the grain and the natural color in the cherrywood.

SOMETIME DURING THE WEEK, it occurred to Suzanne that she'd have to let Tom in her house if he were going to help carry furniture into the kids' rooms. Of course, he *had* already seen her garage, so he was unlikely to be surprised that she wasn't a neighborhood Martha Stewart.

After putting two coats of paint in the front bedroom, she had the routine down pat. Best of all, Wednesday evening Carrie came to help, rolling pale yellow on the walls in Jack's room with abandon while Suzanne wielded the brush alongside moldings and ceiling. Mark had offered as well, she told Suzanne, but she'd told him this was a two-woman job.

"I thought it would be fun with just the two of us, so we have a chance to talk."

Now, Suzanne concentrated as she followed the line of the ceiling. "If I can just figure out how to get the chair railing on straight."

She'd bought the wide molding at the lumber yard and had painted it kelly-green. She intended for it to wrap around all four walls, just below halfway up. Her plan to eyeball it had begun to seem fraught with the possibility of disaster, but she hated to buy a level and a plumb line—whatever that was—if she didn't need them.

"I can rent a miter box," she continued. "You know, to cut the angles for the corners."

"Uh-huh." Carrie's face was spattered with yellow, but she'd heeded Suzanne's warning and tucked her hair, the same brunette as Suzanne's, under an old bandanna. "You'll have to measure *really* carefully."

"Are you doubting me?"

"Maybe. Have you done any woodworking before?"

"I've never used a miter box, if that's what you mean."

"Or installed molding?"

"No," she admitted.

"Maybe you should ask the superhero next door to help."

The temptation was there, but so far she'd resisted. "He's doing so much already."

"Willingly, from the sound of it," her sister pointed out.

"I just don't want to impose." And darn it, she liked the time she'd spent with him too much, this hunger she had to share her day with him. Instinct was shooting off warning flares.

The roller stopped and Carrie twisted precariously on the ladder to look at her. "From what you say, the guy's bored. Give him a chance to help."

"Yes, but..."

"Well, I'll bet he has a level and whatever else it was you needed," her sister pointed out, her practicality unarguable.

"Okay, okay," Suzanne mumbled. "You've convinced me."

"Michael wanted to help. He was dissuaded only because Mark promised to take him out for pizza. Plus, I'm taking him to a play Friday night, so it's not like I'm neglecting him."

"A play?" Suzanne repeated, picturing the six-year-old trying to follow *The Importance of Being Earnest* or the like.

"Seattle Children's Theatre. They're doing *Wind in the Willows.*"

"Wow. I'll bet Jack would love that. I wonder if he's ever been to a real play before?"

"Unless they were in a class that went as a field trip, probably neither of them have been. After we're done, why don't you go online and see if there are still tickets available for Saturday? Seattle Children's Theatre is fantastic. The kids are up close, the sets are simple and the actors have this gift for speaking right to the audience." She dipped the roller in the pan. "It's fun to watch the children's faces."

"I'll bet there's a lot of things Jack and Sophia have

never had the chance to do. Go up the Space Needle, take a ferry ride, go to the zoo…"

"And the aquarium. I still love going there."

"Museum exhibits…"

"Water slides!" Carrie contributed.

Suzanne laughed. "Yeah, Wild Waves. It's expensive, but I'll manage it this summer."

"I have a friend from high school who works for one of the radio stations. They get lots of promotional tickets. I'll see if she'll contribute some."

"Really? That would be great."

"You know, Jack and Michael are only a year apart. And Michael's so confident, I doubt the year will matter."

"I hope they like each other."

"Have faith."

Suzanne gestured with her brush. "You're dripping." Fortunately, they'd covered the worn hardwood floor with several drop cloths.

"Right onto my tennis shoes. Damn," her sister muttered, setting the roller in the pan again and getting down to wipe up globs of paint.

By nine, they were done. After putting the lid on the can and wrapping the roller and brush in plastic to keep them from drying out, they stood back to admire their work.

"It really looks good." Carrie sounded surprised.

"It does, doesn't it?" Suzanne turned slowly to take in the whole effect. "I hope Jack likes the color."

"I thought he approved it?"

"He gave blanket approval to whatever I wanted to do. He'd lost interest."

"Well, it's going to be beautiful with the comforter," Carrie declared stoutly. "And you got a matching valance, right? Maybe you can get a bright rug, too."

Suzanne wished she could afford to replace the off-white blinds to match the color scheme, but knew that was silly. As if Jack would care.

"I'll hang shelves over the desk, and put a big bulletin board somewhere. Maybe that wall." She gestured. "And then posters or something."

"I wish I could come back and help you tomorrow, too, but I really should hear that speaker at the U."

Suzanne shook her head. "The second coat never takes that long. I'll be done in a couple of hours."

After Carrie left, Suzanne went online and bought tickets to the matinee of *The Wind in the Willows.* Saturday morning, she'd start dinner in the Crock-Pot, she decided, so it would be ready when they got home. Having them spend the night was going to be fun. She'd think of it like a sleepover, not a test run, which she suspected it really was. At least, in the caseworker's view.

Thursday, she painted a second coat and cleaned house. Friday night, she hung the valance above the window in Jack's room and put the closet doors back on in both bedrooms. Then she called Tom.

"I wondered if you have a level I could borrow?" she asked. "I'm putting up a chair rail in Jack's room...."

"Need a hand?" her neighbor asked.

"I rented a miter box. It doesn't look all that hard."

There was a moment of silence. Then, with tact she admired, he said only, "I'd be glad to help."

Her determination to do the job herself collapsed. "If you wouldn't mind."

Despite last night's efforts, mainly to get the bathrooms clean, the house was still a disaster. She hadn't done much in the way of bookkeeping or ordering this week, either. She'd planned to vacuum and sweep in the morning, along with putting on a pot roast in the Crock-Pot. Maybe Tom wouldn't notice how much needed doing.

When she let him in the front door, he glanced around, then followed her without comment. No winces. He didn't sidetrack to peer under her bathroom sink. He came, measured, sawed and nailed up the chair rail in less than an hour. Watching him, she had an awful suspicion she would have been struggling well into the night.

"You might want to touch up some spots with paint," he said finally. "But it's looking good."

Once again, she admired the bedroom, bright and fresh. "It is, isn't it? One of these days, I've just got to get these floors refinished. The new paint makes them look worse."

He shook his head. "It's a big job. Usually you have to move out for a while."

"Maybe someday when we're going on vacation." *And* had money to burn. Sure, that was going to happen.

He helped her carry the desk in from the garage, although they left it sitting out in the middle so she could touch up the chair rail behind it.

Stifling a yawn, she said, "I can do that before bedtime."

Tom's lopsided smile inexplicably warmed something inside her. She had the fleeting thought that it was almost tender.

"Looks like bedtime better be soon."

"Melissa implied that if this weekend goes well the kids could move in this coming week. Since Wednesday is the start of Christmas break, we wouldn't have to do anything about school until they'd settled in a little, and they could have Christmas with me instead of in their foster home." She hugged herself. "I can hardly believe it. Christmas with children!"

"It'll be one they never forget," he said in a soft, gruff voice. Then he backed away. "I'd better run. I'll bring over the dresser in the morning, once that last coat of finish has dried."

She faced him. "Tom…thank you."

"No thanks necessary." He backed away as if eager to escape. "Ten o'clock okay?"

She nodded and followed him to the front door, locking it behind him.

On the plus side, so far as she could tell, he wasn't repulsed by the state of her housekeeping. But…why had he suddenly seemed to withdraw like that? Had she said something?

They'd been talking about Christmas. He always put up outside lights, so she knew he wasn't totally opposed to the holiday. Maybe he'd remembered some particularly awful Christmas from his childhood. Had his sister died during the holiday season? That might taint it forever for his family.

Who *did* he spend Christmas with? She tried to recall whether she'd ever noticed a tree inside his front window, and failed. He must go somewhere.

There was no *must* about it, she thought on a rush of dismay. He might very well spend it alone every year. Plenty of people did. Wouldn't that be ironic if they'd both been alone some of those years when she'd declined her aunt's invitation? Two sad people, neither knowing the other was there next door.

Getting the can of kelly-green paint from the garage and going back to Jack's bedroom, Suzanne resolved to ask Tom what his plans were for Christmas. Would he be embarrassed if she invited him to join her and the kids on Christmas eve, or the whole family on Christmas Day?

So what if he was? She'd invite him anyway. The more the merrier.

Besides… She wanted him here to see the joy on Sophia and Jack's faces. He deserved to be there.

She was a little surprised and disconcerted to realize how natural the idea of him joining them was. Especially considering tonight was the first time he'd ever stepped foot in her house.

Clearly, they were going to be friends. If she hadn't been so ridiculously self-conscious around him all these years, maybe they could have been long since.

She got out the brush, dipped it in the thick, semigloss paint, and stroked it over a nail hole. She was smiling, and a moment later began to hum.

I wish you a merry Christmas…

CHAPTER SIX

GARY CALLED SATURDAY MORNING, while Suzanne was peeling potatoes to add to the Crock-Pot. He and Rebecca would arrive on the twenty-fourth, and planned to stay at her mother's house.

"God help me," he added.

Suzanne laughed. "Scared of her?"

"A little. She's a nice lady, but I did steal her daughter away."

"And she's been living in sin with you."

"That, too." His voice held a smile. "On the other hand, Mama Wilson is busy planning our wedding, which seems to make her happy."

Bending to discard peels in the trash can under the sink, Suzanne demanded, "So, tell me the details."

Professing to know nothing, he handed off the phone to his wife-to-be, who immediately said, "Tell me all about the kids!"

Suzanne did, including the plans for today and her hope that they would be coming to stay next weekend.

"That's really fast, but you sound ready."

She laughed, but weakly. "Well, I don't actually have beds for them yet, haven't talked to school officials, don't know the bus schedule... Hey, just a few details like that."

"I meant emotionally."

"Oh, I'm a little nervous, but I think I'd be just as nervous even if we'd had half a dozen sleepovers. And I really like the idea of them being here for Christmas. And for your wedding. Tell all."

The ceremony would take place on January sixth, at the Lutheran Church in north Seattle that her mother and Rebecca had attended. Her mother had rented a mansion in Everett on the bluff above Port Gardner for the reception. "A lot of our friends are in Seattle, but she couldn't find anything there on such short notice. We were really lucky to find someplace this wonderful. This house is huge, and it's furnished like it would have been in 1910 or so. What's more, it'll still be decorated for the holidays. I'm so excited."

Now cutting carrots, the phone tucked between shoulder and ear, Suzanne asked, "What's your dress look like?"

Ivory satin, Rebecca explained, very simple, with seed pearls on the bodice. "Mom kept my grandmother's veil, and it's perfect!"

"And Gary?"

Rebecca laughed. "Well, he wanted to wear jeans and his leather jacket, but has reluctantly agreed to a tuxedo." A muffled voice grumbled in the background, and Rebecca continued, "He's going to be very handsome." Pause, and an exchange that Suzanne couldn't make out. "And miserable," Rebecca added. "I'm compelled to pass on his message. He can't believe anybody wears shoes like that to work every day."

Knowing perfectly well that Gary sold his coffee roast to major grocery stores, his sister said, "Please tell me that he doesn't wear his biker getup when he meets with account representatives."

Again, Rebecca chuckled. "No, the man has half a dozen beautiful suits in his closet, but he complains every time he has to put one on."

Considering everything that needed to be done for the wedding, the holiday and the adoption, they decided not to get together until the whole family gathered on Christmas Day at Carrie's house. In good humor, Suzanne hung up and finished putting ingredients in the Crock-Pot. In the nick of time, because she heard a car in her driveway. She washed her hands and got to the door just as the bell rang.

The kids burst in. "We're here!" Sophia caroled unnecessarily.

Suzanne waved over their heads to Mrs. Burton, still in the car. She lifted a hand and then backed out, leaving Suzanne to close the door.

Jack was already bouncing on the couch and his sister dancing around the coffee table singing a loud rendition of a song Suzanne recognized from the radio, their bags dumped in the middle of the floor.

"Are we gonna get a tree today?" Jack asked. "Huh?"

The song stopped. "Yeah. You said we could," Sophia chimed in.

"I had another idea," Suzanne told them. "We could put up the tree on Wednesday."

Her mouth made an O of shock. "But that's practically right before Christmas!"

"Yes, but you won't be here to see it anyway."

"That's true."

They listened as she told them about the play. Neither seemed terribly interested. She'd no sooner finished than Sophia began to dance again, and Jack to bounce.

"Do you want to see your bedrooms? And bring your bags," Suzanne added.

"Yeah!" They leaped for the bags and then careened down the hallway.

She followed, trying not to be dismayed by their hyperactive behavior.

Jack whooped and disappeared into his room, but Sophia came to a dead stop in the doorway to her bedroom, just staring.

Apprehensive, Suzanne stopped, too. "What do you think?" she asked after a minute.

"It is *so* beautiful," the ten-year-old whispered. "Just like I imagined it."

Suzanne let out a breath of relief. "I was afraid you'd think it was too bright."

"I *like* bright colors." She took a few, tentative steps inside. "Ooh. Is that the dresser we bought?"

If only she'd thought to ask Tom over, Suzanne thought with quick remorse. "Yep. Tom Stefanec—you remember, my neighbor next door—refinished it for you. Isn't it gorgeous?"

She reverently stroked the top and peered at herself in the mirror. "I never thought I'd have anything this pretty for myself."

Ignoring the sting of tears in her eyes, Suzanne gave her

a quick hug. "Just wait until we get a bed and desk in here, and you can decorate."

"Can I put up posters and stuff?"

"Yes, you can."

Across the hall, she found Jack bouncing on the edge of the double bed she'd set up again temporarily. The comforter he'd chosen was spread on it. "Is this my bed?" he asked.

Had he swallowed springs? She guessed that was the effect excitement had on little boys.

She shook her head. "It's too big to leave room for you to play. I'll get new beds delivered this week. So, what do you think of the color?"

"I like it. It's a good color," he declared, thin face serious.

She smiled and sat beside him. "I'm glad."

"We're really going to a play? A real one? Not like the ones we do at school?"

"We really are," she assured him. "In fact—" she glanced at her watch "—we'd better get going."

She herded them out to her car, depressed Jack unutterably by informing him that he wasn't big enough to ride in the front seat but Sophia was, checked to be sure she'd stuck the ticket confirmation in her purse and started for Seattle.

Sophia fiddled with the radio the entire way to the freeway, apparently stunned that Suzanne didn't own a CD player. "Nobody has cassettes anymore!" she protested.

"I have a CD player in the house. Just not in the car. Until I get a new car, it doesn't seem worth the money to me." Suzanne winced at the song on the radio station where Sophia paused. "I don't like rap."

"Why not? It's cool!"

"Some of it may be." She'd save the lecture about violent lyrics that bashed women for another time. "But I don't like it. I'll tell you what." She reached out and turned off the radio. "Let's talk instead."

"Yeah," Jack said from the back seat. "We can talk."

Sophia gave him a slit-eyed glare over her shoulder. "We don't have anything to talk about."

Suzanne was starting to feel desperate. "If we really want to live together, we ought to like to talk, don't you think?"

"You mean, if I won't talk to you, you won't let us move in with you?"

Suzanne forced a smile. "Did I say that? What I was implying is that I'm interested in you two, and I'm hoping you are in me."

Sophia sniffed.

"I don't have very many friends, so I don't think I'm that interesting," Jack informed her.

"Of course you are! You just haven't had a good chance to make friends, changing schools so often." Suzanne glanced sideways. "You, too, Sophia. I'm really hoping you both like your new school."

"Can we drive by it someday?" Jack asked, voice small. "Before we start?"

"Sure." Of course, she'd have to find out which elementary school kids in her neighborhood went to. "Maybe next weekend."

"Do I go to the same school?" his sister asked.

"I assume so." But didn't know for sure. Were Edmonds middle schools grades six through eight? Seven through nine? Another thing to find out. It was entirely possible that

Sophia would be at the middle school next year. Suzanne found she didn't like the idea.

Her gaze slid to the side, and she took in today's outfit. Sophia once again wore jeans that were way too tight and low-cut given the maturity of her figure. The ragged tennis shoes suggested she hadn't had a new wardrobe in too long, so maybe she'd just outgrown her clothes.

Suzanne hoped.

Definitely a subject for another day.

Her head turned suddenly. "Didn't you two bring coats?"

"I have mine," Jack said, lifting a faded blue parka.

Sophia shrugged. "I never wear one."

Her brother couldn't resist telling the whole story. "The zipper is broke on hers."

His sister gave him another evil glare.

"I'll definitely put a new coat on your Christmas list," Suzanne said, with what she hoped appeared as undamaged serenity.

"I got a Christmas list!" Jack bounced. "You want to know what I'm gonna ask Santa for?"

"I thought tonight we could talk about that," she said. "But now, let me think about my driving. We're almost there."

Traffic was heavy for a weekend day, with half the cars on the freeway, it seemed, exiting at Mercer Street in Seattle. It appeared other events were happening at the Seattle Center, built for the 1960 World's Fair. The Key Arena was here, the opera house, and the Northwest Rooms where festivals and shows were staged. A huge fountain occupied the courtyard in the middle, and to the north was the Science Center. A destination for another day, Suzanne realized. Jack would love it, and she thought Sophia would forget she was almost a teenager quickly enough with so much temptation.

Both kids were craning their necks to look up at the Space Needle. Seattle's foremost landmark, it reared high above their heads when she found a parking spot.

"Can we go up?" Sophia asked, as they crossed the street and entered the center.

"It's really high." Jack, still staring upward, sounded alarmed.

"Not today," Suzanne said firmly. "Today, we'll go to the play."

She had another daunting realization, which was that she knew little of their tastes. In the abstract, discovering everything about them seemed fun. In practical terms, she could imagine sneers at what she put on the table at dinner, as well as at the mall when she took Sophia shopping.

More worries to shelve. The shelf, she thought wryly, was starting to groan under the weight of everything she was plunking onto it.

Both kids became quiet when they joined the stream of other parents and children heading into the theater. Suzanne noticed how their body language changed. Jack ducked his head and began dragging his feet, not looking at anyone else. Sophia's expression become remote and irritated, as if she were being dragged here against her will, while at the same time her shoulders hunched as if she were trying to hide her small breasts.

Or her shivers.

Definitely a coat. Suzanne made a mental note to check

both their sizes tonight, when they were in their pajamas, so she'd have some idea where to start.

Once the play started, both forgot their self-consciousness and gazed, rapt, at the actors playing Toad and his friends from *The Wind in the Willows.* It was all absurd and childish and funny. Sophia giggled like the little girl she really was.

During intermission, they looked at each other, dazed, as if they'd forgotten where they were. "It's good!" Jack declared, and a boy sitting in front of them turned around.

"It is good!" he said.

The boy's mother and Suzanne exchanged smiles, and she felt a tiny thrill. It was her very first conspiratorial, we're-mothers-and-aren't-they-sweet? smile. *Wow,* she thought, *I'm a mother.*

After the play, they hung around to meet the actors, then walked to the car. They talked about the play while she drove. Both were excited. Sophia was envious of the actors.

"Maybe that's what I should be," she said. "Although I might like to be a movie actress better. So I could win an Oscar."

"But the nice thing about acting on stage is the audience," Suzanne pointed out.

Her forehead puckered. "Yeah. I wonder if they get as much money?"

Suzanne was pretty sure the Seattle Children's Theatre actors didn't make Julia Roberts type money, and said so. Sophia decided she'd rather be like Julia Roberts then.

Finally, she let Sophia turn on the radio again, and they listened to pop tunes until they got home. Jack, she discovered, was sound asleep, and she had to wake him so he'd be alert enough for dinner.

The moment they finished eating, Sophia asked, "Can I watch TV?"

"Yeah!" Jack agreed.

A little worn out herself, Suzanne gave permission and sat down in the living room as well, automatically reaching for her knitting.

She was already well into a soft, ribbed throw for Tom Stefanec. She'd been able to get quite a bit of knitting done during the day, between customers. The yarn was a heathered blue-gray, and she planned to finish each end with long fringe.

After a while, she noticed that Sophia was sneaking glances at the needles as they whisked in and out of the yarn.

"Do you want to learn a few stitches?" she asked.

"Can I?"

"Sure." So she set aside her own knitting and cast on a row of purple yarn to begin a scarf. "I'll teach you to do that later," she said, "but for now, let's start with the two basic stitches."

Tongue caught between her teeth, Sophia concentrated fiercely on knit and purl, showing surprising tenacity when she dropped a stitch and had to go back. Hard at it, she didn't object when Jack turned the channel to a show he liked.

Finally, Suzanne tucked them in, and heard them whispering and giggling for at least an hour, both getting up to go to the bathroom again before they at last became quiet.

In the morning, she was beating eggs for French toast when Sophia came into the kitchen in her nightgown.

"Jack peed in bed," she announced. "He's crying 'cause he thinks you're going to be mad. Are you?"

"Of course I'm not!" Suzanne set down the egg she'd held in her hand. "Shall I start a shower for him?"

"He's scared of showers. He only takes baths."

"Okay. A bath it is." She started it running before she stuck her head into the bedroom. He sat in the middle of the bed, head hung, face tear-streaked. "Sweetie!" she said. "Don't worry. You can't help it. Grab some clothes and go hop in the tub. I'll wash your pj's this morning along with the sheets."

He lifted his head. "Really?"

"Really."

Sophia watched him race for the bathroom. Then she wrinkled her nose. "Ew! I'm wet. Yuck."

"You can take a shower right after him. I'll wash your nightie, too." Suzanne began stripping the bed, grateful she'd followed Tom's advice and bought a plastic mattress cover. "I shouldn't have let him have that juice so close to bedtime, should I?"

"Uh-uh. Except, I had juice, too, and I didn't have to go that bad."

"Remember that he's lots smaller than you. That means his bladder is, too."

"Are you going to get mad if he keeps doing it?" Sophia asked. She stood in the middle of the bedroom, the wet hem of her nightgown held out from her body.

"Getting mad wouldn't help at all. Besides—" she smiled at the girl "—I don't get mad very often. I can't remember the last time I did."

"Really?" She studied Suzanne with open astonishment. "I get mad lots."

"I haven't seen you yet." Except for the hateful glares, which Suzanne suspected were standard-issue big-sister tools for keeping a younger sibling in line.

"You will," Sophia promised. "'Cause I never know when I'm going to get mad."

"You can learn to hide it when you're mad, you know. That's part of growing up."

Her forehead crinkled again. "Why would you want to hide it? When I'm mad, I want everyone to know."

"Um…" Suzanne paused, the bedding clutched in her arms. "Because people are even less likely to give you what you want when you're rude or violent. That's one reason. Sometimes because you don't want to give another person the satisfaction of knowing they hurt your feelings or made you angry. Sometimes just because you're a better person when you have the self-control not to act on your feelings."

The ten-year-old made a face. "Why would you be a better person? Pretending you don't feel something is lying."

"I don't think it's lying if you choose *not* to tell another person something you're thinking. Lying is the act of deliberately saying something you know to be false."

"Well…" Now she frowned.

"Anyway, just to be practical. Don't you get in trouble at school when you get really mad and act out?"

"Yeah. I get detention."

"Wouldn't you rather not?"

Sounding grudging, Sophia said, "Maybe. I don't know."

"Well, think about it." She tilted her head. "The bathwater has stopped. Why don't you go use my shower? I'll take these out to the garage, then come back for your nightie."

She got the load ready to start but thought she'd better wait half an hour. Her hot-water tank wasn't that big. Then she washed her hands and went back to making breakfast.

Jack was quiet until he realized she wasn't going to say anything about his bed-wetting, then became so ebullient he knocked over his juice.

Just as he had the previous time, he leaped to his feet and cried, "I didn't mean to!"

"I know you didn't." Suzanne stood to get the sponge. "But you were being kind of wild. You're less likely to knock over your drink if you eat without bouncing around in your chair."

His voice dropped to a whisper. "I didn't mean to," he repeated.

She kissed the top of his head. "Don't worry, kiddo. Sit back down and finish your breakfast."

Chastened, he did, eating without saying a word, his shoulders bowed.

The day was too gray for him to go outside, and she had no toys for him. He colored for a while after breakfast, and finally she let him watch TV again while Sophia returned to her knitting. She liked the idea of making her own scarf.

"I won't take it with me," she decided when Mrs. Burton honked in the driveway right after lunch. "I might make a mistake. I'll wait till next weekend."

"Good idea."

Despite the drizzle, Suzanne walked them out to the car, carrying their bags. She wondered if they had much else to bring when they came to stay for good. Clearly, both needed things to occupy them, Jack especially, or the TV would be on ten hours a day. She had asked them what they wanted for Christmas and had written down a long list. She supposed she could suggest some of it to her brother and sister, although neither had asked for ideas. Thanks to her stepson, Carrie knew what boys Jack's age liked, so Suzanne was pretty sure her Christmas present would be age appropriate. But Gary hadn't had a normal childhood himself, and probably didn't have a clue what seven-year-old boys played with.

Honestly—*she* didn't have any idea. Or only the haziest of ideas. The two boy cousins with whom she'd grown up had been quite a bit older than Jack by the time she'd gone to live with them. Jack had given her a list, thank goodness, or else she'd have to go to a toy store and throw herself on the mercy of the clerks. How humbling to realize how little she actually knew about children!

She was about to go back inside when Tom Stefanec's garage door rolled up. This time, it appeared he hadn't been watching for her because his pickup truck backed out. He stopped when he saw her, turned off the engine and got out.

"I was just heading out to grocery shop and to pick up some primer for that dresser. I think we're going to have to paint it."

She pressed her hands to her chest in mock horror. "Paint it?"

He grinned. "Okay, I deserved that. But this one isn't cherry. Come on, you can take a look."

The wood was bare and white, the drawers neatly stacked to one side. But it appeared the front had been singed at some point, the blackened spots probably the reason the dresser had been painted in the first place.

"I sanded, but short of gouging I can't get all the black," he said. "It's a good, solid piece, though."

"You fixed the drawers?"

"Yeah, they'd swelled. All it took was a little sanding." He lifted one of the drawers from the stack and inserted it, demonstrating how smoothly it slid in and out.

"Wow. You're amazing," she said in all sincerity.

"Like I said, I've always enjoyed woodworking."

Suzanne studied the dresser. "I suppose we should paint it the same color as the chair rail. Hold on. I'll run and get the can so you know what color."

She hurried through her house to the garage and returned with the quart can of paint. "Irish Clover," she told him.

"Can I take this so I can match colors? An oil-base paint will stand up better than a latex like this on furniture, and I might not be able to get the same brand."

"Sure." Suzanne sighed. "I suppose I should go do a few errands, too. It sounds like a letdown after the rest of my weekend."

After a moment's pause, he nodded toward his truck. "You want to come with me? We can get that paint, grocery shop, maybe grab a bite to eat?"

The invitation sounded casual, nothing to cause her heart rate to increase, so she ignored her silly reaction and said, "That sounds great. Maybe grocery shopping is more fun if you have company. If you don't mind waiting a minute while I get my purse?"

"Nope. Take your time."

Once more she hurried into the house, this time to brush her hair and capture it in a ponytail, add a little makeup she'd skipped this morning, and grab her purse and grocery list. She slipped on a jacket and went back out, locking the door behind her.

Tom had closed his garage door and gotten back in the truck. Suzanne went around to the passenger side and climbed in. The interior, of course, was spotlessly clean. She'd have sworn it still had that new car smell, even though she knew he'd been driving this truck for at least two years.

"What other errands did you have?" he asked.

She buckled her seat belt. "Oh, I can skip them."

"It's Sunday. I don't have anywhere to be."

"Well, I thought about popping into a couple of secondhand stores I haven't checked yet. I still need a desk for Sophia's room. And who knows? I might find some other goodie."

"Sounds like fun," he said agreeably, turning to look over his shoulder to back out of the driveway.

Sidelong, Suzanne took in the way his shirt stretched across a powerful chest and arms. For an instant, her gaze slipped lower, to well-worn denim pulled taut over muscular thighs. Her belly cramped with awareness she was shocked to recognize as sexual. It had been so long since she'd felt that zing. It apparently didn't take much to capture her attention: a lift to the grocery store and an invitation to share something like a burger or pizza.

Deliberately looking straight ahead, she tried to dismiss

the moment with humor. Hey, nobody could say she wasn't a cheap date!

Her inner alarm, she ignored.

CHAPTER SEVEN

"GET A LOAD OF THIS." Tom shook his head. "I haven't seen anything that ugly in a long time."

He'd stopped in front of a rustic, home-built entertainment center that was painted burnt-orange and lined with mirrors.

"It shouts 1970," Suzanne agreed, laughing. "Can't you just see it with avocado-green shag carpet?"

"Oh, yeah." Still grinning, he wandered over to a tall bookcase.

He kept an eye on her as Suzanne checked out the couple of desks for sale along with sagging sofas, battered, glass-topped coffee tables and folding metal chairs in the thrift store's furniture section. One was made of white melamine that even from this distance he could see was splintered in several places. The other might have possibilities.

"What do you think?" she asked, when he joined her.

This was the third store they'd visited. So far, they'd found zilch.

Tom crouched to open drawers and tip the desk so he could study the underside. Finally, he shook his head. "Lousy construction. We can do better."

"Apparently not today," she said with a sigh.

"You know, there's a place up on Highway 99 I pass every day that looks promising. Why don't we go see if it's open?"

"I'm game," she said.

On the drive up to 99, she smiled at him. "You're either very good at hiding acute boredom, or else you have the soul of a treasure hunter."

"You mean, I'm a scrounger?" He grinned back at her. "I didn't know I was, but, damn, I'm having fun. I keep expecting to turn up an eighteenth-century card table. Maybe a Morris chair made by Gustav Stickley."

A Morris chair? What he was really thinking was that maybe life with her would always be like this. Today, he felt reckless. He'd let himself feel the magnetic draw toward a woman he could—maybe did—love, children, a full, noisy, happy home. Everything he wanted, and everything that scared the crap out of him.

Her eyes narrowed. "You know your antiques."

"Just something I like to read about. What about you?"

"If I could afford them, I'd love to have antiques. Mostly, my house is furnished with whatever I can find at garage sales and secondhand stores. Unfortunately, they're all mid- to late-twentieth century discards."

"Yeah, but that's not such a bad thing. Anyway, that cherry dresser is a beauty."

"It looks like it really is an antique, don't you think?"

He agreed. "I was thinking 1880s or nineties."

"So now I have to worry about a ten-year-old kid damaging it."

Tom winced, earning a laugh from Suzanne.

The store was situated on a crummy section of 99, sandwiched between a tattoo parlor and a tavern. The owner, apparently lacking any imagination or sense of the poetic, called it the Second Hand Store. But, dimly seen through dingy windows, the place seemed to be piled with furniture.

Literally, Tom realized, as he and Suzanne entered to the tinkle of a bell on the door. Desks and dressers were stacked along the walls and throughout the warren of rooms. Prices were good, too, he saw after checking the first few pieces at random—higher than they were at Goodwill and Salvation Army, but dirt cheap compared to antique stores.

The only hard part of getting a desk for Sophia's room was deciding which one to buy. They bought a twin-size shelf-headboard, too, that he thought was solid maple under multiple coats of paint. The proprietor helped him load the two pieces in the bed of his pickup truck.

Slamming the tailgate, Tom said, "I'm itching to get that paint off the headboard. Which room did you have it in mind for?"

"I don't know. It would be nice for either of the kids. Maybe Jack's? He's bound to have more toys and little stuff." She waited while he unlocked the passenger side door. "Um…I didn't mean to assume that you'd refinish these, too."

"I'm having a good time doing it. You're giving me a good excuse." *To woodwork?* he asked himself just a little sardonically. *Or to see her?*

Her teeth worried her lower lip. "Can I say thank you again?"

"You're welcome."

They agreed on Fred Meyer next because they could get

both the paint he needed and their groceries there. He brought the half-used can of paint in with him. The dried drips down the side were perfect for matching.

Tom and Suzanne both took carts, and she followed him to the paint department. She stood so close to him when he studied paint chips, he had to work not to be too conscious of the faint, fruity scent that came from her sleek dark hair. Raspberry?

While they waited for their chosen paint to be mixed, she smiled at him. "This is so much fun. It's like decorating a nursery, except my babies are exceptionally mature."

"And sleep through the night," he agreed.

Her chuckle was the prettiest sound he'd ever heard.

Next stop was linens, where she hoped to find a laundry hamper for the kids to use. Tom wasn't surprised to see her face light up at the sight of colorful towels and ceramic soap dispensers.

"Ohh! I could redo the kids' bathroom, too. It's so boring now." She stroked a nubby, bright red cotton bath mat, then slapped her own hand and put both back on the handle of the grocery cart. "No. Stop me. I have to finish what I've started first."

Taking his cue, Tom said, "Hampers. Looks like they're on the back wall."

She picked out a round hamper along with two wicker wastebaskets, one for each bedroom, then added a simple white ceramic toothbrush holder.

Giving him an apologetic look, she said, "Would you mind if we stop in the toy department before we tackle groceries? I'm still not done with my Christmas shopping."

He couldn't remember the last time he'd enjoyed shopping so much. Did Suzanne have any idea how expressive her face was? Her face glowed with delight when she found what she wanted, dimmed when she didn't. She nibbled on her lower lip while she debated over something, and giggled like a schoolgirl when he ventured a mild joke.

Heck, for the pleasure of watching her, he'd have agreed to browse the cosmetics aisle.

Oh, yeah. He was in trouble.

"Don't mind at all. I usually buy a couple of gifts for the Boeing Good Neighbors Christmas drive. They give them out to food bank families. I think I have to have them in by Tuesday."

"Oh, that's nice. I always donate a hand-knit throw to the Social Concerns Board at my church. They adopt several families and buy gifts for all the members."

When she selected a couple of boxes of LEGO, he followed suit. Tom tended to buy for boys, since the tags for girls always seemed to disappear first from the tree.

Somehow he wasn't surprised when Suzanne got sidetracked a couple more times on the way to the grocery section—once in books, where she chose a couple for Sophia, and once in Christmas decorations.

Putting a box of lights in her cart, she had that glow again. "I'm going to go all out this year. It'll be the best Christmas ever."

He hoped like hell those kids didn't ruin her holiday. They seemed nice enough, but their mother had just died a few months ago and their dad had made plain that he didn't give a crap about them. Seemed as if they couldn't help being time bombs, set to go off whenever Suzanne felt safest.

He wasn't about to spoil her mood by issuing warnings, though. She was a smart woman; she knew taking on kids the ages of Jack and Sophia wasn't going to be a cakewalk.

As if it were the most natural thing in the world, he and Suzanne stuck together while they grocery shopped. His list was pretty limited. He realized what a rut he was in, seeing his cart through her eyes. There were two or three frozen entrées he rotated through every week, a steak for one night, frozen peas and corn, russet potatoes he liked to fry up, beer and soda, packages of cookies.

In contrast, she bought mostly fresh ingredients, obviously with the intention of actually cooking. Fresh broccoli, cauliflower and green beans, salad makings and fruit. She bought whole-wheat flour, several cans of pumpkin, evaporated milk and raisins in the baking aisle.

"I make great pumpkin bread," she explained. "Plus I'm doing the pies for Christmas Day."

"Your brother going to be out for Christmas?" Tom asked. He'd met Gary Lindstrom when he'd visited this fall, and had been impressed with how hard Lindstrom worked to help out his sister. The gutters on her house had been damn near clogged until he'd cleaned them, and he'd built shelves and hung Peg-Boards in her garage, borrowing a ladder from Tom.

She added a half gallon of non-fat milk to her cart. "Didn't I tell you? He's not only coming, but he's getting married right after Christmas!"

Her *Didn't I tell you* sounded so chummy. Seemed she was forgetting that up until a couple of weeks ago, they had exchanged only the barest of courtesies. He knew about the kids and not much else. "Married?"

"Did you meet my first caseworker?" She pursed her lips. "No, I guess you wouldn't have had any reason to. Well, she and Gary fell in love." She told him how they'd met the day Gary had arrived unexpectedly for the visit. "I may be lousy at marriage myself, but apparently I have talent as a matchmaker. Both my sister *and* my brother."

"There's another story I haven't heard."

She laughed. "Carrie married the private investigator I hired to find her and Gary. You've probably seen Mark when he's been over. He does other P.I. stuff, but he specializes in adoption searches. Well, he found Carrie all right."

Tom grinned. "Okay, I'll admit you do have a talent."

With exaggerated woe, she said, "Of course, I lost the chance to have Carrie live with me for a year while she went back to graduate school. She married Mark instead. *And* I lost my caseworker. So maybe I shouldn't be too pleased with myself."

"But you gained a brother- and sister-in-law."

"That's true. And I adore both." She gave him a dazzling smile. "So, you're one of those rare people who sees the cup as half-full."

He wouldn't have called himself an optimist. On the other hand, he didn't let himself get too depressed, either. "What about you?"

He knew already—for someone who'd had as many crummy things happen to her as Suzanne Chauvin had, she still shone with faith and hope. Both had made her an easy mark for her scumbag of an ex. Somehow she'd convinced herself over and over again that he didn't mean what he'd just said, that really he loved her.

"I have setbacks," she confessed, reaching for a box of cereal. "But I guess I do tend to believe, somewhere deep inside, that everything will work out for the best."

"And that everyone has good intentions?"

She made a face at him. "You think I'm foolish, don't you?"

He shook his head. His voice became husky. "I think you're an extraordinary woman."

Her eyes widened and her cheeks flushed before she turned her face away. "Oh," she said softly, then rallied. "That's a nice thing to say. Thank you, Tom."

He cleared his throat. "You're welcome."

After a moment, they started forward down the aisle again, Tom cursing himself. What in hell had gotten into him, to say something like that? He didn't want to scare her off!

After a minute, she asked, "What do you usually do for Christmas?"

"Up until a couple of years ago, I went to a friend's house. We were Rangers together. After I got out, he was stationed at Fort Lewis. His kids think I'm their uncle."

She smiled. "And you happily spoil them."

"Yeah, I do."

Her expression become serious again, even worried. "You said 'up until a couple of years ago'? What happened?"

"He was transferred to Fort Bragg."

They were in the checkout line when she said, "What about your parents? Are they alive?"

"Only my father. He retired in Florida."

They didn't have much to say to each other. Never had. Tom hadn't once heard his father express grief after losing first his daughter, then his wife. Career Army, Roger Stefanec had always been a hard man, closed-in and stern. Although he sometimes regretted having done so, Tom had followed in his father's footsteps when he'd enlisted, but he ran regular self-evaluations to be sure he wasn't becoming like his father in any other way.

Tom helped Suzanne unload her groceries onto the checkout conveyor, then started on his while the clerk rang up her purchases. She in turn waited while he paid for his, and they went out to the pickup together. He'd brought a cooler with a couple of ice packs for their frozen food, so they wouldn't have to hurry home. Then they decided on Pagliacci's for pizza.

Once there, they wrangled like old friends over what to have on the pizza, filled their glasses with soda and found a booth. It was early, and this being Sunday the place wasn't busy.

"Okay," Suzanne said. "I've known you for—what? Five years—and I have no idea what you do for a living."

His mouth quirked. "I think we've known each other for more like two or three weeks."

"Okay, two or three weeks. Here you know all my deep, dark secrets, and I don't know beans about you."

"I work at Boeing. I'm a lead in planning."

Even after he explained, she didn't completely understand what he actually did. Only that somehow planners transformed engineering design into doable procedures.

"Means sitting at a desk all day, but the money is good and there's enough variety to keep me interested." He shrugged. "Don't know what else I can tell you."

Their number was called, and he went to the counter to get the pizza, returning with it and a pair of plates.

Suzanne reached for a piece. "Yum."

For a minute they concentrated on dishing up, with him trying to pretend he didn't find the sight of her curling a strand of cheese around her finger and then nibbling it off erotic as hell.

After eating with apparent gusto for a few minutes, she asked, "Would you have stayed as career Army if you hadn't gotten hurt?"

"I don't know. I was starting to feel like I was getting too old for Special Ops. That's a young man's game. Maybe I was getting disillusioned, or just tired of not staying in one place. So in one way, I was glad of an excuse to get out."

She nodded seriously, her dark eyes grave and sympathetic. The better he knew her, the more beautiful she'd become to him. He didn't just see the perfect curve of her mouth, the delicacy of her cheekbones and jaw, the dark wing of brows and how smooth and white her skin was. Now he also saw the shyness in her gaze, her sweetness and the worry she tried to hide.

Was there any chance when she looked at him she saw anything but a nice guy who'd be a great friend? Tom's gut twisted every time he thought of some other lucky son of a gun persuading her to trust and love him.

Why couldn't it be him?

He realized suddenly that he was staring and that her cheeks were turning pink. A woman in her thirties who still blushed. There was something old-fashioned about Suzanne Chauvin, and maybe that was what attracted him most of all. Maintaining her dignity counted with her, not something you could say about many people these days.

"I'm sorry." He picked up another slice of pizza. "What did you ask me?"

"I was wondering whether you joined right out of high school."

"I got in a couple of years at a community college first. But I didn't know what I wanted to do with my life, and since my dad was Army, joining seemed logical. I guess it was the easiest path."

"Has anybody ever called boot camp easy?"

"Physically, no, but that wasn't an issue for me. I've always been strong." He frowned, trying to figure how best to explain. "It's the part where you hand over all decision making to someone else that's easy. I always felt like it was a cop-out for me."

"You're being hard on yourself. A flunky at IBM doesn't make decisions, either. Or a law-school graduate at a big firm. They scramble to do what they're told. What's any different about the Army?"

"You've got a point there," he admitted. "I guess I've always been a little disappointed in myself for not resisting the pressure to join up. I always said I wouldn't." He gave a grunt of humor. "Mostly to rile my old man, I suspect. But I'd look off the base and see a whole big world out there different from what I knew. I wanted my life to be different. But then I actually got out there and I felt lost, so I went running home to Mama, so to speak."

He'd never articulated it so clearly before, even for himself. The truth was, he'd enlisted because he knew he'd be good at being a soldier, and he didn't know what else he could be good at.

Hanging around with other kids—regular kids—he'd quickly realized that the kind of discipline he was used to wasn't the norm, that they had talked back to their parents without getting the crap whaled out of them. They were used to having opinions and arguing for them. He didn't know how.

Maybe the Army had been a good choice for him at that age. He'd grown up, gained confidence in himself, faced the challenge of becoming a Ranger, where thinking on your feet—yeah, making tough decisions—*was* encouraged. And he was damn good at what he did. The funny part was, from the day his doctor had told him his knee was never going to be stable enough to allow him to return to active duty, he'd reverted and gone back to feeling one hell of a lot like the bewildered kid he'd been when he was eighteen and nineteen. A stranger in a strange land.

"That sounds pretty normal to me," Suzanne said. "Most teenagers go through a phase of rebelling against their parents' values, but then they find their way home, too."

"I never thought of it that way." Could it be that she was right? If so, what did that say about him? Why did he walk through life with a perpetual sense of alienation? The Army had never felt like the right fit for him, but neither did civilian life.

Tom had a suspicion it all came back to his sister's death. His dad never had been what could be called warm, but after Jessie had died, both his parents had withdrawn. Silence had settled over their government-issue house, and it had never really lifted. Boys his age didn't know how to talk about death, so he'd pretended nothing had happened with his friends. It got to be a habit, that sense of standing apart from the people around you, not sharing what you felt.

"I sure didn't know what I wanted out of life when I was eighteen or twenty," Suzanne continued. "I went to college, I got married, I found a job. A boring job. It wasn't until a year ago that I really examined myself enough to understand why I wasn't happy with my life."

"You threw your husband out a lot longer ago than that."

"That's true," she agreed, "but that was just a first step. I kept feeling…empty. Oh, I don't know how to explain."

She didn't have to. He knew exactly what she meant.

"The first step for me was deciding to keep the promise I made myself when I was little that someday I'd find my brother and sister and we'd be family again."

Tom nodded.

"Mark Kincaid—the P.I.—gave me this lecture early about how I shouldn't expect too much from finding my sister and brother. He said people doing that kind of search often imagine they'll be happy once they have family again. That everything wrong with their lives will be right again. They depend on the found person to fulfill them. I didn't think that, not consciously, but I know now that I was guilty of having too high expectations."

"In what way?" Tom asked. "Sounds like you hit it off with your sister and brother."

"I did." She hesitated. "But what I discovered is that I still wasn't very happy with my life. My dissatisfaction didn't have anything to do with having a sister and brother or not. So, of course, I quit my job. Nothing like taking a big financial risk to fulfill yourself."

"And then take on kids, too."

She laughed ruefully. "I don't do anything by half."

"I take it you don't think remarriage is likely?" Tom was pleased with how casual he made the question sound.

"Well, not in the near future, and I'm thirty-two going on thirty-three. I'm running out of childbearing years," she said frankly. "Besides…I liked the idea of adopting. Because of what happened to Carrie and Gary. They got split up, you know, and his adoptive home wasn't a very happy one. So I was a sucker for the idea of taking two kids so they could stay together."

"Yeah, I can see that." He still thought it was a shame she was so determined to be a single mother. As beautiful as she was, he knew damn well there must have been plenty of men interested since her divorce. Yeah, her ex was a creep, but most women remarried anyway.

She pushed her plate away and rested her elbows on the table. "I just hope…"

"It works?"

Her smile wasn't totally convincing. "Read my mind."

"Why wouldn't it?"

"I don't know. Sophia scares me a little. Sometimes she seems…" She paused again, as if struggling to find the right words. "I don't know. As if she doesn't feel the same things most people do."

He leaned back. "You mean about her mother?"

A long breath escaped her. "I suppose that's most of it. I just get the sense sometimes that she's intellectually curious about other people's reactions to her, but doesn't emotionally care. If that makes sense."

"Yeah, it does, but couldn't that be a front?"

"Are ten-year-olds that good at putting up a front?"

He remembered himself after his sister had died, pretending to all his friends that he hadn't changed. "Oh, yeah. They can be."

"She is really protective of Jack, which says something about her. So I'm probably worrying for no reason."

"You're afraid she's like kids who've grown up in orphanages or a string of foster homes and never really bonded with anyone. You know that isn't the case with her."

"That's true, although she's certainly had a weird childhood."

"And she's developed coping skills. Of course she doesn't act like a normal kid her age."

Forehead crinkled, she searched his face as if for reassurance. Then, suddenly, she laughed. "Listen to me begging for reassurance. Has anyone ever told you what a good listener you are?"

Great. She thought of him as a friendly ear.

"Or maybe it's just me." She gave a little nod, as if deciding once and for all. "For some reason, I can talk to you. At this speed, you're going to wish we still barely knew each other."

He recognized that she was once again asking for reassurance, and he had no trouble giving it.

"No. I won't wish that."

For an unguarded moment, their eyes met. He didn't know what his held, whether his voice had changed timbre, but she flushed a little and looked away.

Instinct told him to lighten the moment. Making his tone jocular, he said, "Hey, if we hadn't gotten friendly, I'd be looking for something to do every weekend instead of having a project waiting out in the garage."

As he'd hoped, Suzanne laughed, her self-consciousness forgotten. "Is that a euphemistic way of saying I'm using you?"

"No, it's a euphemistic way of saying I don't mind being used."

"Oh." She nibbled on her lower lip. "Has anyone ever told you you're a nice man?"

A nice man. A good listener. Apparently he was a real exciting guy.

But at least she *was* talking to him instead of scuttling into her house when she caught sight of his pickup coming down the block. Maybe, given his deep wariness about love and ever-after, he should be grateful she still saw their friendship as uncomplicated.

So he took what he could get, said, "I hear it all the time," and was gratified by her laugh.

CHAPTER EIGHT

MELISSA STUART INTERVIEWED both children Monday afternoon and then came to Knit One, Drop In to spend a couple of hours talking to Suzanne—and left her shop with the class schedule after expressing an interest in learning to knit. She declared herself satisfied that all concerned were ready for the big step.

Moving day. She was actually getting her miracle—kids by Christmas.

By Wednesday morning, Suzanne didn't know whether she was more excited or terrified. She'd once again asked Rose to handle the store all day so she could be home.

Melissa brought the kids herself and was opening the trunk when Suzanne came out of the house.

"Hey, guys!" she said. "Guess what? You have beds now."

"You mean, we each have one, in our own rooms?" Sophia asked, as if the concept still amazed her.

"Yep." Suzanne gave Jack a quick squeeze in passing, even though he hadn't rushed to her. At least he didn't reject physical intimacy. She'd better hurry up and teach him to hug now, before he got to the age when he wouldn't be caught dead hugging a parent.

Suzanne joined Melissa at the rear of the car and gazed inside the trunk in dismay.

It wasn't a quarter filled. A couple of duffel bags, a few cardboard boxes, and that was all they had brought of their former life. Suzanne hadn't expected anything else. After all, their life with their mother had been transient. But still…she thought, appalled. Clearly they needed everything, and between the Christmas shopping she'd done this week and the money she'd spent on furniture and getting their rooms ready, her budget was shot.

Quelling the anxiety, she told herself they'd manage with what they had, and they could continue to manage until she could afford more. At least now they did have a real home with their own bedrooms, and that was a big start, wasn't it?

"Nothing heavy from the look of it," she said.

Their bedrooms were almost completely furnished. Last night, she and Tom had carried the second dresser from his garage into Jack's room. With the beds that had arrived yesterday and were now all neatly made up, the kids' bedrooms needed only artwork and messes and sleepovers to make them real, like the Velveteen Rabbit.

Suzanne knew that today Tom was working on the bookcase headboard for Jack's room. He'd been disappointed in the wood once he'd stripped it, so they had decided to paint it kelly-green to match the chest of drawers.

Melissa piled two cardboard boxes atop each other and lifted them. Galvanized, Suzanne took a duffel bag and a plastic grocery bag stuffed full of clothes, and led the way into the house.

Jack, carrying his school book bag, hurried to Suzanne's side to lead the way. "This bedroom is mine," he said importantly, then stopped in the doorway, his jaw dropping. "Oh, wow!"

"You like it?" Suzanne lifted the duffel bag. "Is this yours, or Sophia's?"

"It's mine," his sister said, so Suzanne turned the other way, into Sophia's bedroom.

"Tom's working on a desk we bought for you, but it's not done yet." Suzanne set the bag down on the bed. "But at least you have drawers for your clothes. And I bought a package of hangers for each of your closets."

"Cool." The ten-year-old sat down on the edge of the new twin bed and gave an experimental bounce. "It's new? I mean, brand new?"

"Yep. Do you think it's going to be comfortable?"

She bounced again and then nodded. "I never had a new bed before."

Coming into the bedroom with another bag in her arms, Melissa said, "Wow, this is gorgeous! Did you pick out the color, Sophia?"

She nodded. "I wanted my room to be different. Special."

"You succeeded." Melissa stroked the satiny top of the cherry dresser while looking at the bright comforter and sherbet-orange walls. "It's exotic, like something out of *Arabian Nights.*"

"It's going to be even better, once I hang pictures and stuff. And I'm going to have my own desk, too."

Melissa smiled at Suzanne. "You've gone all out."

"You know who really has is Tom," Suzanne admitted.

"I painted the bedrooms, but he's the one who's refinished the furniture. He's such a perfectionist, he does a beautiful job, doesn't he?"

"I didn't know you two were friends." There was something a little funny in her tone, a stiffness.

Suzanne didn't know what he'd told her about their relationship, but she wanted to make sure Melissa knew he wouldn't have lied about those domestic disturbance calls because he was a friend of hers.

"All the years I've lived here, we've never done more than wave in passing," she said. "But then he met the kids and offered to haul any furniture I bought because he has a pickup. When he saw Sophia's dresser, he offered to strip it for me, and I think he got hooked. He insists that he loves woodworking, and I've been too grateful to argue."

Visibly relaxing, Melissa laughed. "You'd be crazy to argue! This dresser is spectacular."

"Tom's also working on a headboard for Jack's room…"

"He gets a headboard?" Sophia asked, her chin jutting. "How come I don't?"

"Because I haven't found one for you yet. I'll keep looking."

"Oh."

On the way back to the car, leaving the kids in their bedrooms, Melissa smiled at Suzanne. "Their bedrooms are wonderful. What a welcome for them."

"I wanted to make them special, since they don't remember ever having their own before. But I'm a little worried at how few clothes they have. Have they shot up lately?"

The caseworker shook her head. "They came into the foster system with almost nothing. Remember that their mother wasn't in any condition to shop, even if she'd had the money. I think most of what they have came from School Bell. They distribute donated clothes to needy children."

Suzanne looked involuntarily toward Tom's garage. "That's a wonderful thing to do, but it must be humiliating for the kids. What if they wear something that a classmate discarded?"

"That's always a risk, but most of what kids wear is mass-produced, so you see the same shirts and jeans all over the place."

"That's true."

"It's pretty much all the kids have ever known anyway," Melissa continued. "Sophia says she remembers when they lived in a rental house, but I don't think Jack does."

"I get the impression they're more excited about having bedrooms than they are about having an adoptive mother."

"Suzanne…"

They were interrupted, and Melissa left without Suzanne having another opportunity to talk to her privately.

"Forget unpacking," Suzanne told the kids. "Let's go pick out a Christmas tree." Usually she put her tree up two weeks before Christmas. Here they were this year with Christmas Eve only four days away.

They both cheered and raced to the car. She made sure she had cord to tie the trunk closed, grabbed her purse and followed.

At the tree lot, she felt as if she had two toddlers with her, the way they tore around and kept disappearing. After

Jack ran into a man bending over to examine the trunk of a Noble fir, she put a firm hand on his shoulder. "Please tell him you're sorry."

Head hanging, Jack mumbled an apology.

The man smiled. "I'm fine. It's Christmas. Kids get excited."

Nonetheless, Suzanne kept her hand on Jack's shoulder. "Now you need to stay with me. You, too, Sophia," she added when his sister stuck out her tongue at him from between cut trees.

Popping out, Sophia pointed at the aisle she'd been investigating, where the Noble and Grand firs leaned against supports of raw two-by-fours. "These trees are the prettiest."

"*And* the most expensive. We either get a teeny tiny one, or we can get a bigger one of those." She waved toward the Douglas firs.

"Oh." For a moment she looked crestfallen, then went to study the more common, sheared firs. "These are okay, I guess. We should have a big tree."

"Yeah, a big tree!" Jack chimed in.

They finally agreed on one. Suzanne paid and the tree-lot attendant helped load it and tie down the trunk.

The kids chattered excitedly all the way home and trailed her to the garage when she went to get the stand and her boxes of lights and ornaments. She had trouble getting either child to help by holding the tree while she centered it in the stand and tightened the screws. All they wanted to do was take ornaments out of the boxes and say, "I get to put this one on the tree!"

Finally, she wrapped the string of lights around the

branches, plugged it in and made sure no bulbs were burned out. She put in a cassette of Christmas carols and announced, "Time to decorate!"

She sang along happily to the carols as they hung ornaments.

"I don't know the words," Jack said a couple of times.

"You know 'Rudolph.' Everyone knows 'Rudolph,'" his sister said, as if he were stupid for not remembering the words. But Suzanne noticed she didn't sing along, either.

Had they even celebrated Christmas in the recent past? She didn't want to spoil the mood today by asking, and tried not to think of them last Christmas, living in a shelter.

She put the star on top because she was tallest, but mostly she let them decorate. Of course they put too many ornaments on, not wanting to leave any in the boxes, and the lower branches that Jack could reach best were most crowded. There was no color theme, just bright shiny balls next to wooden and felt and tin ornaments she'd acquired through the years. But when they were done, and they all stood back to admire the tree, both of their faces shone.

"It's so beautiful," Sophia whispered.

"It's the best Christmas tree ever," Jack said reverently.

"It *is* beautiful," Suzanne agreed, blinking away tears at the wonder she saw on their faces. She knew forming this new family wouldn't always be as easy as today had been. She needed to store moments like this away to remember.

With determination, she sounded upbeat instead of weepy. "Now, what do you say to some hot chocolate?"

"Yeah!" they both cried and thundered toward the kitchen.

Shaking her head and laughing despite misty eyes, she

followed. Clearly, life in this house would never move at the same relaxed pace again.

JACK WENT TO THE LIVING ROOM to watch TV when Suzanne started dinner, but Sophia sat at the table kicking her heels against the chair leg and watched.

Suzanne took the opportunity to ask, "Does Jack believe in Santa Claus?"

Sophia nodded. "I haven't for years, but he still does."

"Your mom managed?"

"When she didn't have any money, she went to Christmas House. You know, where people can pick out presents?"

Suzanne nodded. Donated gifts were displayed just like in a store, and low-income people could shop there for family members.

"Last Christmas we were in a shelter, and the ladies there helped."

"Did you ever open presents on Christmas eve? Or always in the morning?"

In her best you-don't-know-anything voice, the ten-year-old said, "You're *supposed* to open them in the morning. 'Cause that's when Christmas is."

"When I was really little, before my parents died, we opened some on Christmas eve and then the ones from Santa Christmas morning. I like evening, when the lights on the tree and outside are the prettiest."

"We only got presents from Santa," Sophia said.

"Maybe this year we can open some on Christmas eve and the rest in the morning." Waiting for the pan to heat, Suzanne said, "I was thinking of inviting Tom to join us.

He doesn't have any family to spend the holiday with. Would that be okay with you?"

She shrugged. "I don't care."

"Christmas Day, after we open presents, we'll be going down to my sister's house in Seattle. You can meet her stepson, Michael. He's a year older than Jack. And my brother and his fiancée will be there, too, along with her mom and some other people."

"Is there anyone my age?"

"No, except for you two, the only kid so far is Michael."

"Who's Michael?" Jack asked from the doorway.

She had to explain again about the relatives, and he gave his blessing as well to her inviting Tom Stefanec to join them on Christmas eve and maybe Christmas Day, too.

Both were on their best behavior at the dinner table, although Suzanne discovered that Jack didn't think he liked broccoli. Or, as became apparent when she queried him, almost any other vegetable except for peas.

"Oh. I like corn," he added. "'Specially on the cob."

"I like corn, too," Suzanne said. "But I'll tell you what. I'm going to ask you to try one bite of your vegetable every night, no matter what it is. And one bite of new foods, too. Because lots of what I cook *will* be different than what you're used to eating."

He stared down at his serving of broccoli, his face stricken. "I have to take a bite of *that?*"

"Yep." Suzanne noticed that Sophia was mutilating hers with the fork but hadn't actually eaten a bite either. "That goes for you, too," she said, raising her brows and looking at this child who someday she would think of as her daughter.

"Yeah!" Jack stuck out his tongue at his sister. "It's not just me who hasta eat gross stuff."

Suzanne waited. Both finally, reluctantly, ate a tiny nibble. Jack made horrible faces, then gulped milk.

"So, what did you think?" Suzanne asked.

Sophia looked surprised. "It's okay."

"I think it's dis-gusting," Jack said with relish.

"But good for you."

They were considerably happier with the apple cobbler she'd made for dessert.

After dinner, Suzanne helped Jack put away his small store of possessions. She realized right away that he needed shelves down at his level for toys. And maybe plastic bins to corral LEGO and other small stuff. Besides clothes, all he owned were a few well-worn stuffed animals, two metal Hot Wheels cars, both showing chipped paint, a plastic T. rex that he was proud of, and a couple of puzzles that he said Melissa had bought for him. Suzanne folded his clothes and put them in drawers, then hung his coat in the closet. The room still looked awfully uninhabited.

She left him dumping puzzle pieces on the floor and went to see how Sophia was doing. She'd heaped all her clothes on the bed and was posing, hand on her hip, in front of the floor-length mirror on the closet door. When she saw Suzanne reflected in the mirror, she turned away quickly.

"Getting your clothes put away?" Suzanne asked cheerfully, as if she hadn't noticed the pile on the bed.

She shrugged in that disconcertingly teenage way.

"Can I help?" Suzanne asked.

"If you want," she said without interest. "My clothes are all ugly."

Suzanne picked up a sweater and put it on a hanger. "I bet you haven't had much new in a while, have you?"

Sophia didn't say anything, just wadded up some underwear and stuffed it in the top drawer of the dresser.

"I decided it would be hard to buy clothes for you for Christmas, since fit is important and I don't know what you like yet." Suzanne started folding shirts and handing them to Sophia to put in drawers. "So I thought we'd go shopping the week after. There are always good sales."

Sophia's head came up. "Shopping? For me?"

"Well, of course for you!" Suzanne smiled at her. "I'll get Jack a few things, too, before you two start back to school, but I doubt he cares what he's wearing."

Those disconcerting blue eyes studied Suzanne as if trying to figure out what the catch was. "Have you got lots of money?"

"No. I opened my knitting store this year, and I'm not making much income from it yet. So I'm living off savings. But I can afford to buy you a couple new outfits. And maybe some jeans and T-shirts, too."

"Before I start school?"

"I'll bet you'd feel more confident the first day in a new school wearing something nice."

She nodded.

"Besides, it'll be fun," Suzanne declared. "Now, would you like to help me put some presents under the tree?"

She had Santa's gifts hidden in the garage, the rest in her closet. Both kids carried them as carefully as if they were made of porcelain. When every gift was arranged beneath the tree and they had all admired it again, Suzanne sent Jack to get ready for bed and agreed that, since Sophia was older, she could stay up for a little while longer. Suzanne got her started on her knitting again, then went to supervise his toothbrushing and to tuck him in.

"You know what?" she said, sitting on the edge of his bed. "We need some books for you. We should have a story time before bed. Let's go to the library tomorrow and check some out."

"You'd read to me even if I can read myself?"

She smoothed his hair back from his forehead, feeling a rush of tenderness. "If you don't mind."

"That'd be okay," he agreed. When she started to stand, knowing it was too soon to kiss him good night, he gripped her hand. "Will you leave the hall light on? I'm not scared or anything," he added hastily, "but I might get lost if I have to get up."

"I'll leave it on for now, and when I go to bed I'll turn on the bathroom light instead, okay?"

"Okay."

"Maybe we should get you a night-light, since this house is new for you."

He nodded. "I'm not scared, but...but if I *get* scared, can I get in bed with Soph?"

"I'd rather she got in bed with you, since I didn't put a mattress cover on her bed."

"Will you ask her if maybe she wants to?"

She smiled again. "I will. Now good night." Firmly, she

turned out the light and left his door half-open, so the glow from the hall fell across the hardwood floor in his bedroom.

She sat down in the living room and picked up her own knitting. Not five minutes later, she heard the patter of feet and Jack appeared. "Is it okay if I get up to go to the bathroom?"

"Of course it is."

Sounds of the toilet flushing and doors opening and closing were followed by a few minutes of silence. Then he came out again. "I'm not that sleepy. Can I stay up till Soph goes to bed?"

Suzanne knew he was sleepy; he'd been drooping the last hour. "She'll be along in a little while, but now you need to go back to bed."

"Oh." His shoulders sagged. "Okay."

Five minutes later, she saw him again and pretended not to. The next time she looked up, he was gone.

When once again he appeared, he said, "Isn't it almost time for her to go to bed?"

"Jeez, don't be such a little kid!" his sister snapped.

"I *am* a little kid," he said with dignity. "I just don't think it's fair."

"I'm older, so it is fair."

He sighed heavily and disappeared again.

Suzanne kept hearing rustling and doors creaking, but decided it was best not to make an issue of it.

Finally, she had Sophia put away her knitting and get ready for bed, too. Teeth brushed, she came back out to the living room. "Jack keeps getting up," she announced. "He wants me to sleep with him."

"Are you okay with that?" Suzanne asked.

"Yeah, 'cause he's scared without me."

"Then it's fine with me." Suzanne tucked them in, leaving them side-by-side in the twin bed.

Feeling wrung out, she collapsed in her chair in the living room. Her first day of being a parent, not just a hostess with overnight guests, and she was exhausted! Would she last the first week?

But this time, at least, the house stayed blessedly silent. Jack was apparently content with his sister. Suzanne was almost sorry she hadn't left the double bed in there. Maybe she should put it back. But she hoped he'd start feeling secure enough soon to be able to sleep by himself.

When the phone rang, she jerked, then had to go to the kitchen for the handset.

"So how'd it go, Mom?" her sister asked.

"I'm worn out," Suzanne confessed. "But really it was a great day. We put the tree up, and they had lots of fun decorating. After we were done, and I saw their faces, I almost cried."

"You're doing a nice thing," Carrie said softly.

"Thank you. But that's not why I did it."

"I know. Which doesn't make it any less of a nice thing."

Suzanne made a noise that could be taken as argument or disagreement, whichever Carrie preferred. Then she asked, "Is Michael as hyper about Christmas as they are?"

"*As* hyper? He's uncontrollable. Last weekend he knocked over the half-decorated Christmas tree because he wanted to put an ornament high on it and he wouldn't wait for one of us to lift him. So while our backs were turned, he dragged the ottoman over, stood on it to reach higher, and then—surprise!—fell against the tree, taking it down with him. Of course he bawled because a couple of ornaments broke. The minute we swept up and reassured him that accidents happen, he was all grins again."

"Jack was content with the lower branches. In fact, they just about touch the floor because they have so many ornaments on them."

Her sister laughed. "Oh, and if you haven't put the presents out under the tree yet, I don't recommend it. They're like the polar magnet. He absolutely can't stay away from them."

"Too late. And anyway, isn't that half the fun?"

"I had this amazing ability to guess what every present was," Carrie said smugly. "Used to drive my mother wild."

They talked for a few more minutes. Suzanne had no sooner hung up than Rebecca called for the same reason Carrie had. Suzanne hit End after that conversation feeling amazed and lucky at having family again, people who really cared. What a contrast her life was to a year ago, when she would have been welcome at her aunt and uncle's house Christmas Day but invariably felt like an outsider once she got there. How different this year was!

She should have been content after discussing the day with her sister and her sister-in-law-to-be, but she kept looking at the phone and wishing Tom would call, too. She didn't know why he would or even why she wanted him to. But he was the person she'd confided in most these past few weeks, and she wanted to tell him how she'd felt when they'd admired the tree, about Jack's problem with going to bed and how she'd handled it, about every other little detail of the day.

Of course, she could call him. She'd use the excuse of inviting him to celebrate Christmas with them. She should have invited him long since.

Satisfied with her reasoning, she dialed his number from memory, although she didn't know how she could possibly have memorized it so quickly. She hadn't called him more than once or twice.

He answered on the second ring, and she said, "Tom? This is Suzanne, next door."

"The only Suzanne I know." Pause. "I was just thinking about you."

Her heart stuttered.

"And wondering how the day went," he continued, leaving her feeling foolish.

Of course that's what he'd meant. There was nothing romantic between them.

"It went great. Oh, Tom, I wish you could have seen their faces when they finished decorating the tree! They wouldn't have thought the White House tree was any more beautiful. Getting ready for Christmas was the perfect way to start their lives with me."

"That's appropriate. At its heart, Christmas is about a miraculous beginning, isn't it?"

"Yes." How funny. Her eyes were wanting to water again and her voice was choked up. "It is."

If he noticed, he was nice enough not to comment. "I'm glad Jack is so pleased with his room. Kids being kids, they may not have said it, but they appreciated the effort you went to."

"And your effort," Suzanne reminded him.

"It was nothing, just a welcome reminder of a hobby I've let go. I'm going to get back into woodworking somehow. I've let my tools gather dust."

Would he be insulted if she teased him? She bit her lip and dared. "Dust? Tom! I'm shocked."

He laughed. "You've got me. I did clean them regularly. The dust was, uh, metaphorical."

She laughed with him. "I'm sorry, I couldn't resist."

"No reason to be sorry."

Neither of them said anything. The silence grew a little too long for comfort. Suzanne rushed to fill it. "I actually called to ask if you'd join us for Christmas." When he didn't speak immediately, she hurried on. "If you haven't made other plans."

This silence was almost as long. "You mean it?"

Taken aback, Suzanne said, "Of course I mean it. I wouldn't ask if I didn't."

"But you've got family."

"There's no reason friends can't be welcome, too." Her heart thudded, and she realized how anxious she was. Maybe he didn't want to be that good a friend. They'd only known each other a few weeks. She might be sounding really pushy. Or, heaven forbid, as if she was implying something more than friendship by inviting him to a holiday usually spent with family.

When he spoke again, his voice had a rasp she didn't recognize. "I don't have other plans. I'd love to join you."

"Oh, good," she said, on a rush of relief. "If you'd like to come over Christmas eve, I'm just going to make dinner and let the kids open a couple of presents. Nothing fancy.

Even though it's Sunday, I'm going to have the store open since it's such a big shopping day. Then, late Christmas morning we'll all be going to my sister's in Seattle. You won't be the only person who doesn't know everyone. Carrie's adoptive parents and father-in-law are coming, and so is Rebecca's mother." She reminded him who Rebecca was. "And Mark's partner in his P.I. firm is coming, too. They're good friends."

"This is kind of you, Suzanne," Tom said, sounding formal. "I don't particularly look forward to the holiday. This year, I will."

"I'm glad." She swallowed a lump in her throat. "Shall we say six-thirty on Christmas eve? Unfortunately, my shop is open until five."

"Boeing closes down. I'll be home. Is there anything I can do?"

"Do you mean that?" she asked, then laughed at her echo of his earlier question. "You do, don't you? Um…do you bake?"

"Christmas cookies? Pies?"

"Pies is what I was thinking. I've promised to bring two to Carrie's. I was planning to bake them that evening, after the kids were in bed."

"I'll be glad to. I'll make an extra for Christmas eve."

"Thank you."

"No, thank you for inviting me. Good night, Suzanne," he said, voice husky again.

"Good night," she whispered, and hung up, emotions she couldn't quite identify tumbling in her chest.

CHAPTER NINE

THE PIES, TWO PUMPKIN and one apple, cooled on the counter, their fragrance filling Tom's kitchen. In his refrigerator, cookie dough chilled in a dish towel–covered bowl. He'd never made sugar cookies before, but the cookbook assured him that they were easier to roll out and cut when cold than at room temperature.

He went into the living room for the tenth time to check on whether Suzanne and the kids were home yet. This time he was rewarded by the sight of her car turning into the driveway. Tom turned on his porch light and went out, crossing the strip of lawn that separated his driveway from hers. From the bite in the air, the thermometer had to have dipped below freezing.

"Hi," Suzanne said, getting out of her car. "I hope you're not starving. Dinner is going to take a while."

"I should have invited you to dinner instead of the other way around." He shook his head. "Instead, I have a plan for taking these kids off your hands while you slave in the kitchen."

They were hopping out of the car, too. "We were going to help," the boy said.

Suzanne looked beat, and no wonder. She'd taken Wednesday off, but this had to have been a stressful week.

"Here's my idea," he said. "I figured Christmas wouldn't be Christmas without some cookies. Now, maybe you made some yesterday..."

They all shook their heads.

"I could use help in cutting those cookies out and decorating them. If you two are willing, we could get quite a few baked before we're called for dinner."

"What a wonderful idea!" Suzanne exclaimed. "Do you have cookie cutters?"

"I only have three," he admitted. Which he'd bought yesterday, when he'd conceived the plan. "A tree, a star and a Santa."

"What do you guys think?" she asked the kids. "I can send more supplies with you. I'm sure I have sprinkles, if you don't."

"I do." He'd bought half a dozen colors.

"Yeah, that sounds fun," Jack said. "We cut out Christmas cookies last year at the shelter. Remember, Soph? Mrs. Glass helped us? She was the lady there," he explained to the adults. "You remember, don't you, Soph?"

"Of course I remember!" she snapped. Then, with what Tom sensed was pretend reluctance, she said, "Sure, I guess we can help."

The relief in Suzanne's voice was obvious. "Oh, good. Come on with me, guys, and get some cookie cutters I have. Thanks, Tom."

"You're welcome." He smiled, even if she couldn't see, and waited while the kids went in with her.

They returned in minutes with a cannister filled with what must have been a dozen or more cookie cutters. Somehow he wasn't surprised; a woman who loved knitting the way she did was just the kind to have a cookie cutter for every holiday.

As indeed she did, he saw when Sophia dumped them out on his kitchen counter. He picked up a fat turkey, and Jack studied a shamrock. But she also had a candy cane, an angel and what he was pretty sure was a reindeer.

Tom got out the dough and rolled it out on a sheet of waxed paper. Then he greased the cookie sheet while the kids pressed their chosen shapes into the dough.

Getting them intact onto the cookie sheet turned out to be a bigger challenge than he'd imagined, but they got better at it as they went along.

They agreed to bake the first couple of sheets undecorated and frost them later. Then they decorated the next ones with sprinkles and red hot cinnamon buttons and tiny silver balls. Jack started to get bored, but Sophia embellished her cookies as carefully as if she were being graded on them and really wanted an A.

"Are we almost done?" Jack asked.

"I'll tell you what," Tom said. "Why don't you call Suzanne and see how dinner is coming along? Smelling those cookies baking is making me hungry."

"Me, too!" the boy agreed.

Tom told him the number to dial and watched as he carefully held the receiver to his ear.

"Hi. It's Jack." He giggled at whatever Suzanne said. "We're getting real hungry." Pause. "Okay. We'll bring some great cookies, too."

He handed the phone to Tom, who pushed End and set it back in its cradle. "Suzanne says dinner will be ready in ten or fifteen minutes. She was gonna call us."

"Ah. Well, we'd better make this our last sheet of cookies, then."

He helped decorate the rest to speed them up, then put them in the oven and set the timer. "What say we wash our hands?"

After they'd done so, they put the cookies on plates, and he added a grocery bag with the ready-made frosting and food colorings he'd bought so they could finish later.

Once the last batch was out, Tom asked Sophia to carry the cookies and Jack the pumpkin pie because he had a few other things to bring. They waited patiently at the front door, neither apparently having guessed what he was talking about. When he appeared from a bedroom with his arms full of wrapped gifts, they both gasped.

"Who are those for?" Sophia asked, eyes greedy as any child's would be.

He pretended to think. "The one on top is for Suzanne, and the others… Well, seems to me they might be for a couple of neighborhood kids."

Sophia grinned in delight.

Jack had to work it out before his face cleared. "For us! You mean, for us!"

Tom smiled. "Could be."

They were so excited, he had to remind them to carry the cookies and pie carefully. It would be a shame to have them splat facedown onto grass that crunched underfoot now from frost.

Everyone on the block had turned on their Christmas lights, brilliant, multicolored jewels wrapping trees and shrubs, shimmering white icicles hanging from eaves. This wouldn't be a white Christmas, but frost sparkled on the grass. Every window glowed a welcome, and in most could be seen a lit Christmas tree.

As they walked between his house and Suzanne's, where the welcome was for him as well, Tom was embarrassed to realize he was getting choked up. These last couple of years he'd tried not to get down about Christmas. It was a holiday for kids, he told himself. Too commercial, anyway. He put up outside lights because everyone else did, and was glad to take them down on New Year's Day.

But this year…this year, he'd been like a kid himself, after Suzanne had invited him. Even though he'd already had something for both Sophia and Jack, he'd gone out to buy more gifts as well as the cookie cutters and baking supplies. He'd darn near counted the hours. Today had seemed interminable. He didn't think he'd been this excited since the last Christmas when his sister had been healthy, and he'd been only eight that year.

They opened the front door to be greeted with the wonderful smell of ham baking. Wearing an apron, Suzanne appeared from the kitchen. She was radiant with her cheeks rosy and her dark hair slipping from the scrunchie meant to hold it atop her head.

"Oh, good, you're here. My goodness, look at those cookies. They're beautiful." When she saw what was in his arms, she said, "You shouldn't have," then laughed.

"But since you did, go ahead and add them to the heaps under the tree."

He did, then followed her and the kids to the kitchen to find her table laid for the holiday with candles and a pinecone centerpiece.

"Cookies here." She directed the operation. "You already washed your hands? Oh, good. Tom, could you slice the ham when I put it on the table? Thank you."

She lit the candles and produced bowls of baked russet potatoes, applesauce and green beans. She offered him wine, but he chose the milk she'd already poured for herself and the kids.

Tom sliced the ham while they all watched, then held out their plates to be served. Sophia and Jack looked perplexed when Suzanne announced, "I'll say grace." She had to explain the tradition, then said a few words of gratitude for all their blessings and this food they were about to eat.

During dinner, they talked about Christmases past, with Suzanne encouraging the children to recall those they'd spent with their mother. Jack talked readily about the ones he remembered, but Tom noticed that Sophia stayed silent. Her expression was one of indifference, though he doubted that was the way she felt.

He saw Suzanne had noticed as well, but she gently responded to Jack's comments and said nothing to make Sophia uncomfortable. She wasn't the only one silent, anyway. Tom couldn't think of an uplifting story to contribute.

It was the nicest dinner Tom could remember having in years. Good food, good company, and a sense of warmth that he knew radiated from the gentle, dark-haired woman who had invited him to be part of her family tonight. She included him as if he belonged here, and he was shocked by how naturally he'd stepped into the "dad at the head of the table" role.

He'd always wanted to try it out. He guessed tonight was his chance.

Too bad tonight and tomorrow would be over in the blink of an eye. For him, this holiday was make-believe. He wasn't Dad anchoring his end of the table; he was a guest.

With the force of a blow, Tom realized how much he wished none of this was pretend. He wanted not just to be a husband and father, but to have *this* woman, these children.

Christmas made everyone sentimental, he told himself. Even his parents had tried at Christmas. This wasn't reality.

He was glad to be pulled from his brooding by Suzanne smiling and saying, "Seconds, anyone? No? Shall we have dessert now, or open presents first?"

"Presents! Presents!" the kids chanted.

She looked at Tom as if he had a meaningful vote, and he smiled. "Presents."

The kids raced to the living room and dropped to the floor beside the tree. Suzanne joined them, sinking gracefully to sit cross-legged where she could read the tags and distribute gifts.

Tom had brought a couple that were for him, one from his father and another from his Ranger buddy and his wife.

"Let's take turns," Suzanne said. "So we can all see what we each got. Jack first, since he's youngest."

Sophia was too agog to argue, for once. She watched as Jack ripped off paper to find a big box of LEGO.

For a minute he just stared. "Wow! Look at that castle!"

"That's cool," his sister agreed. She accepted a present from Suzanne and opened with only a little less haste. Her breath rushed out.

Tom leaned forward from his seat on an ottoman to see what she'd gotten. It was an exquisite porcelain doll, an Indian or Pakistani girl dressed in a vivid sari.

"It's so beautiful," she whispered. Her stunned gaze rose to Suzanne. "Thank you."

Suzanne smiled with such tenderness, Tom's chest burned. "You're welcome."

She handed him the envelope from his father and said, "You next."

He shook his head. "I'm betting you're younger."

Her chin tilted up. "How old are you?"

"Thirty-five."

"Oh. Okay. Fair's fair." She tore hers open almost as eagerly as the kids had, saying, "This one is from Rose, the lady who works for me when I have to take time off." It was a tapestry tote bag that depicted kittens chasing balls of yarn. She laughed. "How appropriate!"

Tom opened next, the envelope from his father. He already knew what it contained: a check. That's what he got every year, although he made a more substantial living already than he needed. But gifts by definition meant you had to know the recipient, and his father had never known him. "Money," he said, and set the envelope beside him.

When he saw which of his gifts Suzanne was handing to Jack for the next round, Tom cleared his throat. "I probably should have discussed this one with you first."

Jack was already ripping, though, and stared in puzzlement when he found only a photo inside.

"I'm going to build you a climber this spring, as soon as the weather clears up." Tom looked at Suzanne. "With your permission."

"Oh, Tom!" Her eyes filled with tears that she quickly blinked away. "That's so generous of you. I've been wishing I could manage one…."

"Hey, now that I've gotten the dust off those tools…"

She laughed, but in a watery way. "Jack, thank Mr. Stefanec. This is a truly incredible present."

"You're going to build one like this?" the boy asked, his eyes wide with amazement. "With a slide, and a fort, and everything?"

"That's the plan," Tom agreed, feeling pretty good about his idea. "It's for Sophia, too, if she's interested, so it can't be a boys-only fort."

"Aw," Jack pretended to complain.

His sister elbowed him, then snatched the picture to look. Sounding awed, she said, "That's like…like at a *playground* or something."

"My presents for you aren't nearly as good," Tom admitted.

He hadn't done badly, though. She seemed pretty happy with the kit to paint finger and toenails that included tiny stickers of stars and peace signs and rainbows, and with the glass-fronted curio cabinet he'd bought for her to display cute collectibles.

"How convenient," Suzanne said, handing her a package. "This ought to go in it nicely."

This was a big-eyed ceramic puppy figurine, poised to pounce.

"To hold you until we decide to get a real dog," Suzanne told her.

Tom held his breath when Suzanne picked up the gift from him, the buying of which he'd agonized over. He hadn't wanted anything too impersonal, but it couldn't be too intimate, either, or too expensive. He'd ended up choosing a necklace that he thought was pretty.

She tore off the paper, then opened the jeweler's box and stared silently for a moment while he waited, tense. When she lifted her head, her eyes were misty and her mouth had a soft curve.

"It's exquisite. Oh! I have to put it on." She lifted out the necklace. Garnets clustered around a tiny diamond to form a cheerful flower pendant on a delicate gold chain. "Shoot," she said, groping behind her neck. "Can you fasten it for me?"

She scooted over so she sat right in front of him. He looked down at her bare nape and slender shoulders. Transfixed by the realization that she wanted him to touch her, to brush his fingers against the silken weight of hair and the skin that he knew would be just as smooth, just as silky, he couldn't move for a moment.

Then he swallowed and reached to take the ends of the fine gold chain from her. Feeling clumsy, he had to concentrate to get the catch fastened. It was with reluctance that he said, "There, got it."

She twisted in place to say, "How does it look?"

As delicate and old-fashioned as she was, it nestled at

her throat just as he'd imagined it. He had to tear his gaze away from the long line of her neck and the hint of cleavage above her T-shirt. "Beautiful," he said hoarsely.

"Thank you," she whispered, laid a hand for a moment on his knee, then turned back to face the kids. "Tom's turn," she said. "Sophia, can you bring him that big one?"

The girl scrambled to her feet to carry a plump package to him. It felt like a pillow when he took it from her.

Tom pulled the ribbon off, then carefully opened the paper to expose something he knew instinctively she'd knit. He spread out a blue-gray throw with eight-inch-long fringe, incredibly soft and fluffy.

"It's a silk-angora mix, so it has to be dry cleaned when it's dirty," Suzanne said. "But I think that yarn is luscious."

Damn it, he had a lump in his throat. He stroked the throw to regain his composure, finally lifting his gaze to hers. "You knit this for me?"

She nodded, and for the first time he realized that she was anxious, just as he'd been when she'd opened his gift. She didn't know how much this meant to him.

"I was afraid to use a bright color, since all I've seen is your living room. I hope you don't think this blue is boring."

"Boring? This is..." He had trouble finding words. "It's stunning. It's really nice of you to do this."

Nice. If that wasn't the most inadequate word he knew.

"After everything you've done for us? Are you kidding?"

Of course that's why she'd done it. She wanted to pay him back. Not feel in debt to him. Hiding his disappointment, he smiled. "Call it even."

They'd made a fair dent in the heap of presents under

the tree by the time Suzanne said, "I'm afraid that's it, kids. Well," she laughed, "until morning. But enough to make visions of sugarplums dance in your head tonight, right?"

"What are sugarplums?" Jack asked, predictably.

She went on all fours and kissed the top of his head before sitting back. "I have absolutely no idea, but they sound sweet, don't they?"

He nodded. "Can I open my LEGO?"

"Of course you can. I bought a plastic container just for them." She stood and went to her bedroom, returning with a bright green lidded box. "So we don't sweep them up by accident."

"O-kay!" He happily tore and dumped a cascade of small plastic blocks into the container. Then he got out a flat square that Tom realized was a base and went to work.

Sophia went to put her doll in her bedroom, so it wouldn't get broken. Suzanne went with her, and they returned to say that it looked perfect on the dresser.

Eventually she dished up pie, which they ate in the living room.

Watching the kids and Suzanne, Tom was dizzy with an emotion so unfamiliar, he had trouble identifying it as undiluted happiness. The boy was building with his new LEGO, Sophia sorting her gifts, Suzanne touching the necklace at her throat as if to be sure it was there and also watching the kids.

Finally she turned her head. "Would you like a cup of tea or coffee? Wine?"

"I'm good," he said.

Her mouth curved. "Me, too."

Sophia tried on the hat Suzanne had knit her and went to seek a mirror. She attempted to persuade her brother to play a new game, and when she couldn't drag him away from his construction, she became immersed in one of her new books. Christmas carols played in the background and Jack chattered about what he was building.

Tom knew it was time for the guest to bow out, but he couldn't seem to make himself move. He wanted this life, this family. Tonight he wasn't letting himself be scared. In refusing to leave, he was holding on with both hands like a kid who'd opened someone else's package by accident and didn't want to give back the toy he'd found inside.

Suzanne stretched languidly, pulling her shirt taut across her breasts. "Oh, dear. I'm afraid I have to clean the kitchen."

"I'll help," Tom offered. It was a world-class excuse to stay.

"You don't have to…."

"Sure I do. You cooked."

"If you mean it, I won't say no."

He cleared the table while she emptied the dishwasher, then rinsed dishes and began to load it again. As she put away food and he scrubbed pans, shirtsleeves rolled up, Tom said, "How's it going with the kids?"

"Mostly good." She took a roll of clear plastic wrap from a drawer and covered the ham. "On the surface, Jack is adjusting easily. Well, you've seen him. But I know he can't just unplug from one home and plug in here instead without a glitch. Of course, there's the bed-wetting."

"Every night?"

"I was excited because Jack made it through the first

night dry, but he wet his bed every single night since. Sophia slept with him the first night, but she doesn't like waking up wet. And who can blame her? You wouldn't believe how much laundry I'm having to do."

"Is she afraid to sleep in her own room?" He rinsed a pan.

"I don't think so, although I'm not sure. Really it's Jack. Getting him to bed is like…like trying to stuff an unhappy cat into a carrier to go to the vet's. He keeps popping out with excuses. Then I'll see him peeking around the corner. Then he has to use the bathroom. Then, then, then." She sighed. "I know it's hard for him when he's never had his own bedroom. And I haven't objected to the two sharing a bed. I've even thought of putting the double bed back in there temporarily, but Jack wants *his* bed."

"I was a lot older than he is, and I was scared to go to bed by myself after my sister died." Now, where had that come from? Tom wondered. He hadn't thought about that in twenty years.

"Really? Did you two share a bedroom?"

"Yeah, we were in base housing," he explained. "The place only had two bedrooms. When she got really sick, my parents had me sleep on the couch in the living room. Then, suddenly, she was gone, and I was supposed to go back into that bedroom and be by myself in the dark."

"How did your parents handle it?" she asked, stopping with the dish towel in her hands and her head tilted to one side.

As matter-of-factly as he could, Tom said, "My father said he'd use his belt if I came out of that bedroom before morning." *That goddamn bedroom,* was what his father had really said.

"Oh, Tom!" She laid her hand on his bare forearm and then snatched it back quickly, as if embarrassed. "How awful."

Not many days after his father's ultimatum, Tom had puked in bed and been afraid to open the door to ask for his mother. He'd lain rigid in bed until morning, when he'd lied and said he must have been asleep when he'd thrown up.

"Not much help to you, I'm afraid. I don't recommend his technique."

"No wonder you're not close."

"He's a hard man. In fairness," he said, although he didn't like to be fair where his father was concerned, "I think he was raised that way himself."

"Was he nicer to your sister?"

Tom thought back as he set another pan in the drainer. "She was a girl. She didn't have to be toughened up."

She looked directly at him. "How on earth did you manage to turn into such a kind man?"

He grinned, if crookedly. "I rebelled."

She opened her mouth, probably to chide him for making light of something so grim to judge from her indignant expression, but Sophia wandered into the kitchen just then, requesting Christmas cookies.

"Me and Jack are hungry."

"How on earth could you be?" Suzanne shook her head, but poured two glasses of milk and allowed the girl to take two cookies apiece out to the living room.

When Sophia was gone, Tom said, "You want my

advice? I think you're doing the right thing with Jack. He'll get used to having his own room. And don't make too much of the bed-wetting. He's had a hard time."

"I know he has. Oh, phooey!" she exclaimed. "I shouldn't let him have milk this close to bedtime."

"Does keeping him from drinking during the evening make any difference?"

Suzanne made a face. "Not so far as I can tell. Honestly, I don't know if anything does. He saw a doctor in November, who couldn't find a thing wrong with him and felt it was not unusual for the circumstances."

"Then don't worry about it." He turned off the water after rinsing the last pan and took a look around to realize the kitchen was clean. They were done. His excuse was used up.

He let the soapy water out of the sink, dried his hands and stretched in his turn, almost touching the ceiling.

"I should be getting on home."

She hung up the dish towel. "And I should be getting them to bed. You know they're going to be up at the crack of dawn."

"Santa?"

"Despite the lack of chimney." She lowered her voice. "Santa is bringing him a B-I-K-E."

"He can probably spell that word."

"I suppose he can. I haven't seen him read yet. Melissa said he's good in math but struggling with his reading. I read stories to him at bedtime last night, but I'll wait until he starts school and I can talk to his teacher to see what I can do to help."

Tom nodded. "Makes sense. So, what's the plan for tomorrow?"

"I thought we'd leave about noon."

"Works for me. Suzanne, thank you for including me tonight." *Let me stay. Let this be real.*

"It was a much nicer Christmas with you here." She flashed him a grin. "I'd still be scrubbing pans if you hadn't been here to do it."

"I can be a handy fellow," he agreed, half joking and half not. He could be indispensable if only she'd keep him around for good.

"It felt right having you here tonight. And your presents for the kids…and me—" she touched her necklace "—were wonderful."

"I'm glad you liked them." He never felt he was great with words, but he tried. "That afghan you made for me is special. One of the nicest presents anyone has ever given me."

"I'm glad," she said, too, her voice soft. "Isn't it funny…"

"Isn't what funny?" he asked when she didn't finish.

"Oh, I was just thinking how far we've come in only a few weeks. How is it we managed to live next to each other for so long without getting to know each other?"

He told the truth. "You always looked scared of me."

"Oh, dear." She pressed her hands to her cheeks. "It was that obvious?"

"Afraid so," he said with gentle amusement. "I saw you scooting into the house at the sight of my truck turning the corner enough times."

She lowered her hands, leaving her cheeks pink. "You know I wasn't scared, don't you? Just embarrassed."

"I wish I *had* known and could have told you there wasn't any reason for you to be."

"The kids are a blessing in more ways than one."

He saw it that way, too. "I'll just go say good night to them...."

He collected his gifts from the couch and said his good nights. Suzanne went to the door with him. When he turned back to thank her one more time, she stunned him anew by rising on tiptoe and kissing his cheek.

"Merry Christmas."

Tom managed to say a gruff, "Merry Christmas," and headed home, hearing the door shut behind him.

Thank God he hadn't seen that coming, he thought, stumbling across the dark lawn. Because if he had, he didn't know if he could have resisted the temptation to turn his head and meet her lips with his.

CHAPTER TEN

SUZANNE DIDN'T HEAR THE KIDS get up the next morning, but Jack's whoop of joy jarred her out of sleep and to a sitting position. What…? And then she remembered. Christmas morning. The bike with a huge red bow tied to the handles.

Smiling, she got up, put her bathrobe on and went out to the living room. Jack stood astride his bike, pretending he was steering it.

And he had on the same pajamas he'd gone to bed in, and they were dry.

"I never had a bike before," he said when he saw her.

Sophia was quiet, watching him. Suzanne worried that she was hurt that nothing so grand was under the tree for her. She'd been a lot harder to shop for. She probably still enjoyed playing with Barbie dolls, but had to be starting to notice boys. Her interest in toys was bound to be short-lived, but teenage stuff was probably premature. And when Suzanne had floated the idea of a bike, she hadn't seemed interested.

"Let's see what else Santa brought," Suzanne suggested.

Jack ripped paper and flung it in heaps, apparently delighted with the superhero figure he'd put on his Christmas list, an addition to his LEGO set and a soccer ball.

Sophia opened her presents more slowly, head bent. Suzanne, having realized it would be the perfect size, had given her a sweater she'd knit for one of the patterns she'd sold. Sophia had said she liked to draw and paint, so her big present was a drawing set with charcoal and colored pencils and a fat book of blank, creamy paper.

She unlatched the wooden case and touched all the pencils, thumbed through the paper, then closed it up again. "Thank you."

This was a child who was usually volatile, not withdrawn. What was bothering her?

All Suzanne could do was smile and say, "You're welcome."

Sophia offered to frost the cookies left undecorated yesterday, and Suzanne left her to it while she showered and got dressed.

She asked Jack if he'd like to go try his bike, but he was engrossed in his LEGO and a movie and said, "Maybe later."

When mid-morning came and she sent them off to get dressed, she wished belatedly that she'd bought them some new clothes so they would look their best today. Chances were nobody in the family would get really dressed up, but she didn't know for sure. And even relaxed on a holiday didn't mean grungy jeans and sweatshirts.

To think, the last Christmas she and her brother and sister had spent together, she'd been five, Gary two and Carrie a baby, fascinated by the bright lights on the tree. Now, finally, they would all be together again today.

When she saw Jack, she didn't say anything about his choices because his wardrobe had no better alternatives.

Sophia emerged from her room wearing her new sweater over jeans and shoes even more tattered than Jack's.

"Do you like the sweater?" Suzanne asked. "It looks really cute."

She shrugged. "Yeah, it's cool."

Hiding her disappointment at the lack of enthusiasm, Suzanne said brightly, "Let's go see if Tom is ready."

He was, and offered to drive. His pickup was an extended cab, and the kids were enthusiastic.

"I wish we could ride in back," Jack said wistfully.

His sister curled her lip. "That's dumb. We'd freeze."

"I'm afraid it's not safe," Suzanne said. "Sophia, we don't have to call each other's ideas 'dumb.'"

"Well, it is," she muttered, and climbed in.

Sophia sighed and met Tom's sympathetic gaze.

The drive passed quickly, thanks in large part to Tom, who made pleasant conversation, answered Jack's incessant questions and got Sophia to talk about her art after she told him about the drawing set.

"A teacher last year sent this picture of mine to a contest, and I won a ribbon."

"Really?" Suzanne turned in her seat. "That's wonderful!"

"Your teacher must have really thought she saw talent," Tom said. "Do you enjoy drawing?"

"Yeah, I do it a lot. Sometimes when I'm supposed to be doing other things."

Tom laughed. "Tempting, isn't it? After all, you've got a pencil in your hand, paper in front of you…"

"That teacher was nice about it. The one I had while we lived with Mrs. Burton wasn't."

"I'll tell you what," Suzanne said. "When we go into the school, I'll ask whether there's a fifth-grade teacher that has a particular interest in art whose class you could be in."

"I wish we didn't have to go back to school," she mumbled. "You could homeschool us."

"Not and run a business. Besides—" Suzanne cast her a sympathetic smile over her shoulder "—I think it's healthier for us if I'm not having to be the bad guy about schoolwork. And you need to make friends besides."

She hunched her shoulders. "Nobody'll like me. They never do."

"I like you," her brother piped up.

"Big deal." She shrugged.

Suzanne wanted to talk to her about being nicer to her brother, but she wasn't sure yet how much of what she observed was normal sibling interaction and how much was Sophia's way of taking out her feelings of being scared and angry on the only target she knew was safe: the brother who adored her. And Suzanne had to balance the occasional grumpiness with Sophia's generous willingness, despite Jack's bed-wetting, to sleep with him so he felt safe.

"Take the Forty-fifth Street exit," she instructed Tom, and gave directions to the narrow, tree-lined street in the Wallingford district of Seattle where Carrie and Mark owned a 1920s-era brick home.

They were fortunate enough to find parking barely a block from their destination. Carrying cookies, pies and a box of wrapped presents, they walked to Carrie's.

It was a charming house that Suzanne thought of as Hansel and Gretel's cottage, with a peaked roof, old multipaned windows, a wrought-iron railing along the street and a doorway that led only to the garden in back. The kids gaped and hung back when she rang the bell.

The door swung open and warmth and noise spilled out. Carrie hugged Suzanne, then smiled at Tom and the kids. "Welcome. I'm Suzanne's sister, Carrie. In case you couldn't tell."

Anyone could tell because the women looked a great deal alike. So much so that they'd agreed that, if they had met by chance before they'd been reunited, they would have recognized each other instantly. Carrie was a tiny bit shorter, and her dark hair had curls Suzanne envied, her face a hint of the pixie while Suzanne's was more placid.

"I'll be Aunt Carrie to you," she said to Jack and Sophia. "And you have a cousin now. Michael could hardly wait until you got here."

Her husband appeared behind her and pulled her back. "Maybe we should let them in," he suggested good-naturedly.

"Oh, pooh. They could have pushed me out of the way. Here," she said, reaching for a covered dish, "let me take the pies to the kitchen while you put those under the tree and say hi to everyone else. How many pies did you make?"

"Only two. The rest are cookies the kids and Tom made."

"Ohh. Christmas cookies. Michael, they're here," she called.

"He's right behind me," her good-looking, dark-haired husband said.

In the entry, shedding their coats, Suzanne introduced the two men and Sophia and Jack to Michael, who was being inexplicably shy. The two boys hardly looked at each other, just mumbled, "Hello."

Suzanne was glad to see that her kids' clothes weren't too great a contrast to Michael's stiff new jeans, sneakers and T-shirt.

Suzanne's brother came out of the kitchen then. "Did I hear the doorbell? Suzanne! Hey." He submitted to a hug with better grace than he had the first time she'd met him as an adult, when he'd seemed like a wild creature unused to human touch. Rebecca rushed from the back of the house at the sound of voices, and more embraces ensued.

"Mom says she's met you at your shop. Although she didn't know then that you were going to be my matchmaker. Hi," she said, holding out a hand to Tom, "I didn't catch your name?"

As it turned out, Suzanne remembered Mrs. Wilson. They chatted briefly about knitting and the classes she offered. Then Carrie's parents arrived and introductions had to start all over again.

Suzanne watched Gary closely, wondering how hard this was for him. He knew that Carrie's adoptive parents had had the opportunity to adopt both Carrie and him and had chosen not to take him. They'd also told Carrie they'd regretted the decision ever since. Carrie's mom had cried, explaining how lacking in confidence she'd been, how frightened she'd been that she would fail with the angry little boy who was so traumatized by his parents' death and foster care that he'd taken to biting. But Gary had reason to feel bitter, and this was the first time he'd met the couple who could have saved him from a miserable adoptive placement.

To his credit, he was polite if rather expressionless, and Carrie anxiously filled silences. Within moments they were all past the first awkwardness, and people began to break into groups. Suzanne pretended not to notice that Carrie's mother had to blink hard when she turned away.

Carrie and her mom went off to peel potatoes. Mark's father, an older man who looked remarkably like him—no, probably it was the other way around—collected coats and took them to a back bedroom, and Gary raised his eyebrows at the sight of Tom.

"We've met," he said, holding out his hand.

"That's right. Tom Stefanec." They shook.

"Didn't realize you two were friends."

Suzanne cringed at the memory of the things she'd said to her brother about her obsessively neat next-door neighbor. For the first time, it occurred to her that everyone would assume she and Tom were a couple. They'd be, well, *assessing* him, and judging her taste.

"Tom's been my salvation recently," she said hastily. "Wait'll you see the beautiful job he's done refinishing furniture for the kids' rooms. Speaking of..." She turned. "Have you met Sophia and Jack yet?"

He said his hellos. "Michael called me Uncle Gary. Shook me up," he said humorously. "Marriage, okay. But I'm already an uncle?"

Mark returned. "Michael, why don't you show Jack your room? Sophia, too, if she'd like."

"Um, sure," she agreed, obviously choosing the lesser of two evils.

Both followed Suzanne's nephew up the stairs.

"I hope Jack and Michael hit it off," Suzanne worried.

"Why wouldn't they?" Mark asked, surprised. "Boys aren't shy for long."

Tom did look shy, or perhaps just overwhelmed by the sheer number of strangers. But before long the men were talking about the Seattle Seahawks' amazing season and their chances in the play-offs, and he'd accepted a glass of wine. Suzanne was able to relax and seek out her sister and Rebecca in the kitchen.

The women all ended up congregating there, most of the talk concerning the upcoming wedding. Rebecca kept saying, "I can't believe how fast this has happened!" but she laughed and blushed when she said it, so everyone knew she wasn't suffering from cold feet.

Suzanne excused herself after fifteen or twenty minutes and went upstairs to see whether the kids needed rescuing. Not halfway down the hall, she could already hear Sophia's voice ordering the two younger boys around. Smiling, she stopped in the doorway.

"Get some great new stuff for Christmas, Michael?"

He looked up from where he was kneeling by a miniature pirate ship that was crewed by tiny pirates with eye patches and wicked swords at their sides. "Yeah!" he said. "I'm showing Soph and Jack what I got. Look. These are Playmobils. I got the island, too. We're gonna have a battle."

Jack barely glanced up, so engrossed was he in setting the crimson sails on the ship.

Only boys, Suzanne thought in amusement. Or maybe not. Sophia, sitting cross-legged and holding a miniature cannon, had a bloodthirsty look in her eyes.

"See, the pirates left behind the chest with their gold," she said, holding it up. "And these *other* pirates won't give it back. So they have to fight for it. Plus, there's a skeleton. We're making him like a ghost. He's going to scare *everybody.*"

"I see. Well, I'll leave you to it. Dinner should be ready in half an hour or so."

All three heads came up then. "Can we open presents after dinner?" Sophia asked.

"I'll leave that up to Michael's mom and dad. It's their house."

"I'm sure they'll let us," he assured his new friends. "I'll tell Dad he's gotta let us."

Laughing, Suzanne went back downstairs. None of the men noticed her coming, and she paused for a moment with one hand on the bannister to see…well, whether *Tom* needed rescuing even if the kids didn't.

In interests and temperament, they were an odd conglomeration, these men. Julian St. John, Carrie's adoptive father, was a dignified and highly respected cardiac surgeon, nearing retirement. Mark Kincaid was a former homicide detective and now private investigator. His father had been a police officer, too, and with both men it showed in their rugged builds and stance. Suzanne's brother Gary, looked like the biker he was with his shaggy hair, but he was also a highly successful coffee entrepreneur. And then Tom, a former Army Ranger, now Boeing planner. She was glad to see him looking comfortable and nodding with the others at something Carrie's adoptive dad was saying.

Tom stood beside Mark, Carrie's husband, and Suzanne realized that even though they didn't actually look alike, there was something similar about them. They were both big men, broad-shouldered and somehow tough, but it was more than that. A way of standing, perhaps, a sense that neither was completely relaxed. Maybe a cop and a soldier weren't that different?

The doorbell rang. Who was missing? Suzanne wondered, mentally counting noses.

"Must be Gwen," Mark said, separating himself from the group, and Suzanne remembered that his partner at the P.I. agency had been invited today as well.

Both Tom and Mark saw Suzanne as they turned toward the door. Tom's brows rose in a silent question—*How are the kids doing?*—and she smiled and gave a thumbs-up. She felt a funny little lump in her chest when he gave a pleased nod. That exchange had felt so natural, as if they really were a couple and used to communicating without words.

"Let me introduce you to Gwen," Mark said.

His partner proved to be a tall, gorgeous woman with short auburn hair and a mannish directness about her. Even her handshake was firm.

"Suzanne. Good to meet you. Mark was right, you do look like Carrie."

"She looks like me. *I* was around first," she said, smiling.

"Yeah, goes without saying. We big sisters have to stand up for ourselves."

They both laughed.

"Isn't your family local?"

"No, my parents retired to Houston of all places and my sister is married with umpteen kids in a Detroit suburb. I usually fly back, but this year two of them have chicken pox, which I *haven't* had. Seemed like staying away was the better part of valor."

"Coward," Mark taunted.

"Have *you* had chicken pox?"

"Ruined my sixth birthday party."

"And I don't want it to ruin my thirty-fifth." She appraised the men in the living room. "Thanks for having me, everyone."

Mark made introductions, then escorted her to the kitchen for round two.

Clearly alarmed by the talk of weddings and florists and photographers, Gwen edged toward the kitchen door as soon as manners allowed. A woman who'd succeeded as a cop and then P.I., she must feel more comfortable with men.

Not more than a minute after she'd rejoined the men in the living room, Suzanne heard them all laugh and felt a tiny pang of something that was horribly uncomfortable. Would Tom be attracted to Gwen? He was one of the few men who topped her near six feet, and with his years in Army special operations, he and she would have quite a bit in common.

Suzanne was saved from a ridiculous attack of jealousy by Carrie's announcement that it was time to carry food to the table. Suzanne took rolls that had been heating in the microwave, put them in a basket on the table and then went to call the kids down. Everyone gathered, and she was amazed to see that somehow her sister and brother-in-law had lengthened their table and found enough chairs for everyone to eat together. No segregated adult and children's tables in this home.

"She's going to be so beautiful in a few years," Carrie

murmured in Suzanne's ear when Sophia and the two boys reappeared. "Those eyes."

"You ought to see how fiercely she can stare out of them," Suzanne said with a small laugh. "And yes, it's occurred to me that boys are going to be after her in no time. I mean, she's already…" She hesitated.

"Voluptuous? Or on her way to being? Yep. Chain her in her bedroom now."

Suzanne grimaced at her sister. "Oh, thanks."

Sophia and Jack hung back shyly until Michael, supremely confident, said, "You can sit with me. Okay?"

They both flashed glances at Suzanne, who smiled and nodded, choosing a seat herself at their end of the table, across from Mark's dad who'd chosen to sit near his grandson. She was surprised and pleased when Tom moved around the table as if it was a given that he would sit beside her.

"Sorry to abandon you," she murmured.

He lifted his brows in seeming surprise. "I've enjoyed myself."

Once they were all seated, Carrie shushed everybody. "This is a special occasion, and I'm going to ask everybody to hold hands while we give thanks for this chance for our entire family, past and present, to be together."

Just like that, Suzanne's vision was blurred by tears. This *was* an extraordinary gathering—beginning with the three siblings reunited after having lost each other for twenty-six years, *and* one of the sets of adoptive parents, plus a new husband, a fiancée, and now Suzanne's children who would also be Chauvins.

She took Sophia's smaller hand in hers, gave a quick

squeeze, and felt her other hand in turn be engulfed in Tom's large, reassuring grip.

"We all know this gathering would never have been possible were it not for Suzanne's determination, persistence and love," Carrie continued, smiling down the table at her sister. "She made a vow to reunite us, and she did. It's thanks to her that we not only found each other, but I found Mark and Gary found Rebecca. Two more families within the family, and another in the making now that Sophia and Jack have joined us. We've lost nothing—" she turned the smile to her adoptive parents "—and gained so much. I feel blessed today."

There were murmurs from around the table, although Suzanne couldn't make out faces. Tom's hand tightened, as though he too was moved by Carrie's quiet words, and Suzanne was grateful for the strength of his grip.

Carrie then said a more conventional if still heartfelt grace, and they all finished with "Amen."

Suzanne was sorry to let go of her new daughter's hand, and of Tom's. She dried tears with her napkin and hid new ones behind it, aware that Tom had laid his hand on her back and rubbed gently even as he asked Dr. St. John a question as if to deflect attention from her.

When she finally took a deep breath and laid her napkin on her lap, Tom smiled at her. "You have quite a family here."

"I do, don't I?"

"I'd say you're lucky, but luck doesn't have much to do with it. Carrie's right. You wouldn't be together today if not for you."

Her eyes filled, and she sniffed. "You're making me cry again."

He laughed, patted her back and removed his hand. Somehow that laugh, a low, sympathetic rumble, restored her poise, and she was able to accept the plate of sliced turkey that Sophia passed to her.

She participated in conversation during dinner, but later couldn't have repeated a word of it. She kept looking at faces—Gary's, relaxed and amused, a glint in his dark eyes when his gaze turned to Rebecca; Carrie's, so like her own and yet reflecting a personality so different; the pride on Carrie's adoptive mother's. A smile here, a private glance there, a laugh, a way Gary and Carrie both had of turning their heads in response to a question.

With sudden, throat-tightening emotion, Suzanne thought of her parents. *Can you see us?* she asked them. *We're back together, the way we always should have been. And you must have done something right, because we love each other despite the years apart. We* fit. *Oh, if you can't see us, I wish you could. Gary looks so much like you, Dad. You'd be proud of the man he's become. And Mom, I only hope I can make Jack and Sophia feel as loved as I felt.*

"You okay?" Tom murmured in her ear, voice rich with concern.

She gave him a tremulous smile. "Yes. I'm just happy."

"As you should be. Although, you might want to know that a rather large portion of Jack's dinner is making its way under the table since Michael slipped away to open a door. I'd swear that he had company when he came back."

She turned her head to see Jack palm a clump of the

hated broccoli and ease his hand down to his lap and then to his side.

Did Daisy *like* broccoli? Or, after dinner, would they find a discarded heap under the table if they lifted the cloth and peeked? A bubble of laughter caught in her throat, and she leaned closer to Tom.

"That would be Daisy, the world's sweetest and most spoiled mongrel."

"He's going to want a dog more than ever now," Tom observed.

He was, wasn't he? One more thing to think about.

Everyone moved to the living room to open presents. They'd all exchanged separately within their smaller family units, but still it took ages, with them oohing and aahing over each others' gifts as they were opened.

It seemed everyone had brought Jack and Sophia gifts as well as Michael, including Carrie's adoptive parents, Mark's dad and Rebecca's mom. Even Gwen Mayer had brought small presents for each child. Most were fun things, but Carrie's mother gave both kids gorgeous, expensive parkas, and Rebecca's mother gave them winter boots.

"You did tell me sizes," Carrie whispered, "and I passed them on. I hope everything fits."

Toward the end, Gary slipped Suzanne an envelope. "This is to help you out. No argument this time." He moved away before she could open it.

When she did, she stared, stunned, at the check included in the card. The zeros on it blurred and persisted in moving around, but she finally understood that her brother had just given her ten thousand dollars.

Mouth hanging open, she turned her head to seek him out, but the moment their eyes met, he shook his head even though a smile played around his mouth.

Darn it, she wanted to cry again. She'd bought so much for the kids, and they still needed so much. Of course, Rebecca had undoubtedly known the state they'd be in; she had helped place many children from similar circumstances.

And Gary had offered before, while he'd been staying with Suzanne earlier in the fall. She'd turned him down, hurting his feelings, she knew, but through Rebecca she'd sent him the message that she'd accept help if he offered again. The truth was, he could afford to give checks of this size. She still teased him by calling him a coffee "mogul," but it was true. After running away from home at sixteen, he'd worked as a mechanic until someone had asked him to build them a coffee roaster. Ultimately, he'd gone into business with one coffee shop in Santa Fe. At last count, he owned twelve or thirteen, she thought, in New Mexico and now Arizona. And he sold his roast in distinctive packaging to major grocery chains. He owned a beautiful home in Santa Fe, but otherwise his wants had been few. As he'd put it, shrugging carelessly, "The money's just piling up."

And he, of all of them, knew what it felt like to be in the foster system, to be viewed and rejected by prospective adoptive parents, to go to a new home, full of hope. His placement had been unhappy. His adoptive mother had left when he was a young teen, never even writing or calling, and his adoptive father had been abusive.

He hadn't said much, because Gary never did, but Suzanne knew he saw the symbolism in her willingness to take Sophia and Jack so they could stay together. She was doing it partly for him, even though it was too late, and he wanted to help make it work.

She couldn't say no to this check. She'd spend it on the kids, and be grateful.

Thank you, she mouthed to him, and he grinned and dipped his head.

Leaving the wrapping paper in heaps in the living room, everyone accepted coffee, tea or milk, handfuls of cookies or servings of pie. Conversations were quiet, contented; Daisy wandered despite Mark's rolled eyes and collected offerings and scratches under her silky chin. Tom stayed close to Suzanne now.

Eventually, the kids bundled up in their new coats and gathered their hoard. Suzanne accepted packages of leftover turkey and trimmings, empty and washed pie pans and cookie plates, and she hugged everyone and tearfully thanked them.

"Merry Christmas!" followed them out into the crisp night, made bright by stars and by the lights on every house up and down the street.

Jack heaved a happy sigh. "That was the best Christmas ever!"

Suzanne felt the same, and Tom, laden with a Navajo rug Gary and Rebecca had given her and a rather large, remote-controlled car that someone had given Jack, said quietly, "It just might have been."

But Sophia stayed silent, and Suzanne felt apprehension stir. Although any child would enjoy the deluge of presents, she had to be thinking about her mother, mourning the loss of what had been, and wondering whether Suzanne would really want to keep her forever. They had a long road to travel, she knew they did, but they'd made a good beginning, hadn't they? What was it Tom had said Christmas was? A day for miraculous beginnings?

Taking a deep breath of sharp, wintry air, she thought, *I won't let worry ruin today.* How could she? Not when she'd dreamed about this exact Christmas since she was six years old, and had seen her brother and sister taken away.

Since she'd become an adult, part of that dream had always been a man beside her. Her chest heavy with the emotions of the day, she was glad that today it was Tom.

CHAPTER ELEVEN

CHRISTMAS NIGHT, SUZANNE turned out the lights and started down the hall to bed. She was just passing Sophia's closed door when she heard a stifled sound from behind it. She tensed. The kids had gone to bed together—in Jack's room.

But another soft gasp came, and another. No, not a gasp. A sob. Sophia must have slipped away as soon as her brother had fallen asleep, and was now crying in her own bed.

Suzanne hesitated. Should she respect Sophia's privacy? She had a right to mourn her mother. In fact, it was healthy for her to do so. Suzanne had sensed this coming.

But there was no way she could keep walking down the hall, brush her teeth and go to bed, leaving her ten-year-old adoptive-daughter-to-be sobbing her heart out alone.

Without second-guessing herself, Suzanne knocked lightly. When there was no answer, she opened the door. "Sophia?" she murmured. "Honey, are you okay?"

"Go away!" came a fierce whisper from the bed.

Standing in the half-open doorway, the light streaming around her, Suzanne said softly, "Sometimes it helps to have someone to talk to when you feel sad. Especially when you're missing someone. It's easier to remember out loud. That person—your mom—seems more real and less like somebody you've only imagined."

She paused, and when there was no response, took that as encouragement. She made her way into the dark room, stopping beside the bed. "All of this is lots easier for Jack, isn't it? Did it make you mad today, because he seemed so happy? As if he didn't remember your mom at all?"

"Yes!" This acknowledgment bubbled with the anger so readily apparent whenever Sophia lashed out at her brother.

Suzanne sat on the edge of the bed, making no attempt to touch the girl. "He's struggling in his own way, you know. His bed-wetting…"

"He did that even when Mom was alive." Her voice was choked.

"But you both knew she was slipping away, didn't you? That must have been terrifying."

Silence.

"And his being afraid to go to bed alone…"

"He's just scared of the dark!"

"That's right. But he doesn't feel safe, because he know's the world *isn't* completely safe. You and he will know that forever."

"Because you do?"

Suzanne nodded, then wasn't sure Sophia could see her. "Yes. It…has an effect. It makes you afraid to take risks sometimes, and other times to cling when you should let go." Would a child her age understand what Suzanne was talking about? she wondered. "Like me. I stayed married too long to a man who didn't treat me very well because…oh, I guess because the known was less scary than the unknown."

"So we're gonna be sad forever?"

She let herself laugh a little. "No, of course not. Haven't you been happy some of the time since your mom died? Maybe even last night, and today?"

"I shouldn't have been!" Sophia wailed. "Mom just died!"

"Oh, honey." This time, Suzanne did reach out, laying her hand on the bed-covered lump that was a grief-stricken child. "I know she'd want…"

The lump lurched and flipped away from her touch. "It's your fault!"

Suzanne froze, hand outstretched. "What?"

Voice laced with venom, Sophia cried, "You're trying to make us forget her, aren't you? Like…like she never was. Suddenly *you're* our mom. Only you're not!"

She felt as if her rib cage were being crushed. Her hand fell to her side. "You think that's why I gave you presents? To make you forget your mother?"

"Mommy couldn't buy us stuff, or make nice meals! But just 'cause you can doesn't make you better."

It was all Suzanne could do to squeeze out words. "I never thought I was better."

"Then why'd you do all this?" *This* was unnamed in the piteous cry.

"I wanted you to feel welcome. And I did want you to be happy."

"We're not ready to be happy! Okay?" Sophia flipped over, back to Suzanne. Now her voice was muffled by the pillow and perhaps by tears. "I want you to go away."

Her eyes burned and she had to swallow to be sure she could control her voice. She stood. "All right. I'm going.

But we'll have to talk about this again. About how you feel, and your mom, and everything."

"I don't want to talk about it! Not with you!"

The first tears leaked out as she retreated, following the band of light to the door. There, she paused, not turning around. "I know one thing. Wherever your mom is, she wants someone to love you, and for you to be happy. More than anything in the world, that's what she wants."

"How do *you* know?" The anger, the rejection, were perilously close to hate.

"Because..." She swallowed again. "Because, if something were to happen to me now, that's what I'd want. Good night, Sophia." This time, she slipped out, leaving the door open a hand's width, and continued down the hall to her bedroom.

There, her legs failed her and she sank into the rocker, covering her face with her hands as hot tears escaped.

She only let herself weep for a few minutes, knowing as she did that it was a pathetic kind of luxury. Had she really believed that adopting children the ages of Jack and especially Sophia would be *easy?* She had joked with Melissa about the honeymoon period. The truth was, she was lucky there'd actually been one, that Sophia had been sweet—within her abilities—and cooperative for almost an entire week.

She should be glad that Sophia mourned her mother. Hadn't she worried when the ten-year-old seemed unfeeling? So, now she was admitting that she felt all the surging misery and grief and loneliness Suzanne remembered quite well, even though it was filtered by the years.

And maybe, she admitted as she wiped tears, she *was* guilty of trying to make Sophia and Jack forget their mother because they had it so good now. She hadn't consciously done that, but she'd sure gone overboard on making their bedrooms perfect, and she'd bought extravagantly for Christmas even though she really couldn't afford to spend so much.

And maybe it would have been better if the whole process *hadn't* been rushed, if she'd been able to give them gifts but not felt the pressure to create a perfect Christmas. It had given her an excuse to say implicitly *See how wonderful your lives will be, now that you're my children?*

And she wondered that Sophia felt as if Suzanne were trying to buy their love. Maybe... She swallowed. Maybe she had been.

She'd meant to ask to see a picture of their mom, to talk to them about her, to find out where she was buried and take them to visit her grave if possible. Show them her album of photos of her own, long-lost family, remind them that she knew how they felt because she, too, had lost her parents in a blinding instant that had changed her life.

But not, she thought, as disorienting as theirs had been. She had had the comfort of living with family she knew. She'd been held by her aunt, who had cried with her. She hadn't had to go to a foster home, where people came and inspected her like a calf up for sale, shaking their heads and walking away as if she were too scrawny. She, at least, had known security and familiarity if not love.

So maybe she didn't understand as well as she'd thought she had.

She lay in the dark, hurting as she examined herself and her best intentions. The clock passed midnight, and Christmas was gone before she sank into a troubled sleep.

FRIDAY OF THAT WEEK, TOM WAS out salting his walkway when Suzanne got home from work. Boeing shut down for the week between Christmas and New Year's, and he'd been at loose ends with Suzanne and the kids gone every day. Rain had fallen for a few days after Christmas, followed by sinking temperatures that promised to descend into the low twenties today. By morning, weather forecasters promised, the roads would be black ice.

His porch light was on as was the motion detector above the garage, but neither reached to his neighbor's driveway. He saw Suzanne get out of her car, but no other doors opened and closed.

"Hey," he called. "Lose the kids?"

"Hi, Tom." Suzanne circled the car and came over to his driveway. "They're at Carrie's. She called last night and suggested picking them up this morning. Mark's agency is closed this week, and of course Carrie isn't in school. This way they didn't have to go to work with me today and tomorrow. I know it's boring for them. I'll pick them up tomorrow night." She gazed up at the dark, cold sky. "Weather willing."

"Roads are supposed to be dangerous tomorrow." He studied her closely, trying to see if she looked as tired as she sounded.

"Oh, dear." She bit her lip anxiously. "My tires aren't the greatest."

"If we have black ice come morning, there's no point in you opening. The state patrol will be asking people to stay home."

"I suppose that's true. Fortunately, I don't have any classes scheduled tomorrow." Even with a jacket on, she shivered.

"If need be, I'll drive you to Seattle to pick the kids up. If you're absolutely determined to open shop, I'll drive you there, too."

"You're always doing something nice for me," she said, in a funny, quiet voice. "I wish I had some way to return the favor."

He straightened, the bag of salt in his hand. "You don't think you did? By having me for Christmas?"

"That's not quite the same thing as the hours and hours of hard work you've put in."

Tom let a word escape him he rarely used. She stared.

"I'm sorry. But that's..." He struggled. "I did something for you I enjoyed. You...shared your family. You gave me the best Christmas I've had since..."

"Your friend moved," she said softly.

Since I was a kid was what he'd been going to say, but he didn't correct her.

"Still..."

"Still nothing." He frowned, wondering why she was so intent on beating herself up. "You have dinner plans?"

"Oh, I can find something." She sounded dispirited.

"If you don't mind sharing a steak, I can put on an extra potato. I'd enjoy the company."

"I'll feel guilty if I take part of your steak...."

"I asked," he reminded her.

"Well…what if I contribute a peach pie?"

"Peach?" At the end of December, peaches seemed like a distant memory.

"I sliced and froze some last summer."

"You can have the whole steak," he told her.

At last, she laughed. "Okay. Let me go drop my purse off and get the pie."

He was done and had closed the garage by the time she got back. Letting her in, he said, "I'll microwave the potatoes to speed them up. Here, let me hang up your coat." She shrugged out of it and he put it on a hanger next to his parka in the closet. "Why don't you come on back to the kitchen."

She followed, looking around, and he realized she'd never been past his living room even though he'd become comfortable in her house. He was embarrassed by the sterility of his. The dining room held a table, chairs and one painting he'd spotted in the window of a gallery downtown and had bought on impulse. That was it. There was plenty of room for a china cabinet, but he didn't own any china so what was the point?

He hadn't changed much in the kitchen since he'd bought the house. Even the stools that pulled up to the breakfast bar had been left by the previous owners. He kept it neat, the counters bare, and thought of it as a functional room. He cooked here; he ate here. But her kitchen…her kitchen was warm, homey, cluttered, fragrant with things like that peach pie baking. It was a room where kids could do their homework, hang around to talk while she cooked, whisper as they sneaked midnight snacks. It didn't feel industrial.

"Have a seat." He got two big russet potatoes out of the bin, washed them and stabbed them full of holes, then put them in the microwave on high. Then he took asparagus from the refrigerator, rinsed it and cut it into short lengths. "Those potatoes are going to take a while. I could make a salad."

"I'm not starved. More exhausted. I'm really grateful not to be standing in my own kitchen staring at the cupboards wondering if it's worth making something."

Appraising her, he realized she had paused long enough to brush her hair and put on a touch of lipstick before she came over. He'd like to think she'd bothered because she wanted to look nice for him, but chances were she was just trying to hide her exhaustion.

He pulled up the second stool and straddled it, hooking his heels over the rung. "I'm surprised they were willing to stay over."

"Jack was excited about seeing Michael again. Apparently they were in the middle of a pirate battle." Amusement colored her voice, but disappeared when she said without expression, "And Sophia... Well, she's trying very hard to reject me."

"Ah."

Her eyes narrowed. "You expected it."

"Yeah, I guess I did."

Her shoulders sagged and the fight left her. "Why didn't I?"

He would have liked to hug her, but he didn't know if they were on those terms. Touching her the way he had Christmas Day, that had just come naturally. Too naturally. It would be easy to pull her into his arms and never let her go. Trouble was, she hadn't invited any physical intimacy.

In answer to her question, Tom said, "Because you hoped she wouldn't. You want to love her, and you want her to love you."

She looked at him, her face vulnerable. "Do you think she ever will?"

God. He was supposed to stay on the other side of the bar?

"Yeah," he said in a gritty voice. "I think she will. I think maybe she's already starting to, and that's what scares her."

Hope stole slowly over her features, taking them from pretty to spectacular. "Really?"

"Is she upset, or genuinely indifferent?"

"This all started Christmas night with a storm of tears. I was trying to make her forget her mom. She implied that I'd thought I could buy her affection. She made sure I knew that I couldn't."

"Ah," he said again.

She tilted her head in exasperation.

"So she's upset. Which means she was tempted."

"You mean, to be bought?"

"No," he said gently. "To let herself forget."

Naked hope again shone on her face. "I thought that's what it was. But then I was afraid I was trying to fool myself."

"I doubt it."

"Why are you so easy to talk to?" she wondered. "When anyone else asks, I pretend everything is fine. But I can always talk to you."

"Maybe it's this homely mug," he suggested, only half kidding.

Expecting polite protestation, he was surprised when she studied him with a crinkled forehead.

"Maybe if you looked like…like Mel Gibson, I wouldn't feel comfortable talking to you. But it's funny…." She stopped, her frown deepening. "I just don't see you the same way I used to."

He went still. "And how was that?"

"Really, I never saw you at all. I paid attention to things like the way you edged your lawn or the fact that you power-washed your driveway."

"Another of those neighbor-from-hell stories."

She rolled her eyes. "I'm trying to explain something here."

He grinned. "Yeah, yeah."

"What I mean is, my whole impression of you was determined by how inadequate I felt in comparison."

"Wow." That floored him. He'd always figured she was happy with her casual style of gardening. "You thought I was trying to make you look bad?"

Her "No, no…" was weak.

"Don't worry. You can't hurt my feelings."

Yeah, she could. More than anyone else he could think of, she could. But he needed to know how she felt about him.

Forehead still creased in perturbation, she said, "I think maybe it was all symbolic. What I was really embarrassed about was the fact that you'd overheard those awful fights. So then I imagined you saw me as some kind of white trash, an impression I wasn't doing anything to counter when my lawn was ragged, my flower beds weedy, my car rusting. So I had to resent you a little, or I would have felt even crummier about myself."

"I wish I'd known. I'd have let dandelions grow in my lawn."

She smiled, but then got serious again. "But then, I actually met your eyes one day. And I guess I've never seen you the same again."

A jackhammer took up residence in his chest. "Yeah?"

"I thought… I thought what a *nice* face you have."

Nice?

"It's your smile," she continued. "So don't call yourself homely."

"All I know is, they passed me over for the fire-fighter's calendar."

"But you aren't a firefighter!"

He grinned.

She whacked his shoulder. "If you *were* a firefighter, they'd choose you in a heartbeat and you know it! They don't care about faces, they go for beefcake."

The jackhammer coughed and took a tap or two, as if warming up. "You calling me *beefcake?*"

"Well," she said, looking suddenly prim, "you *are* well built."

"Thank you."

"I've seen you run." She frowned again. "And you don't limp or anything. Why did you have to retire from the Army?"

"My leg was hit by shrapnel. I've got a hell of a scar." He gestured from mid-thigh toward his calf. "The knee isn't totally stable. I'm okay unless I turn wrong or try to cut and run. I haven't joined any adult soccer or basketball leagues, I can tell you."

"Does it hurt?" Her big brown eyes were soft with sympathy.

"It aches a little when the weather is cold. No big deal."

"I'm sorry."

He shook his head. "Nothing to be sorry for. Everyone gets some aches and pains along the way."

"I suppose." Suzanne sighed.

"Hey, I never offered you anything to drink. I have coffee, pop, beer and wine."

"Do you know, I think some wine would be good."

He had a rack on his kitchen countertop. From it, he selected a Napa Valley merlot and poured two glasses. While up, he checked the potatoes and turned the oven on to broil.

"Are you sure I can't help?" she asked.

"This dinner is about as easy as they come. I'm on it." Handing Suzanne a glass of wine and sitting again, Tom asked, in part to distract her from her desire to leap up and do her share and more, "How's business this week?"

"Not as bad as I expected, but I think it's because Boeing is closed and a lot of other people are off, too. I'm told that January will be deadly."

"Can you handle some months like that?" What he really wanted to say was *Are you hurting for money?*

She nodded. "I saved enough to cushion me for this first year, while I'm getting established. And Gary, bless his heart, gave me some money for Christmas. He's offered before, and I turned him down, but now with the kids, I really appreciated his help."

"What does he do?"

The minute she told him, he recognized the name of her brother's coffee company. He'd bought some himself.

"He claims to have no use for most of his income. Rebecca tells me that he's been donating a whole lot to a shelter for teenage runaways in Santa Fe. Which makes sense, since he was one himself."

Tom raised his brows in surprise, and she told him her brother's story.

With a sigh, she concluded, "I always hoped my brother and sister at least had happy, loving homes."

"Carrie's adoptive parents seemed like good people."

"They're so nice. I know you weren't aware, but Christmas Day was a little touchy because Gary had never met them."

The microwave beeped and Tom rose again to check the potatoes. "Touchy how?"

She explained then concluded, "But Gary was gracious. It won't be as awkward the next time. I'm so glad. They've practically adopted me, too, now that they know Carrie has a sister, so I'd hate for us not to be able to include everyone in family gatherings."

"Didn't look like that would be a problem." Tom put the steak under the broiler.

"I think the kids were overwhelmed with so many people."

A little dryly, he said, "They seemed to deal with so many presents just fine."

Suzanne gave her low, throaty chuckle. "You have a point. Jack has been gloating all week. *And* getting greedy. He wants some of the toys Michael has."

"Normal for a kid that age, I imagine."

She sighed. "The one present that's been a resounding failure so far is the bike. I don't know if you've noticed, but he hasn't tried it yet. I mean, he hasn't had an awful lot of opportunity, what with having to go to the shop every day, but it turns out he doesn't actually know *how* to ride a bike."

"He hasn't wanted to try?"

"I told him I'd get training wheels, but I haven't had a chance yet."

"At seven and a half?"

"Do you think he can learn without?"

"Sure. He just needs a little help." He got up again to turn on the asparagus and refill their wineglasses.

"What kind of help?" Suzanne asked.

"Don't you remember learning to ride a bike?"

"I think I taught myself. But I was older."

He could see her trying to remember, and had gotten enough hints about her childhood to guess no one had ever offered to help her. She'd probably learned on a bike one of her cousins had outgrown and therefore no longer wanted.

"You hold the bike up until he's ready for you to let go. Simple as that."

"Oh." She pursed her lips. "I can do that."

On her only day home? "I'd be glad to help," he said. "Your Sundays are going to be tough now that you have the kids."

"No more than any parent's."

"You're single, and you're starting up a business. Most parents have it cushy compared to that."

"When you put it that way…I'd be thrilled if you'd help teach Jack to ride a bike."

"Good." He smiled at her. "Now, how'd you like to set the table? Looks like everything is about done."

He told her where to find silverware, plates and, when she asked, place mats and napkins. The fact that the table was bare probably gave away the fact that his usual dinner was eaten on a TV tray in the living room or here at the breakfast bar.

"This is so nice," she said, sitting down. "I like to cook, but not when I get home from work. I've been known to have cereal, or nothing but a bowl of ice cream. Maybe," she said hopefully, "Sophia will turn out to love to cook."

"Be a prize-winning chef by eleven."

Another delicious chuckle. "Why not?"

"We all have our fantasies."

She opened her mouth, then closed it and blushed.

Damn. She'd been about to ask what his fantasies were. Right this minute, he couldn't think of a one that didn't involve her.

Pretending he hadn't noticed, Tom said, "I gotta tell you, Sophia doesn't strike me as the domestic kind."

Looking grateful, Suzanne argued, "I don't know about that. Did I tell you she's already learning to knit? She's almost done with a muffler."

"Did you notice your throw out on the couch? It looks good there."

"I'm glad you liked it." She smiled at him, her brown eyes warm and direct.

If he kissed her, would she ever smile at him like that again? Or would she go back to slipping into her garage to avoid having to talk to him?

Was it worth the risk to find out?

He let her turn the conversation to local politics—city councils seemed to brew more controversy and downright nastiness than state or national government, maybe because everyone knew everyone.

The peach pie was incredible. His pleasure was so evident, Suzanne said, "I'm just going to leave the rest for you." She didn't let him argue. "No, really. I have bags and bags of peaches in the freezer. I'll make another. The kids probably won't eat it anyway. They're not so sure they like most of what I put in front of them."

"Well, then, thank you."

She insisted on helping clear the table and load the dishwasher, and he let her just to prolong her visit and enjoy the sight of her bustling in his kitchen. With her coloring and fine bones, she looked as French as her name suggested. He imagined her behind the counter in a Parisian *boulangerie,* flour dusting her cheek, her quick smile and laugh delighting the customers.

"Do you speak French?" he asked.

She turned, startled, from the sink where she was rinsing plates. "Yes, but not well. Why?"

"I was just thinking that you really do look French."

"Oh." Her gaze shied momentarily from his, as if she was disconcerted to know that he'd been studying her. "My parents spoke both French and English. We kids learned, but Uncle Miles didn't speak it, of course, so my aunt Jeanne never did and I forgot every word really quickly after my parents died. I took four years in college, thinking I'd get a chance to visit France, but I never made it."

"I'm sorry you didn't," he said. "Or maybe not, because you might never have come back."

"I would have, because of my siblings. I couldn't have left them behind." She shook off the shadow that had dimmed her smile. "Now, I could move to Rouen, and they could visit."

"Why not?" He wiped the counter and saw with regret that the kitchen was clean. "We're done. Go home and get a good night's sleep, Suzanne."

She gave a huge yawn, then laughed. "After the wine, I think I need to. Thank you, Tom. This has been such a nice evening."

Nice was becoming his least favorite word.

"You're welcome." He walked her to the door. "I'm an early riser. Call me in the morning if you want a ride."

She put on her coat but shivered nonetheless the minute he opened the front door. "It *is* cold, isn't it?"

"It is. Be careful if your steps are icy."

"I will." She flipped a hand and was gone before he could debate whether to risk that kiss.

Despite the cold, he stepped out on his own porch in shirtsleeves and watched until he saw her go safely in her front door.

"Damn," he murmured, wishing he'd taken a chance. Afraid of losing her friendship, he'd been a coward. But he might not get many chances to have her alone.

Her friendship was going to turn into a kind of hell for a man in love with her. Yeah, he was going to have to take that risk.

CHAPTER TWELVE

WHEN HER ALARM WENT OFF the next morning, Suzanne surfaced reluctantly, thought, *Oh, I hope Jack didn't wet his bed last night,* then remembered. No children. She was shocked to feel a momentary twinge of relief. But it *was* momentary. Any parent enjoyed a day off.

The strain of dealing with Sophia had worn her out more this week than had the everyday necessity of changing Jack's bed, making breakfast for the kids, planning dinner, organizing them so that they brought enough to keep them entertained all day at the shop—and then getting herself ready for work. Sophia had remained sullen and almost insolent whenever Suzanne asked her to do anything, Jack puzzled at his sister's mood. And, of course, after three days stuck at the shop, they were getting bored. Carrie's offer to take them overnight had been a godsend.

Suzanne thought how lovely it would be to close her eyes for just a tiny bit longer, then stretched and sat up, putting her feet on the floor.

It wasn't until she was in the shower that she remembered what Tom had said about the weather forecast. And that made her think about dinner, the things they'd talked about, the way he'd joked about her calling him *beefcake,* the odd expression on his face when she'd admitted to not seeing him quite the way she used to.

The other day Carrie had teased her about her gallant suitor, and she'd known she'd been blushing when she'd tried to claim they were just friends.

She wished she knew whether he was thinking about the possibilities, too. She wished she was better at reading signals from a man.

If she just weren't so inexperienced. Josh had been her high-school sweetheart, her college sweetheart, her husband. She'd dated since her divorce, but not successfully. She'd come to the conclusion that she didn't know how to flirt, didn't always notice when someone else was, and she was agreeing to have dinner with men she wasn't attracted to just because they'd asked and she didn't know how to say no.

Thirty-two years old and she wasn't sure she'd be able to tell if a man was interested or not, short of him sweeping her in his arms. Which Tom certainly hadn't done. Last night, she'd almost hoped…

Embarrassed at how vividly she imagined him kissing her, she ducked her head under the hot spray. It had been so long since she'd had more than vague fantasies triggered by a romantic movie or book, she hardly knew how to react to the idea of the real thing!

Finally turning off the shower, stepping out and wrapping her hair in a towel, Suzanne half wished she hadn't ever thought of Tom that way. She liked having him as a friend. What if he realized she was attracted to him, and he wasn't to her?

In the middle of drying herself, she stopped to stare in the mirror. Heaven help her, what if he *was?* Did she even want to think about having a relationship, never mind actually have one? What about the kids? How would she find the time?

Maybe, if she didn't encourage him, she'd never find out if he felt the same. Which was certainly safer. They could go on being friends without awkwardness.

But Suzanne kept remembering Christmas Day and the way Gary and Rebecca had looked at each other, the intimacy and sexual energy every time Carrie and Mark's eyes had met. She'd envied them. She wanted that closeness with someone, the knowledge that she didn't bear every burden alone. Lately she'd felt that with Tom, without having identified the sweet sense of relief.

Suzanne put on a bathrobe and slippers and went to the living room. She turned on the television to the picture of what appeared to be a dozen-car pile-up on the freeway.

"Overpasses are particularly treacherous," the newscaster was saying. "Seattle city police are asking that commuters be extremely cautious when approaching hills. Roads appear deceptively clear until the motorist brakes." The TV picture changed to show an SUV sliding inexorably down a steep road in Seattle, finally smashing against a parked car. "State patrol are asking that you stay home if at all possible. Many government offices will be closed today…"

Suzanne stood for a few minutes, watching the chaos out on the roads with horrified fascination. Early commuters hadn't heeded yesterday's warnings, and it appeared that highways were sheet ice.

Well. She wouldn't be opening her shop today. Even if the weather warmed up enough for the ice to begin to melt, she couldn't imagine that anyone would go shopping. And since this was Saturday, that gave her two whole days off.

"Oh, no! The kids!" she exclaimed aloud. How would she pick them up? Tom had offered, but she couldn't ask him to go out unless conditions improved a whole lot.

She'd have to call Carrie. But not yet. Chances were their whole household was still sound asleep.

She could go back to bed. Suzanne had a seductive image of burrowing back under her covers, closing her eyes, drifting… Oh, yes. Definitely back to bed.

But she'd call Tom first, to be sure he wasn't waiting to drive her downtown if she insisted.

"Hey," he said, when he answered the phone. "Have you turned on the TV?"

"Yes. What a mess out there!"

"Convinced you not to go to work?"

"Convinced me to go back to bed."

He laughed, a low, intimate sound that made her wonder what it would be like to go back to bed with *him.*

"You deserve a snooze. Give me a call later and we can figure out how to pick the kids up."

Feeling daring, she asked, "What do you plan to do today?"

"I wish I could finish that headboard, but it's too cold out in the garage." Suzanne could all but hear his shrug. "Probably read."

"Would you like to come over for lunch later?"

"After you get up, you mean?" Amusement deepened his voice.

"I figure by noon, I should have had enough sleep."

He laughed. "It's a deal."

She hung up, smiling and able to feel the heat in her cheeks. If she didn't want to encourage him, she probably shouldn't have suggested lunch. But it would have been a little strange if they'd both spent solitary days right next door to each other, given that he'd offered to drive her to Seattle later.

Oh, Lord. She was overanalyzing. An invitation to lunch was *not* equivalent to an invitation to bed. She hadn't been self-conscious before, not even last night when he'd suggested dinner. She was just being silly. He probably wasn't even interested in her. He was a nice man who was a little bit lonely and glad to feel needed. That was all.

Is that really what you hope? asked an annoying voice in her head.

"Shut up," Suzanne told it, and went back to bed.

When she woke up again at ten-thirty, she felt fantastic. And the experts claimed you couldn't catch up on sleep. What did they know?

She got dressed with slightly more care than she might otherwise have, wearing jeans and a coral-colored cotton-and-silk sweater that draped beautifully, then called Carrie's house.

Mark answered, saying, "I hope you stayed home today."

"I did. I turned on the TV to see how bad it is. How are the kids?"

"They're having a great time, Suzanne. It should warm

up this afternoon, if you want to pick them up, but they can just as well stay the night."

"I miss them."

"Want to say hi?" He muffled the phone and called their names.

A moment later, a small voice said, "Hi."

"Jack? How are you? Are you having fun with Michael?"

"Yeah, but you are coming to get us today, right?"

"You scared last night?"

"No-o." At least, he wasn't going to admit he'd been. "But I like my new bed."

"I'm glad," she said. "I miss you guys."

"I miss you, too," he said, melting her heart.

"Can I talk to your sister?"

His voice became more distant. "Here, Soph."

"Hello?" his sister said.

"I hope you haven't been bored," Suzanne said.

"I'm making banana bread with Aunt Carrie."

Suzanne felt a funny little squeeze. She couldn't be mom, but Sophia seemed to have no qualms about accepting an aunt and uncle.

"Well, good. I'd like to pick you two up today. I wanted to take you shopping tomorrow. It's our last chance before school starts."

"Oh. Okay." The tone suggested, if not enthusiasm, at least acquiescence. Or maybe, Suzanne thought wryly, greed.

"Tom said he'd drive me if the roads are still icy. So tell Aunt Carrie and Uncle Mark that I'll plan to be there between two and three."

"Okay. Bye."

Hearing dead air, Suzanne made a face and hit End herself. Apparently when a conversation with Sophia was over, it was over.

She went out to explore her cupboards, eating a banana to hold her until lunch. Realizing she'd have to grocery shop soon, she had a flash of remembrance. Shopping with Tom wasn't the most romantic outing in the world, but she couldn't remember enjoying a day more than she had the one with him.

So? She liked him. It didn't have to mean more than that.

And she was putting together an apple cobbler because he appreciated her cooking. Period.

Well, it would also dress up the otherwise ordinary soup and sandwiches she'd have to feed him.

He rang the doorbell just after noon and entered with a chilly blast of air.

"Brr," she said, shivering. "That doesn't feel like it's warming up."

"Still icy." He sniffed. "Something smells good."

"Apple cobbler. To make up for the peanut-butter-and-jelly sandwich you get for lunch."

Tom grinned, making his rough-hewn face handsome. "Happens I like peanut butter and jelly."

Hoping her voice didn't sound breathless, Suzanne led the way to the kitchen. "I was kidding. I do have cold cuts. Unless you prefer peanut butter."

They bantered while she dished up split-pea soup and sliced and set out the whole-wheat hazelnut bread she'd bought at the bakery that was only a block from Knit One, Drop In. It sounded, she began to think, an awful lot like flirting. Had he noticed? She sneaked a peak at him, met his eyes and felt her cheeks warm. For Pete's sake! Thirty-two, and she couldn't even flirt without blushing.

She couldn't remember the last thing he'd said. "I called the kids."

"Yeah? They having fun?"

"Jack said he was, but he likes his own bed. I promised to pick them up around two-thirty. If you think we can, safely."

"Sure. The major roads will be sanded." He began to put together a sandwich as she sat down across the table from him. "We'll want to get home in plenty of time to avoid the crazy drivers."

Suzanne relaxed. He sounded the way he always did. Not as if he'd noticed that *she* was sounding any different than usual. Probably it was all in her imagination.

She told him her plans for tomorrow. "I know the malls will be mobbed this weekend, but the kids really need some new clothes before they go back to school."

Tom said thoughtfully, "You know, maybe Jack would rather stay with me. He could help put that last coat of paint on his headboard, and if the weather's good, we could have a bike-riding lesson." He raised his brows. "Unless you'd intended to make him try on clothes, too?"

"I like that." She pretended to indignation. "*Make* him try on clothes."

There was that incredibly charming, even sexy, smile again. "Well, we are both guys. And, uh, guys don't usually go much for shopping."

"You claimed to enjoy shopping when we went a couple of weeks ago."

"That was for materials for a project."

"You mean, furniture."

"Right. See, that's different. Clothes…" He shook his head. "When I have to go, I buy two or three of everything that fits, so it lasts me a long time."

She laughed. "I don't believe you."

"Believe it." He grinned.

"I'll have you know, one of my cousins is a clotheshorse. His wife told me she doesn't like to iron his shirts, because he criticizes how she does it."

"To every rule, there's an exception." He continued to eat. "Good soup."

She laughed again, then took a bite of her sandwich. When she looked up, it was to find him watching her with…well, she couldn't decide. It was as if he'd just noticed something about her and was trying to fit it in context.

"What?" she asked.

He shook his head slightly, as though he was clearing it. "Nothing. I was just thinking that until the last few weeks, I'd never heard you laugh. Not in all the years we've lived next to each other."

"Never? But…I laugh."

His voice was quiet, a little gruff. "Not often enough. You're…beautiful when you laugh." His mouth twisted. "Actually, you're beautiful all the time. But more so when you're happy."

"I…thank you." Suddenly shy, she looked down at the sandwich she'd lost interest in. "I'd never heard you laugh, either. It didn't seem like you ever had anyone over. I don't think people by themselves *do* laugh."

"I embarrassed you. I'm sorry. I'm glad to hear you laugh. That's all."

"No." She risked a glance up. "It was nice of you to say."

Tom sounded matter-of-fact, but his eyes were warm. "That you're beautiful? You must know you are."

"That sounds so narcissistic! Honestly, I don't much think about how I look. Or at least, I haven't in years. I know I've never thought of myself as more than pretty, on a good day."

Trust him to jump on the most revealing thing she'd said.

"Why 'in years'? Do you mean, since your divorce?"

She hunched her shoulders, recognized what she was doing and consciously straightened them. "Probably long before that. I guess, since Josh, I haven't been that interested in starting anything."

There was a long silence. Then, voice quiet, Tom said, "Are you warning me off?"

Her breath caught. "I didn't know I needed… I mean, that you were… Oh." She squeezed her eyes shut.

After a moment, he said, "Yes or no would do. I won't push, Suzanne."

She had to open her eyes and meet his. He was watching her very seriously. No, more than that. He looked wary, guarded. He expected her to say she was warning him off.

Until this second, Suzanne hadn't known what she would decide. Maybe it was his expression, the sense she had that he was bracing himself, that finally did give her the courage to say "No. I wasn't. Truly, I didn't know that you were, um…" Losing her nerve, she looked back down at her plate. "You see, I haven't actually dated much. Josh was my only serious boyfriend. And husband, of course."

"Only?" Tom sounded incredulous.

"We went together in high school. I suggested we date other people in college, but he was so upset, I backed down and…well, we got married, and you know what happened."

"So that bastard is your only real experience with men."

"Well, the uncle who raised me. Who is actually kind of a jerk. And my cousins. They're not much better."

"Good God."

"I mean, Roddie isn't that bad. I like him better than Ray. And of course I've known nice men. Friends' husbands. Oh, and Mark, and now Gary." She was babbling, and couldn't seem to stop. "It's not that I think all men are awful. Really."

"Suzanne." His chair scraped back. "Look at me."

Knowing her cheeks must be bright red, she lifted her head.

Tom stood, his hand outstretched to her. He wasn't smiling, but his eyes were so kind she stood without a second thought and went to him. His hand gripped hers, and with the other one he tilted her chin up.

"Would you mind if I kissed you?"

Her voice didn't seem to want to work. Maybe she'd worn it down. Shyly, she shook her head.

He bent his head slowly, as if he still expected her to pull away. He was going to kiss her. She *wanted* him to kiss her. Even if she suddenly wasn't quite sure what to do. It might be different than it had been with Josh. She hoped it would be. But not so different that she didn't know how to respond.

His lips brushed hers. "Relax," he murmured against her mouth.

She closed her eyes. "I'm nervous."

Now his voice was a low, soothing rumble. "I know. But you don't have to be."

"I'll…I'll try."

He made a sound that might have been a chuckle, but sounded more like a groan, then pressed his lips to hers again.

She felt like a mannequin and was probably as appealing to kiss, but the excitement low in her belly began to radiate warmth that felt very, very good, and after a moment her mouth softened.

He gently sucked her lower lip, then touched it with his tongue. She drew in a sharp breath, then timidly kissed him back. The large hand that had held her chin up slid to her nape, and she let her head fall back. He kept the kiss slow, undemanding, intoxicating.

Suzanne heard herself sigh with pleasure. Or moan. She didn't know, but Tom's fingers bit into hers and he deepened the kiss, his tongue stroking hers. It felt heavenly. Already on tiptoe, she swayed toward him, gripping his shoulder.

Now he was the one to make a rough sound deep in his throat. He dropped her hand and wrapped his arm around her, pulling her against his big body. No longer sure she could have stood without his support, she only felt. And such amazing things. Josh had always been demanding, even rough, never tender and slow like this. Tom's hand squeezed her neck, while his other one kneaded her lower back and hip. His arousal was unmistakable, but he was also patient, as if he had all the time in the world for her to become confident.

Suddenly he lifted his head. “Hey!”

Dazed, she opened her eyes.

He grazed his knuckles over her cheek. “You’re crying.”

“I’m not!”

“Yeah, you are.”

“Really?” Wondering, she drew back and touched her own face. “I’m so sorry!”

The worry in his eyes wrenched her heart. “I didn’t mean to upset you.”

“You didn’t. I just…I suddenly thought how nobody has ever been as patient and kind and *nice* to me as you are.”

He didn’t move much, but she felt his withdrawal. “You know, I’m starting to hate that word.”

“What word?”

“Nice.”

“But…”

Tom shook his head. “Never mind. Forget I said that. What I hate is that your uncle and your husband were such jackasses, you think it’s extraordinary when some guy is decent to you.”

Made brave by the anger in his voice, Suzanne stroked his hard jaw. “More than decent. Offering to lend me your lawn mower would have been decent. Actually mowing my lawn was generous. Spending days and days working on furniture for kids you didn’t even know was extraordinary. But mostly, it was the way you kissed me. As if what *I* felt was way more important than anything you wanted.”

“I want you,” he said clearly, the expression on his face all but stopping her heart. “I want you to be happy.”

"I never knew," she said in amazement. "I just thought..."

"I was *nice?*"

"Well, um, I guess so." She sounded dim-witted. "When...?"

"Did I start wanting you?"

She nodded.

"I don't know. I always thought you were beautiful. I was glad when you kicked your ex out. But I didn't know you."

"And I acted like I was scared of you, besides." She grimaced.

"That is a little off-putting." The skin at the corners of his eyes crinkled when he smiled.

"I've barely admitted to myself that I was attracted to you," she confessed. "I guess I'm a little slow."

"That's why you've been eyeing me today?"

"See? I'm an open book!"

His hand caught her chin. "That's one of the things I like best about you. You're direct, gentle and clearly puzzled by other people's agendas."

"You're making me sound like a child."

"No. Just a lovely woman who's an anomaly in the modern world."

"Um...thank you. I think."

They stood there smiling at each other, rather foolishly, she suspected. Finally, still smiling, he bent his head again and kissed her.

This one heated up with astonishing speed. The soft brush of mouth against mouth metamorphosed into the tangle of tongues, his hands gripping her hips to lift her higher into his arms until she was pressed as tightly against him as the barrier of clothing allowed. When they surfaced for air, he nipped her earlobe and she nuzzled his neck before he groaned and kissed her again.

He was the one to eventually lift his head and say raggedly, "I hate to mention it, but aren't we supposed to pick up the kids?"

Awash in the most wonderful sensations, she blinked. "Pick up…" Comprehension flooded back. "Oh! What time is it?"

He turned his head. "One-thirty."

"I said two-thirty."

"Ah." His grip loosened. "Unless you want to have a quickie…" He grinned at her expression. "Didn't think so. You, Suzanne Chauvin, are not a quickie kind of woman."

Her sniff might have been more effective if she weren't nestled up against his erection. "I should hope not. Although…"

Her sentence trailed off wistfully.

He kissed her hard. "Not the first time. Tempting though it is."

When he loosened his grip, opening inches between them, she had the first reawakening of self-consciousness. She'd never even shaken hands with this man a few weeks ago, and now they were talking about sex!

Knowing her face must be hot and her hair disheveled, she said the only thing that came to mind. "Um, would you like some apple cobbler?"

"As an alternative to you?" Tom asked politely.

She scrunched her face in embarrassment. "I guess this isn't a great moment for me to play hostess, is it?"

He kissed her lightly. "I'm just kidding. No, save the cobbler for dinner. The kids'll enjoy it."

"But you'll have dinner with us, won't you?"

Sounding like his usual kind self, he said, "Don't feel like you always have to ask me, Suzanne."

She said simply, "But I like it when you're with us."

"God." His hands, lingering at her waist, tightened momentarily, and something intense flashed in his eyes. Voice gravelly, he said, "You're not making it easy to let you go."

"Well, I wish you didn't have to," she admitted. "We're going to have to sneak around behind the kids' backs, aren't we?"

"You think we'd succeed? Sophia has an all-knowing look."

"Mark did say the kids could stay until tomorrow."

Tom raised his brows.

Suzanne blushed anew. Had that sounded as if she was implying…? *Was* she implying…?

With an effort, she corralled her muddled thoughts and asked the real question: Was she ready?

Her body apparently thought so. But she had responsibilities. A history. Good reasons to hesitate about starting a relationship at all, never mind racing into one. So…no. No, she wasn't ready.

Besides… "Jack really wanted to come home. He was worried that I wouldn't come today."

Tom's hands fell to his sides and he stepped back. "They both need to know you keep your promises."

She nodded.

"We have plenty of time, Suzanne. It took us five

years to do more than wave in passing. We can sneak kisses for a while."

They had better sneak them, she thought practically. The kids weren't hers yet, and the caseworker might get suspicious if they were suddenly getting married.

Married? Wow, there was a big jump.

And yet, it didn't feel like one. It felt…right. She examined the word, and the contentment the idea brought her. She'd said that before, about bringing home Jack and Sophia, and despite Sophia's anger, she still knew they belonged with her. Now, without the slightest doubt, she knew Tom would be a wonderful father and husband.

Still, they shouldn't rush too much. And stealing some kisses—that should be fun.

She smiled at him. "What do you say we head for Seattle?"

CHAPTER THIRTEEN

NEW YEAR'S EVE WASN'T ONE of Suzanne's favorite holidays, but the kids started talking about it the minute she and Tom picked them up at her sister's house.

Michael was going to his granddad's house while his mom and dad went to a party, Jack informed them. "Michael gets to watch fireworks over the lake. I wish I was gonna see fireworks. Are we?"

"Mostly there are lots of loud booms at midnight. I don't always stay up," Suzanne admitted.

"Not stay up?" Tom exclaimed in mock horror.

"I can watch the ball drop in Times Square at nine o'clock our time. That's good enough for me most years."

"This year, we'll have our own party. What do you two say?" Tom asked, cocking his head toward the back seat.

"Yay! We're gonna have a party!"

"Do I get to drink champagne?" Sophia asked.

Tom looked at Suzanne. "Do we *have* champagne?"

"Afraid not."

"No champagne. Sorry. But we'll have time tomorrow after we get home from shopping to make something special and maybe we could order a pizza."

More cheers from the back seat.

The kids seemed happy enough to be home, although Sophia predictably disappeared to her bedroom.

They all slept late, even Jack. She made pancakes for breakfast, pouring them in some approximation of animal shapes to Jack's delight.

It was early afternoon before she and Sophia were ready to leave. Jack ran next door to get Tom, who wheeled the new bicycle out of the garage and called, "Have fun," when Suzanne and Sophia got in the car.

"Yeah. Have fun!" Jack agreed.

They looked like father and son, standing side-by-side, Tom's hand on Jack's thin shoulder. Jack had happily agreed to stay behind. He didn't like to shop. If Suzanne bought him some clothes, that was okay. She could tell he didn't care. Nor, probably, would the other boys in school notice one way or the other what he was wearing at this age. Michael sure didn't.

Suzanne started the car and backed out. She half wished *she* were staying behind, too. Sophia was quiet, head bent, hair screening her face. With no idea what her mood was, Suzanne couldn't relax and have fun.

"I hope Jack doesn't fall off," she said.

Sophia shrugged. "I did. I got this big bump on my head. Like my brains were oozing out." She said *oozing* with positive relish.

At least they were talking.

"You must have had a concussion. Did you go to emergency?"

"Course I did!" She shot Suzanne an impatient look. "Mom thought I was going to die."

"I had a concussion when I was a kid. Mostly I remember throwing up."

"I puked lots."

Suzanne cleared her throat. "Sophia, there's something I've been wanting to say all week."

The ten-year-old retreated behind her screen of hair.

"If I gave the impression I was trying to make you forget your mom, I'm sorry." Suzanne drove as she talked, knowing it was better not to be searching Sophia's face for reactions. "Maybe I was trying too hard. I don't know. I just… I want you to be happy and feel safe and loved with me. When I spent so much on your bedrooms and on Christmas, it wasn't because I wanted to show you that I could give you nicer things than your mother could. It was because…" She paused. "Well, you know I went to live with my aunt and uncle after my parents died, right?"

Sophia nodded.

"I knew they didn't really want me. My cousins were mad that they had to share a bedroom so I could have one, my uncle was irritated by the disruption and by changes in routine, and although Aunt Jeanne was nicer, she didn't make any special effort, either. I overheard my uncle grumbling about his paycheck having to stretch for me when I wasn't even theirs. In all the years there I never felt I belonged or was wanted. Anyway, I might have been clumsy with you two—I know how recently your mom died—but I was trying to show you that you *are* wanted."

Those vivid eyes stole a glance at Suzanne. Sophia's voice was small when she said, "I guess I know that. I was mostly feeling sad."

Stopped at a red light near the mall, Suzanne reached out and squeezed her hand. "I wanted this Christmas to be the best ever, but for my sake, not yours. Because last year, I spent Christmas Eve with friends and then didn't go anywhere Christmas Day. I felt really alone. Then, this year, I not only had you two, I'd also found my brother and sister at last, and it all seemed magical. But you weren't ready. I should have known you wouldn't be."

Sophia snuffled. "It *was* the best Christmas I remember. Lots of the time I didn't think about Mom at all. But then I'd remember, and I kept thinking I shouldn't be happy!"

"That's a hard one, isn't it? Sometimes you forget, and you didn't think you ever would. And you feel guilty for being happy."

"I don't want Mom to know I am!" she wailed.

Suzanne didn't say anything for a minute. They'd entered the mall lot, and she turned gratefully into the first empty parking slot she saw, even though it was a long walk from the entry. She set the emergency brake, switched off the engine, then turned in her seat to face Sophia.

"I've never been sure in my own mind whether people who have died can watch over us or not. Sometimes it would be a little uncomfortable, and sometimes really comforting. Christmas Day, when I looked around the table at Carrie's, I had this little talk in my head with my parents. I asked if they could see us all together again. I really wished they could."

"It's okay to talk to someone who's dead?"

"Sure it is." She smiled at Sophia, her own face wet now, too.

"Oh." Sophia swiped at her tears.

Suzanne opened the glove compartment and took out the small box of tissues she kept there. She took a couple herself, then handed the box to her daughter. *My daughter,* she thought in fresh amazement. Okay, maybe not officially, but in every way that mattered to her.

After blowing her nose, she said, "I think one of the things we have to do is make sure you do remember your mom. Why don't we buy a photo album today, so you can put your pictures in it? And you could pick out a favorite and we could get it framed, so you could have it out on your dresser or desk."

"You wouldn't mind?"

"Of course not! Some night this week, I could show you pictures of my parents, and maybe you'd show me yours of your mom. I'd like to know whether you look like her, or your father, or some great grandmother."

Sounding shy, Sophia said, "Mom said I looked like my father. I don't really remember him. I guess maybe Jack looks more like her."

"Do you have a picture of him?"

She nodded. "Mom said to keep it even if he was a jerk, because he was still part of us."

Suzanne gave a choked laugh. "That's true. Did you know *his* parents?"

"Huh-uh. I don't think even he knew them." She sounded uncertain. "He wasn't ever adopted, either. He had lots of foster homes. That's why I thought…" Her throat seemed to close.

"You thought that might happen to you, too?"

Suddenly sobbing, she flung herself against Suzanne and held on hard. Suzanne cried, held her and murmured, "I am so glad I found you. So glad," over and over.

Finally, Sophia drew back, her face wet, her eyes swollen and her nose running. "I got snot all over you. I'm sorry!"

Suzanne reached for more tissues and laughed. "Oh, sweetie, it's okay!"

The ten-year-old blew her nose hard. "Can we still go shopping?"

"Of course we can!" She smiled despite the fact that her face probably looked awful, too. "And we're going to have fun, aren't we?"

"Yeah. I guess Mom wouldn't mind."

Suzanne squeezed her hand one more time. "I know she wouldn't."

They did have fun. Suzanne was disconcerted to find that, with Sophia's height and figure, they had to shop in the junior department rather than the children's, but the clothes *were* cute if a whole lot sexier than she was comfortable with a ten-year-old wearing. She was relieved to find that Sophia didn't especially want skintight jeans or T-shirts, and they were able to find some that looked stylish without making her look sixteen. Choosing a dress for her to wear to Gary and Rebecca's wedding the next Saturday took longer, but at the third store they found one they both liked. They also bought a couple of bras, pajamas and socks, as well as two pairs of jeans, a pile of sweatshirts and shirts and a wedding outfit for Jack.

"I'm going to have to take him shopping for shoes,"

Suzanne said. "Oh, well. He'd be bored to death today, wouldn't he?"

Carrying two bags, Sophia nodded. "He'd be whining, 'Aren't we be done?'"

"You bored yet?"

"No! Do I get shoes, too?"

Looking down at the tattered sneakers, Suzanne said, "Yes, you do."

They bought running shoes, sandals with a wedge heel to go with the dress and a pair of stylish boots to wear under jeans, then called it a day.

Suzanne drove up their block to the sight of Jack pedaling down the street with Tom trotting along holding him up. Her heart gave a bump in her chest, and she almost laughed at herself. Give her a man who was great with kids any day. As far as she was concerned, Tom could forget the chocolates and flowers if he never disappointed Jack or Sophia.

Sophia giggled. "He looks funny, doesn't he?"

"You mean Tom?" Suzanne said, trying to sound non-chalant. "Actually, I think he looks sweet."

"Are you going to marry him?" Sophia asked.

They both waved at Jack and Tom, then Suzanne turned into the driveway. "What makes you think I'm going to marry him?"

"I saw you kiss him last night."

Suzanne lifted her brows. "How could you have?"

"I sneaked down the hall. 'Cause you were talking, and then it got really quiet." She grinned. "And you were smooching."

So much for sneaking around.

"You shouldn't spy on people, you know."

"I like to know things."

Suzanne considered and rejected the idea of lecturing about privacy. Instead, she asked, "Would you mind?"

Momentarily hesitant, Sophia said, "He'd…well, want us, right?"

Suzanne smiled. "What do you think?"

"Yeah, because he's really nice." Her face worked as she thought. "I guess it would be okay," she finally decided. "Jack especially likes him."

"I noticed. It's important for a boy to have a role model."

"So, are you?"

"We haven't gotten to that point," Suzanne said, a little primly. "So promise me you don't say anything. But…I hope we do."

"Yeah! If you do, do I get to be part of the wedding? With a fancy dress and everything?"

"I promise, if I ever get married you will definitely be part of the wedding. Both of you," she said firmly. "Now promise. That includes Jack. You didn't tell him about the kissing, did you?"

"Not yet. How come I can't tell him?"

"Because I don't want him disappointed if Tom and I decide we don't want to get married."

"Oh." Sophia thought. "Okay."

Suzanne fixed a stern look on her face. "Cross your heart…"

She rolled her eyes. "Hope to die. I promise!"

"Thank you. Now let's carry your loot in."

Jack was pushing the bike up the driveway, Tom right behind him, when they got out.

"I almost told Tom to let go," he said excitedly. "'Cept I wasn't sure."

"Today was your first time ever on a bike." Suzanne hugged him and smiled over his head at Tom. "You haven't been riding ever since we left, have you?"

"Nope," Jack said, tilting his head back to look up at her with sparkling eyes. "I helped paint, too. And we watched football and had pie."

"Peach pie," Tom murmured.

"I can stay awake tonight. Right?"

"I don't see why not."

He peered into the trunk of the car. "Boy, you bought a lot of stuff."

"Some of which is for you. In fact, I'd like you to try it all on now."

His eyes widened, and his voice rose to a whine. "Do I hafta try *everything* on?"

"Yes, you do. How else will I know if I bought the right sizes?"

His shoulders sagged.

Tom clapped him on the back. "You're on your own, big guy. The second half of that bowl game is starting."

"No fair! I was watching, too. Can I...?"

Suzanne grinned at him. "Not a chance. Here, you help carry, too."

Sophia was already laden and heading for the open garage.

Suzanne loaded Jack and sent him off, then turned to Tom. "Thank you. We had a great time."

He smiled at her. "We did, too."

"Sophia saw us 'smooching' last night. She sneaked down the hall."

He laughed. "Told you. No way you can keep a secret from that girl."

"But we didn't even make it twenty-four hours!"

"Just think," he said. "When she's sixteen and trying to make out with some boy in the driveway, you can return the favor."

An involuntary shudder racked her body.

Tom laughed harder. "This is going to be fun."

She punched him in the arm. "Hey, I haven't had ten years to get used to the idea of having a teenager! Give me a break."

"Don't worry, I'll pop out of my house as soon as I hear her boyfriend's junker pull into your driveway and escort her to the front door."

He'd pop out of *his* house? Was that how he saw them six years from now? Still sneaking kisses and probably a whole lot more?

Hiding her dismay, Suzanne laughed, then agreed on what time he'd come over for their New Year's Eve party before grabbing the last bags and heading into the garage herself. Tom pulled it closed behind her.

She took the bags to Jack's room and insisted he try the new clothes on now.

"Yes, this very minute," she repeated, after the third protest.

On the surface, she approved the clothes he tried on, stuffed one shirt that needed to be returned back in the bag, and told him he looked handsome in the khaki slacks and button-down shirt she'd chosen for the wedding. Inside, she kept reexamining Tom's teasing remark, trying to decide if she was taking it way too literally. *And* too seriously.

He probably hadn't meant anything by it. Anyway, he could hardly say, *Since we'll be married,* I'll *deal with Sophia's boyfriends.*

On the other hand... Maybe *she'd* been making some big assumptions. He'd kissed her, and said he wanted her and he wanted her to be happy, but they hadn't talked about the future at all beyond the whole sneaking-around idea. He had, after all, reached the age of thirty-five without ever getting married. Maybe he was perfectly happy single. Okay, so he'd implied that he was lonely; maybe he just wanted dinner invitations and to have her in his bed for a not-so-quickie on occasion. Maybe the whole idea of permanently taking on a messy woman and noisy children held zilch appeal.

If that was true, she couldn't even get mad at him. She was the one who'd made a huge leap from a first kiss to their inevitable wedding. She'd done that partly because he seemed to like the kids so much, but marriage did not necessarily follow.

By the time Sophia twirled into Jack's bedroom to show off her dress, Suzanne had convinced herself that she was looking too far ahead, considering that Tom and she had kissed for the first time just yesterday.

Tom came over at six, and they had a fun evening watching the celebration in Times Square on TV, eating pizza and then cobbler and drinking pop. Jack was sleepy by the time midnight arrived Eastern standard time, and Tom carried him to bed half an hour later, teeth unbrushed.

Then Tom sheepishly produced an unopened Seattle edition Monopoly game someone had given him a couple of years before, and the three of them played until the fireworks burst from the Space Needle on TV.

After tucking Sophia in, Suzanne returned to the living room for a private celebration before going to bed in the wee hours.

She couldn't remember a better beginning to a new year.

The next evening at dinner, she said, "Just think, school tomorrow."

The previous week she'd looked up the school district on the Internet and studied the boundary lines, so she knew which school they would be going to. She also knew that most of the elementary schools were K-6, thank goodness. Sophia would have another year there before moving on to the middle school.

Once Suzanne had tucked both kids in and was sitting down to pay bills her phone rang.

"Any chance you want to sneak around right now?" Tom asked.

She gave a choked laugh. "How far do I have to sneak?"

"Your front porch?"

"It's cold!"

"Not too cold for a good-night kiss," he coaxed.

"Let me find my slippers and put on a coat."

"Deal."

Two minutes later, she unlocked and stepped out onto the dark porch to find Tom already waiting.

A little light fell from the living-room window, but without the porch light on he was mostly a dark hulk.

"Hey," he said softly. He must have kept his hands in his pockets because they were warm when he cupped her face. "I missed you."

"I missed you, too," she admitted, a tiny bit dismayed to realize it was true. Despite her resolve to enjoy being a mom on her own the way she'd intended, she'd kept thinking, *I'll have to tell Tom what Sophia said,* or her gaze would stray to the place at the table she'd started to think of as his, or the laugh at Jack's knock-knock joke would seem thin without Tom's heartier guffaw.

"I'm here now," he murmured, and bent to capture her mouth.

The kiss was sweet and sensual, and Suzanne lost herself in it despite her qualms. He was warm and solid, and awfully skilled with his lips and tongue and hands for a man who claimed to be surprised she'd be attracted to him.

"You're a fraud," she said when she came up for air.

"Huh?" He nipped her earlobe.

"All those things you said about having an ugly mug. You wouldn't be so good at kissing if plenty of women hadn't thought your face was handsome."

Voice a pleased rumble, he said, "So, I'm good at kissing, huh?"

Breathless, Suzanne tilted her head back to let him explore her neck. "Tut-tut. You're sounding like Jack, angling to hear every compliment twice."

"A man's got to take it where he can get it." He trailed kisses up her throat, nuzzled her chin and hovered above her mouth. "So, if it wasn't a compliment, what was the point?"

"Women have not been lacking in your past."

"There are a lot of single women at Boeing. Not so many single guys my age."

"Don't sound so smug."

He chuckled, his chest vibrating under her hands. "I'm kissing you, not my co-workers."

"Mm. That's true."

And she enjoyed every minute.

By the time Suzanne slipped back inside and locked up again, she had no interest in the unpaid bills. Heck, maybe she'd just go to bed and dream.

She'd turned out lights and was on her way down the hall when Sophia's sleepy voice came from her room.

"Smooching again?"

"Nosy."

Sophia's giggle followed her to bed, where Suzanne lay wondering about Tom's past relationships. Eventually she relaxed and decided they didn't matter. Of course at his age he'd had some, maybe serious. But they had plenty of time to talk about things like that.

MAYBE GOOD-NIGHT KISSES *weren't* such a good idea. Tom groaned and rolled over in bed. Damn it, he wanted Suzanne in bed with him.

But he knew darn well Suzanne wouldn't invite him into her bed with the kids down the hall, and they weren't old enough to leave by themselves.

There was, of course, a legitimate way for him to share her bed, but he was afraid to rush her. Despite the fact that they'd known each other for five years, their relationship was already moving fast.

So fast, it had been all he could do despite the cold not to start ripping her clothes off on her front porch. So fast that, despite the fact that they'd hardly talked until six weeks ago, he knew most of her worries and the things that had made her sad in her life as well as the ones that made her smile. They'd spent Christmas together, New Year's together. He'd baked cookies with the kids, had a part in furnishing their rooms, was helping Jack learn to ride his bike. He thought the kids had accepted him already as part of their lives. And Suzanne was the kind of woman who would be thinking about marriage, because she was unlikely to be interested in a casual sexual relationship.

But that had to scare the crap out of her. The fact that she'd dated so little in the two years since her divorce was telling. Tom had wondered about that, until he'd found out that she'd had literally no experience with men before the crud she'd married. No frame of reference. Nothing to make her *want* to try again. Clearly, she'd had no interest in husband-hunting.

He'd ambled into her life through a side door, so to speak. And he'd obviously met her primary criteria, which was being good father material.

But whether she was anywhere close to ready to think about marriage in anything but a *gee, this might head there down the line* way, he had no idea. He was hoping to bring her around to his way of thinking a little more quickly than *down the line.* In the meantime, it looked as if he was going to suffer one hell of a lot of sexual frustration.

Of course, her brother's wedding might bring the topic of marriage to mind. He'd received an invitation in the mail

Friday. It was taking place this coming Saturday. Presumably Gary or Rebecca had asked Suzanne if she'd like Tom to escort her, and also presumably she'd said yes. That was a good sign, wasn't it?

Strange that, of all people, he felt so ready to take the plunge. Maybe even stranger, when he thought about it, that he'd always assumed he *would* someday. Remembering the chill between his parents should have been enough to put him off the whole institution.

But in a hazy way, Tom knew things had been better before Jessie had died. When memories flicked into his mind, he immediately classified them as Before or After. Considering he'd been eight when she'd got sick and ten when she'd died, he should have more clear Before memories than he did. He could conjure enough, though, to know that things had once been different. His father had still been a stern taskmaster; Tom remembered scrubbing floors on his hands and knees when he couldn't have been more than six or seven because he'd made a mess. But they'd had fun as a family, too, and Tom's mother had been softer. His father would kiss his mother goodbye before he left for work, sometimes lay an arm around her shoulders when they watched TV in the darkened living room, caress her casually in passing. And Tom did remember how much he'd liked having a sister. Jessie had looked up to him, followed him around, had been willing to play whatever role he'd wanted her to in whatever game he'd chosen.

So he guessed that was when he'd formed the default opinion that when he grew up, he'd get married and have kids. But maybe it was the After that had tripped him up when he got close. He knew how bad it could get, and he'd wanted to be absolutely sure that he and the woman he married would never end up hating each other because grief—or something else unforeseen—had torn them apart.

For the first time in his life, with Suzanne, he was sure—if only about his part. He'd always been attracted to her, of course, and was still in awe at the way she returned his kisses. But that was only the beginning. He'd fallen in love with the woman he saw beneath the delicate and beautiful surface; with the Suzanne who was vulnerable, gentle, stronger than she knew, determined and possessing of an extraordinary ability to love.

Staring up at the dark ceiling, his body more relaxed but no closer to sleep than ever, Tom thought, *And there's the real question.*

Suzanne enjoyed his kisses; she trusted him with the kids; she relied on him, she thought he was a nice man. All of which might incline her toward marriage.

But had he really touched her heart?

Maybe, he thought, he shouldn't push for marriage. To get them through the years to come, any couple had to have something special. Liking, physical attraction, convenience, those were the kinds of things that could sour.

He was sure, but he needed to be equally sure that she felt the same. And right now...Tom didn't think she did.

CHAPTER FOURTEEN

OUTSIDE THE CLOSED CLASSROOM door, Suzanne hugged Jack and whispered, "I hope Ms. Lopez is the best teacher you've ever had," then gently set him away from her.

Eyes wide and scared, he looked incredibly cute and brave when he squared his shoulders and marched through the door the vice principal opened.

She smiled at Suzanne, said, "He'll love Ms. Lopez, I promise," and went in after Jack. Once inside, she announced, "Class, I'd like you to meet a new student."

Left in the deserted hall of the elementary school, Suzanne blinked away tears and found her way blindly toward the front entrance, outside of which she'd left her car.

The last thing Sophia had said this morning before they'd gotten out of the car was "I bet this school is going to suck, too." She'd walked in with a mulish look on her face, her shoulders hunched in that way she had of closing herself in. The only thin ray of hope Suzanne had was that Sophia had gotten up extra early on her own to get ready. She'd put on brand new jeans, boots and her favorite of the new tops. And when Jack hadn't appeared after Suzanne's first wake-up call, Sophia had gone into his bedroom.

"Get up! We gotta go to school today. Remember?"

The *words* weren't encouraging, but her voice had sounded...excited.

Suzanne had made sure they arrived before the first bell that morning, and was glad to find that their previous school had sent the kids' records. Melissa had let the school know the kids would be starting here after Christmas break, so they were expected.

Rather than taking them directly to their new classes, the vice principal had spent the time talking to both of them, reassuring Jack and coaxing a flicker of a smile from Sophia. As it happened, the principal had seen the note Sophia's teacher had written about her artistic talent and had been able to put her into a classroom with a teacher who particularly enjoyed nurturing that kind of ability.

"He's an exciting teacher," the vice principal had assured them. "He loves using video—the kids all learn to use the camera and edit. They integrate art and the television shows they create themselves into their other lessons." Her eyes met Suzanne's. "He enjoys kids with strong opinions and voices."

Suzanne was more reassured by that than anything else she'd heard. The administration had noted Sophia's tendency to speak out bluntly and to get mad, and had tried in response to choose a teacher who'd be most likely to channel her strong personality appropriately.

The school secretary had called another student in Sophia's classroom to escort her, and Sophia had barely acknowledged Suzanne's, "Have a good day!" before leaving with the other girl. Of course, both kids were used to first days at new schools.

Now, Suzanne smiled somewhat blindly in the direction of the school secretary, who'd no doubt seen tears before, and went out into the cold, hurrying to her car.

Once behind the wheel, gripping the steering wheel, Suzanne thought, *Please, please, let them be happy here.*

Then she put the car in gear and pulled out of her parking spot.

At the shop, she had time to make herself a cup of tea and drink it before she turned the Closed sign to Open. Last week, she had posted her new days and hours, and had concluded quickly that her customers weren't going to mind.

By mid-afternoon, when she started listening for the school bus that would stop just a block away, she was thinking, *What customers?* She'd barely seen a handful of people all day. Her take so far was the worst of any single day since she'd opened last summer. Even her one class had been poorly attended, with half the students registered failing to appear. Apparently rumors of how dead retail could be in January were accurate.

The kids burst in just after three, and she set down her knitting and jumped to her feet.

"Tell me everything! How did it go?"

They both talked at once.

"It was okay." Sophia's shrug didn't look as nonchalant as she intended.

"I had fun!" Jack said, his thin face alight. "Ms. Lopez is really nice! And I kinda made a friend today."

"A friend? Really?" Suzanne drew them back to the sitting area where she held her classes.

"Yeah! His name is Dylan. Ms. Lopez asked him to

show me around today, and he did a real good job. He picked me to be on his relay team in P.E. an' everything."

"That's great!" She smiled, thrilled at the enthusiasm shining from him.

"I got homework, though. They made me take tests today. Ms. Lopez says I did real good on the math."

"Melissa told me your last teacher said you were really good at math, too. What homework do you have?"

The school had loaned him flash cards, it developed, although apparently Suzanne was expected to buy some, and he was supposed to read for twenty minutes. Plus, there was a program on PBS tonight about whales that Ms. Lopez had encouraged them to watch.

"Are you done?" Sophia finally said with sisterly disgust, stemming the tide of words. "So I can tell about *my* day?"

"Um..." His forehead creased. "I guess. Mostly."

"Thank you," she said with masterly sarcasm.

"Did you make any friends?" he asked.

"On the first day?" She rolled her eyes. "Yeah, right."

"How do you like your teacher?" Suzanne asked.

"He's okay. I learned to use a video camera. It is *so* cool! We filmed this weekly news show. Mr. Schroder says I can be the anchor next week."

Jack thought that was hilarious. "An anchor? Are they going to drop you to the bottom of the sea?"

"That's what the person who tells you the news on TV is called." The curl of her lip expressed how exquisitely pained she was to be related to this boy. "Dummy."

Suzanne cleared her throat. They'd had talks about calling names.

"Well, he is."

"No, he's seven years old."

"Yeah!" Jack jumped in. "I bet *you* didn't know everything when you were seven, either."

Sophia decided to abandon the argument. "Can we get a video camera? It is so fun to use!"

"I'm afraid you'll have to enjoy using the one at school for now." Suzanne smiled at her. "Did they make you take tests, too?"

"I think I'm going to tomorrow." She frowned. "We started a spelling unit, and the words are a lot harder than I'm used to. Like *annihilate* and *retribution.*"

Surprised, Suzanne said, "Those are depressing words."

"We're talking about world news."

Well, that explained depressing.

"Do you have homework, too?"

"Tons of it!" she exclaimed. "Can I start it now?"

"I hope you will." Suzanne looked at the seven-year-old. "Jack, since there aren't any customers right now, why don't we do flash cards?"

One more customer wandered in about four o'clock and left without buying anything. Suzanne didn't bother to close out the till. She resolved, though, to be positive about the time she now had on her hands. She would use it to design patterns and to knit items for sale. She hadn't intended them to be more than an occasional sideline, but the Christmas season had demonstrated how profitable they could be. She could use yarns that were about to be discounted because they weren't selling well, and turn them into gorgeous afghans, sweaters and scarves that would fly out once she displayed them in her window.

Tom had invited them all to dinner that night so he could hear about the kids' day, too, so once home they dumped their belongings in their bedrooms, locked the front door and went to his house.

Over black bean and corn burritos, he listened as they talked over each other in bursts.

"This girl asked where I bought my shirt…"

"Dylan asked if I play Little League. He was really surprised when I said I never have. So can I this year?" He turned hopeful eyes on Suzanne.

"The sixth graders are, like, really snobby. Like *they're* better than everyone."

"There's this other guy in my class who's shorter than I am. *Lots* shorter," Jack said with satisfaction.

Sophia suddenly fixated on Tom. "Do *you* have a video camera?"

He blinked. "No. Why? Are you going to take up something I should videotape?"

"Take up something?"

"Yeah. Like ice skating, or ballet, or you're going to have a solo in the school concert."

"No, I just wanted to borrow it if you had one." She told him about her day's adventures. "So now I really, really want my own."

"But borrowing mine would be an adequate substitute."

Sophia gave him a dazzling smile. "If you decide to get one…"

"You'll be the first to know," he agreed. To Suzanne, he murmured, "Pity the boys someday."

She laughed and shook her head. "She's shameless."

"So can I be in Little League?" Jack persisted. "Huh? Can I?"

"If we can figure out transportation, sure."

He cheered, and she worried about his disappointment if she couldn't. What did other working parents do? Depend on stay-at-home moms to ferry their children everywhere? Or would practices be in the evening once days became longer?

After dinner, Suzanne insisted that they all help clear the table and load the dishwasher. Afterward, Sophia grabbed the keys and the kids ran ahead to the house, squabbling over who got the TV.

Suzanne called after them, "Schoolwork trumps even favorite shows! Jack has to watch *Nova.* Tape your show, Sophia."

"No fair!" They disappeared into the house, leaving Tom and Suzanne on his porch.

His easy smile vanished, and he pulled her back inside and closed the door. She found herself backed up against the door, his hands flattened on it to each side of her head.

"What…?"

"I missed you."

She barely had time to say "Oh," before his mouth claimed hers with none of his usual gentleness. His kiss was urgent, his body crowding hers. That raw male hunger drove her response. She all but melted, kissing him back, forgetting she even *had* children, never mind that she needed to follow them home.

When he finally lifted his head, she stared him, dazed. His face was stark with a need she'd never seen on it before, his chest rising and falling hard, his eyes dark.

"What…what was that about?" Suzanne whispered.

"Over dinner, I just kept looking at you and thinking how much I wanted to touch you."

"But…you looked so patient!"

"With them, yeah. I didn't feel patient where you're concerned." His jaw muscles flexed. "But I have to be, don't I?" He backed away, releasing her. "In fact, you'd better get home now and head off World War III."

"Yes, I…" She shook her head, trying to clear it, hoping her knees were sturdy enough to hold her. "I suppose I should."

Furrows between his brows made Tom's face forbidding, different from the kind one she'd thought she knew so well. She couldn't tell if he was irritated at her, or himself. He opened the door.

"Good night, Suzanne."

"Thank you for dinner."

He dipped his head.

She hesitated, but had no idea what to say. *I want you, too?* But he could tell from her response that she did. *Does this mean you're not happy sneaking a few kisses? It has to be more, or else?* But what would *else* mean? Anyway, he hadn't actually said that.

"I'll see you tomorrow?" Her voice rose slightly, uncertainty creeping into it.

His face softened a little. "I'm sure you will."

Did he sound resigned rather than pleased? Or was she imagining things?

She stumbled over the doorjamb. Righting herself, Suzanne said, “Good night, Tom,” and retreated into the darkness between their houses.

“HOW BIG DID YOU SAY this wedding was?” Clearly, they weren’t going to be parking anywhere near the mansion.

“I don’t think over a hundred.” Suzanne peered ahead. “But if the house doesn’t have much parking…”

Tom grunted. “Looking at those heels, I’d better let you ladies off in front and then go find a place.”

Suzanne smiled at him. “A gentleman to the core.”

Ever since she’d come out her front door, he’d been trying not to regret the fact that the kids were behind her. He’d wanted to sweep her away to a romantic evening, the kind they’d never had.

Made of some kind of crinkly gold fabric that also looked whisper-thin and clung in all the right places, her dress also bared plenty of leg, enhanced by strappy black high heels. She’d pulled back strands of hair from around her face, included thin gold ribbon, and had somehow created intricate, interlocking braids that formed a kind of net over the back of her head. From it, sleek hair flowed down her back. Her eyes looked huge and mysterious, her lush mouth exotic with lipstick, her face even more delicately sculpted than ever.

He’d almost gotten used to thinking of her as Suzanne, the woman he kissed every night on her front porch. Much as he wanted her, Tom had quit feeling intimidated by her beauty. This afternoon, every time he glanced her way, she dislodged his breath afresh.

He turned between the open, wrought-iron gates and followed the curved driveway that led under a portico at the front of the elegant mansion. The double doors were flung wide, and beautifully dressed people were squeezed onto the porch. A couple of cars in front of him took turns pausing to let someone out, then continued. In his turn, he stopped.

Suzanne squeezed his hand, gave him a brilliant smile and said, "Hurry back."

"Can I go with you?" Jack asked.

Tom shrugged. "Fine by me."

"If you're sure." At two male nods, Suzanne got out, as gracefully as a woman in heels could from a two-ton pickup truck, then opened the back door to let out Sophia. As soon as they'd reached the porch, Tom started forward again.

"Shall we come back in a couple of hours?" he kidded.

"Yeah! I don't want to go to any wedding. Dylan says they'll *kiss*."

Tom laughed. "Yeah, I bet they will. But it's not so bad. And I want to see the inside of that house. I'll bet the woodwork is something special."

He got lucky and found a parking spot not a quarter of a mile along, and he and Jack walked back. The kid looked cute today in chinos, a button-down shirt and a tie, his face fresh-scrubbed. He held Tom's hand as if by matter-of-fact, the trusting warmth of that small grip tweaking something in Tom's chest.

Cars were still disgorging passengers, but Suzanne and Sophia waited just inside the front door. As far as Tom was concerned, no one else was even there, not with Suzanne's smile lighting at the sight of him.

No, that wasn't quite true. He'd noticed what a beauty Sophia was today, too. Suzanne had probably hoped the simple dress was childlike, but the effect was far from it. Dotted with a print of tiny flowers, the blue fabric made the blue of her eyes more vivid, and however gangly she was in what was probably her first pair of shoes with any heels, they showed off long, coltish legs. Her dark hair looked in danger of escaping whatever arrangement was holding it on top of her head, but Tom suspected that impression was deceptive. Seemed to him actresses in movies often had similarly disheveled dos, even walking a red carpet. Yeah, Sophia was going to be a beauty all right.

"We have the two prettiest ladies here," Tom told Jack, who gave him a look of astonishment.

"Two?"

"Hey, look at your sister."

His face scrunched up. "I guess she looks okay."

Tom laughed, clapped him on the back, and then kissed Suzanne on the cheek when he reached her.

"Thanks for waiting for us."

She chuckled. "We've been serving as an informal receiving line. We've met half a dozen of Rebecca's friends. Oh, and Jagger, Gary's partner in Chimayo Coffee Company. He's best man, you know."

Tom didn't, but that was okay.

They peeked into the downstairs rooms where the reception would be held, then followed the traffic up the sweep of stairs to the top-floor ballroom. Folding chairs had been set up, leaving the traditional aisle down the middle.

"No ushers," a cheerful young man told them. "Seat yourselves. Bride's family to the left, groom's to the right."

Rebecca's side had the numbers, not surprisingly, since she'd grown up locally and gone to both college and graduate school in the Northwest. Except for half a dozen people Tom didn't know, the rest of Gary's side seemed to be family. The turnout, though, was impressive, including the whole contingent from Christmas, even Carrie's adoptive parents and Mark's father, and a large group that had Suzanne murmuring under her breath, "Oh, dear," then, "I mean, wonderful! Uncle Miles made it."

Uncle Miles was apparently the florid-faced fellow beside a woman who was obviously Suzanne's aunt. She was a dead ringer but for the streaks of gray in her hair and the lines in her face.

Suzanne laid hands on both the kids' shoulders and stopped them. "Aunt Jeanne, Uncle Miles." She laughed. "Everyone."

Which presumably included the two younger men who must be her cousins, their wives and the horde of kids that accompanied them.

"We can talk later, but I'd like you to meet the kids. Jack, Sophia, this is the aunt and uncle who raised me. And folks, this is Tom Stefanec, my next-door neighbor."

All said hi, but the crowded aisle forced them on. They slipped into the third row right behind Carrie, her adoptive parents, Mark, his father and Michael.

Tom joined the general greeting, but was thinking, *I'm*

her neighbor? That was the best she could do in the introduction department?

They said their hellos, and Mark refused permission for Michael to sit beside Jack on the grounds that they wouldn't be able to resist whispering if not wrestling.

Tom sat back at last and took a look around the ballroom. A high, coved ceiling, tall, multipaned windows and Adams-style, white-painted paneled walls made it visually spacious and reminiscent of a more elegant, formal era. Huge vases of white and pale pink lilies resided in niches designed for them. The early lumber barons had apparently lived like kings.

"Isn't it beautiful?" Suzanne whispered.

"Makes me want to sweep you onto the floor for a waltz," Tom agreed.

"Oh." Her eyes became soft, even misty. "Do you know how to waltz?"

"As it happens, I do."

Her nose crinkled endearingly. "Unfortunately, I don't. I'd step on your feet. I've always wanted to take a ballroom dance class."

"Why don't we someday?"

Mark turned in his seat. "Damn it, man. I heard that. We don't volunteer for things like that. We pretend to go reluctantly. To make them happy."

"Sorry," Tom said solemnly. "I'm new at this. Won't happen again."

Suzanne punched his arm. Sophia giggled.

A woman seated herself at the organ to one side and began to play. Tom thought he recognized Handel. Behind them, the shuffling of feet suggested a few people were still seating themselves.

Finally, the minister appeared at the front, beatific smile in place, joined by Gary's bulky, bearded friend and by the groom himself, expression so reserved he was probably wishing himself not on display. On the other side, a blond woman with cropped hair stepped to the front. Apparently the maid of honor wasn't coming up the aisle with the bride.

Suzanne gave a soft sigh. "Gary's so handsome. He looks eerily like my father in my parents' wedding pictures. I wish…" Her voice faded away.

Tom knew what she wished. He took her hand, but she didn't look at him. He heard her give a small sniff.

A murmur through the crowd made them turn to see Rebecca coming down the aisle beside her mother. Tom gave a nod of approval. He was glad she hadn't asked a male friend to take the part of the parent who had been both mother and father.

"She's so pretty," Sophia exclaimed.

Jack rolled his eyes and slumped in his seat.

Once upon a time, Tom would have done the same. Today… Damn it, today he was getting a lump in his throat. More even than Christmas, this day represented the extraordinary reunion of a family that would have been forever lost if not for the determination and steadfast love of the woman beside him.

Love he wanted for himself.

He glanced at the groom, to see the way his face had relaxed at the sight of his beloved. Gary Lindstrom had had a crummy life, abused by his adoptive father and abandoned by his adoptive mother. Now, dozens of people who were family crowded his side of the aisle to celebrate his marriage, his ability despite everything to trust to a future and to the beautiful, copper-haired woman gliding toward him.

Only a seven-year-old boy could *not* feel something.

Tom waited for Suzanne to turn her glowing smile on him, the one that said, *Soon, that will be me. And* you *will be waiting for me, your hand out.*

Disquiet crept beneath his breastbone when that didn't happen. He tried to ignore it.

Rebecca reached Gary, who kissed her mother's cheek and took her hand.

The ceremony proceeded, a more traditional one than Tom might have anticipated. Was Gary a churchgoer? Tom didn't know, but guessed Rebecca, at least, must be.

Some of the words struck home.

"…and therefore is not by any to be entered into unadvisedly or lightly, but reverently, discreetly, advisedly, soberly, and in the fear of God."

Light-headed, Tom thought, *I can do that.*

But could she?

"Gary, will you have this woman to be your wedded wife, to live together after God's ordinance in the holy estate of matrimony? Will you love her, comfort her, honor and keep her in sickness and in health and, forsaking all others, keep only unto her, so long as you both shall live?"

Gary found a smile for his bride. "I will," he said clearly.

"I will," she said in turn, when asked.

They repeated their vows in steady voices. The bearded

friend—Jagger?—produced a ring, which Gary slipped onto Rebecca's finger.

With this ring, I thee wed.

What was Suzanne thinking? He stole a glance at her, to see her watching raptly, tears flowing apparently unnoticed down her cheeks.

Of course she would cry at her brother's wedding. She was that kind of woman. She'd probably cry at any wedding.

Tom laid his arm over the back of the chair. She gave him a distracted, watery smile, without ever quite tearing her gaze from the bride and groom.

"I pronounce you man and wife," the minister said with a smile. "You may kiss the bride."

"Eew!" Jack buried his face in his hands.

Everyone else sighed and murmured when Gary swept his wife into his arms and kissed her passionately. A laugh began when they didn't surface for a good minute.

Finally, the organist played a beautiful, delicate piece of music and the two of them, flushed from their kiss, walked down the aisle to applause and smiles.

Suzanne swiped at her cheeks. "That was lovely."

Face wet, too, Carrie turned in her seat. "It was, wasn't it?"

The two hugged over the back of Carrie's folding chair, and then, talking, they all joined the exodus.

"You didn't cry at our wedding," Mark complained.

"That's because I was so happy."

"And now you're miserable?"

"No, I'm crying now because I'm so happy." She laughed through her tears. "And, no, it makes no sense. It doesn't have to."

Tom looked around, to see that darn near every woman was at least misty eyed. He put a hand on Sophia's shoulder. "Don't grow up and cry at weddings."

She lifted vivid, awed eyes to meet his. "But it was so-o beautiful."

"He looked so much like Dad," Suzanne said to her sister. "It's uncanny."

"I thought he did," her sister agreed.

"But then, I kept seeing Mom in you at your wedding." Suzanne wiped her eyes again as they moved slowly toward the stairs.

And so it went. When she met up with her aunt, the two of them hugged and wept some more, Uncle Miles standing by with ill-concealed impatience. When they finally reached Gary and Rebecca, he drew her into a fierce hug.

Tom heard his rough whisper.

"Thank you. If it weren't for you…"

"This is my happy ending," she told him tearfully.

Tom's disquiet sharpened, began to feel jagged.

He congratulated Gary and kissed Rebecca on her cheek.

They stood in line to get plates of food, then began to circulate, meeting a small cluster of Gary's co-workers from Santa Fe, Rebecca's maid of honor, an artist who had just been featured in *Seattle Magazine,* and finally the aunt, uncle and cousins.

Juggling his drink and plate, Tom shook hands with Ray and Roddie and found that his preconceived dislike of Uncle Miles hadn't been intense enough.

Before Tom had even met him, Miles muttered to his wife, "Taking in kids that age is asking for trouble." Neither

Suzanne nor Jack heard, but Sophia stiffened, not relaxing until Tom drew her a few feet aside and murmured in her ear, "This is the man who couldn't even find it in his heart to take in his own niece and nephew."

"Suzanne says he wasn't that nice to her."

"Yeah, that's what I understand. She's only polite because she loves her aunt."

"Do *I* have to…" the girl began.

"Yes. For Suzanne's sake."

"Oh." She scowled. "All right."

He smiled at her. "Good girl. Oh, and did I tell you how spectacular you look today? You're going to be breaking hearts before you know it."

Delicate color crept into her cheeks, and her smile was the softest he'd ever seen from her. "Um…thank you."

Eventually the party moved back upstairs for dancing, once the chairs had been cleared out. In the middle of the floor, locked together, Rebecca and Gary rocked from foot to foot. Tom got one intoxicating dance with Suzanne before he and Mark switched partners, and then he led Sophia out while Suzanne and Carrie tried to teach their sons a few steps.

Finally, leaving the couples without children to dance the night away, a general exodus began.

Getting Suzanne out the door wasn't easy, though. First she had to hug her brother and his new wife again, her sister, her aunt, Carrie's adoptive parents, even her cousin's wives.

"This is the best day!" she was still exclaiming when Tom pulled up with the GMC and she and the kids climbed in.

"Wasn't that fun?" she asked them, buckling herself in.

"Yeah, it was. I've never danced before." She had several times tonight, first with Tom, then Mark, and last with a boy who'd looked about fifteen and probably hadn't realized how much younger she was.

"The food was real, real good," Jack contributed.

Suzanne laughed. "I don't know if I tasted a bite."

"I did. It was good." Tom had finally realized there was no meat, but the caterers had done such a good job, he hadn't cared. He wouldn't mind having the recipe for that mushroom ravioli in a light cream sauce.

Suzanne raved the rest of the way home. Rebecca's dress! Wasn't it exquisite? Did he know the processional music had been "Rondeau" by Jean-Joseph Mouret?

No, he'd never heard of Mouret.

The honeymoon! Did everyone know Gary was taking Rebecca to New Zealand? She'd always wanted to go, and of course it was summer there right now, and wasn't that romantic? They were going to be gone for a month!

Sophia ate it up. Jack began to hum tunelessly and stare out the side window. Tom felt a headache begin squeezing his temples.

"I want a wedding like that," Sophia declared. "Only with lots, lots more people. Like maybe six hundred. So I have this long way to walk with everyone looking at me."

Suzanne laughed. "Honey, you'd better start making friends now." She turned to Tom. "You weren't bored, were you?"

He sent her what he hoped was a significant smile. "No, I found it inspirational."

No blush, no meaningful flash of those big, smoky dark

eyes. Nope, all she did was gush, "It was uplifting, wasn't it? The way Gary looked at Rebecca…"

Blah blah blah.

Tom made his good-nights short. As the garage door rolled down behind his pickup, the headache tightened and his earlier disquiet became flat-out heartburn.

Either Suzanne was incapable of thinking about her own wants and needs, so focused was she on the happiness of other people, or her thoughts hadn't even begun to turn to marriage—at least, not with him.

Oh, yeah, or choice number three: she'd gone out of her way today to make sure he didn't start hearing wedding bells of his own.

Shoulders slumped, he sat in the empty pickup in his dimly lit, silent garage, making no move to get out.

Was he the one jumping the gun? Or did love come quick if it was going to come at all?

He wished he'd had to work today and could have bowed out of the wedding. Wished he weren't putting pressure on himself and Suzanne.

Tom finally got out and went into his house, turning on the TV just to hear voices that weren't full of doubt.

CHAPTER FIFTEEN

EVER SINCE THE WEDDING Tom had been different. Quieter, more withdrawn. Sometimes Suzanne caught a fleeting look of...something. Frustration, irritation, more anger? She wasn't sure.

She'd given hardly a thought to his past, to the dysfunctional childhood and the years as a soldier. Not just a regular soldier, but an Army Ranger. Weren't they trained in all kinds of horrible things? Tom had seemed so nice, so gentle, she'd taken him at face value, forgoing any analysis of what she'd learned about his past.

But now...now she was starting to wonder. Was he not quite what he seemed? Or had he just been in a bad mood for some reason?

She didn't want to think he had a capacity for anger and violence she hadn't seen, but knew he must. He'd spent ten years as a soldier. The gentle, considerate man she knew would be a really bad soldier. He must have hidden layers.

She felt silly even thinking that, because of course everyone did. But it did make her realize how much she *didn't* know about him. For example, he'd never once talked about his experiences in the Army. Wouldn't it be normal to at least tell funny stories? They hadn't shared first loves, first kisses, that kind of thing. Really, when she thought about it, he was awfully close-mouthed.

What would his Army friends be like? Would they be hard, crude men? What would she talk to them about? And would she ever have the chance, anyway? He hadn't introduced her to any of his friends from work, even though he'd mentioned having drinks after work, or bowling with some of the guys.

The week after the wedding, they didn't see quite as much of him as they had been, although he had dinner with them a couple of nights, and she did slip out onto the porch several times for late-night rendezvous.

Even though she was nervous about the next step, Suzanne was beginning to find it frustrating that they couldn't do more than make out like a pair of teenagers. Maybe it was time she asked Carrie to take the kids again. Not this week—she and Mark were driving over to Leavenworth, leaving Michael with his grandfather. But next weekend, Suzanne decided. Saturday at the shop was especially boring for the kids anyway.

She hadn't asked Carrie yet when, on Monday night, Tom declined her invitation to dinner. Was he offended because, on Sunday night, she'd been distracted when he'd called because Jack had had trouble going to sleep?

On Wednesday he asked them all out for pizza, and at first she felt a wave of relief. But then, in the noisy pizza parlor, they never really had a chance for private conversation, even when the kids played arcade games. They kept running back for more quarters, or to exclaim about how great some game was, or to get a drink. Tom talked about checking out lumber for the backyard climber he was planning, about features he could add. Suzanne wanted to hear about something deeply meaningful to him, not the difference between putting bark and some kind of shredded rubber down beneath the monkey bars.

Suzanne knew she wasn't in the world's best mood because of business being so slow. She loved to knit, but that was pretty much all she was doing. All day. Every day. It was beginning to scare her, and they were hardly into January. Gary's money would go really fast, if that's all she had.

Tom did kiss her good-night, after shooing the kids in the door, but as troubled as she felt, she wasn't as responsive as she could have been.

"Are you okay?" he asked.

The gentleness in his voice, the reemergence of the Tom she knew, brought tears to her eyes. "I'm sorry. Things haven't been the same, have they?"

His expression just…closed. He might as well have pulled a mask over it. Voice just as expressionless, he said, "We need to talk."

Apprehension burned in her chest. Was it her tears? But he'd seen her cry before. Plenty of times. And she hadn't said anything. Had she?

"I…"

"You say business is slow. I can get away at lunchtime."

"But…"

"If you're busy, I'll just wave and we can find another time." He opened her front door and said, "Good night, Suzanne."

What could she say but "Good night, Tom."

She closed the door slowly, not even having to turn off the porch light—she left it off when they met out there, so they didn't become the talk of the neighborhood. She turned the dead bolt, then sank down on the sofa.

How had everything gone so wrong?

Their friendship had blossomed so naturally. She enjoyed his company, he was great with the kids—Jack would be crushed if Tom suddenly didn't have time for him—and Suzanne had loved feeling herself revive as a woman.

What could she have done wrong? she wondered in a panic, hating the necessity of asking the question. How many times had she asked it during her marriage? Searching, searching for the magic answer that would make her be what Josh needed.

Two years out from her divorce, she had almost convinced herself that she wasn't at fault for the failure of her marriage. It had taken her a long time to start looking at Josh and thinking, *I didn't do anything to deserve this.* Even on the day she'd carried his stuff out to the driveway, barricaded the door and waited breathlessly inside for him to come home and find it, her confidence had been no stronger than tall grass that flattened under a strong wind.

She'd really begun to believe in herself this past year, after reuniting with Carrie and then Gary, and when business had seemed to be going so well despite her lack of know-how. She was making a success of her new life. She was.

But maybe…maybe she didn't know how to read men. Maybe she was boring Tom…

If so, she couldn't change herself. She was who she was.

Maybe he'd assumed they'd fall right into bed and he'd run out of patience…

But then why hadn't he invited her to a romantic weekend getaway or something like that?

Maybe the wedding had scared him off. Starting with the fact that she'd made sure he'd been invited. Had he seen it as a hint?

She let out a strangled sound and covered her face with her hands. Maybe, maybe, maybe. She had no idea!

But an insidious thought emerged.

Maybe something about *her* was lacking. Maybe she wasn't meant to have what her sister and brother had both found. Maybe Josh had been right, when he'd blamed so much on her.

She slept poorly that night. How could she help it?

The next morning, she dropped the kids at school, then opened Knit One, Drop In. The day started off slightly better than the last few. She had a ten o'clock class that was better attended than the ones last week, and several of the students made purchases. Otherwise—she knit.

She'd meant to work out some new patterns, but hadn't started one yet. She found herself too tense, always lifting her head when shoppers went by outside but didn't come in. So she was knitting a whole bunch of sweaters for children in sizes 2T to 6T. The few she'd offered for sale had sold well.

No customer had darkened her door in almost an hour when Tom entered to a tinkle of the bell.

So few men ever came in here, he looked immediately out

of place. Too big, too masculine. He wore a suit, and her first, heart-squeezing thought was how handsome he was in it.

How far she'd come, to think *handsome*. No, he'd never really be that, not with his blunt features and crooked nose, but he was always compelling.

She jumped to her feet. "Oh! Hi. You know, nobody would miss me if you want to go grab a sandwich at the bakery around the corner. I can just put a note on the door…."

"No, I was just hoping to talk." He looked around. "The place looks great."

"Thank you. We can sit down back where I hold classes."

He fingered a few yarns on the way, but his expression remained serious.

Suzanne wanted to chatter brightly, but her stomach knotted with anxiety and she knew she couldn't.

So she sat down, locked her hands together on her lap and asked, "What did you want to talk about, Tom?"

"Us." He choose an upholstered chair, too, sitting gingerly, as if afraid he'd sink too deep in it.

Her laugh sounded fake. "Isn't it women who are supposed to want to talk about the relationship?"

He just looked at her.

She swallowed. "What?"

"I'm wondering if we should have started this."

Oh God, oh God, she'd been so afraid he would say that. Was she so inadequate?

"Why?" she whispered.

"I really liked being friends with you."

"But you don't like…" What could she call what they had? "…dating me?"

"Oh, I like it." He cleared his throat. "Maybe I'm too impatient. Maybe I should let things unfold. I don't know."

"Let...*what* unfold?"

"Our relationship." He gestured. "The trouble is, I kiss you on your front porch and go home to an empty house and wonder what the point was."

"The...the point?" Suzanne was all but paralyzed.

"I'm frustrated."

She bit her lip. "Um... I thought, this weekend I could ask Carrie to take the kids Friday or Saturday night."

What was she doing? *Bribing* him? *Saying, Don't abandon me, I'll give you myself?*

Pure heat showed in his eyes, stealing what little ability she had left to breathe. But the next second, he'd banked it.

"I didn't mean that. Well—" one corner of his mouth lifted in acknowledgment "—I'm frustrated that way, too."

Too. They were back to the fact that somehow she wasn't satisfying him. Drearily she asked herself why she was even surprised.

"Where did you see us going?" he asked.

What was the point in being shy? "I hoped we might end up married," she admitted.

"You didn't even glance at me during your brother's ceremony."

"I tried really hard not to look at you. We haven't been dating that long. I thought it was too soon to hint at any kind of expectations."

His fingers were working, tightening on his thighs, loosening, the knuckles once letting out a cracking sound. Voice hoarse, he said, "I had them, too."

Stunned, she faltered, "Then…then why?"

"Let me ask you something." He paused, his gaze steady. "Why did you want to marry me?"

"The first time I really met your eyes, I saw how kind you were. I think I knew then that you would be a wonderful husband and father."

"So I'm nice."

"I know you seem to hate that word, but is it so awful to be nice?"

He didn't answer. "Have you been frustrated? When you went to bed, did you lie there wishing I'd come into the bedroom with you?"

Until she ached.

When she wasn't worrying. Too often, she'd quit thinking about him as soon as she shut the door, already preoccupied with the bills she'd paid out of her savings, about the fact that Dylan seemed to have lost interest in Jack as a friend, about the overhead she was paying to knit somewhere besides her living room.

"Yes."

But she could tell she'd been silent too long.

Tom stood up, as if he could no longer contain his tension. He shoved his hands in the pockets of his slacks and looked down at her.

"Do you love me, Suzanne?"

She actually let out a soft gasp of shock. And yet… How could she not have been prepared for him to ask her? Or to say, *I love you,* and anticipate a response?

"I… I hadn't put it into words, but…"

Her floundering was as bad as silence.

Tom's jaw flexed. "That's what I thought. You see, I have fallen in love with you, Suzanne. And my gut feeling is, you either do right away or not at all."

She'd have stood if she'd been sure she could. "Because I haven't said the words…"

"Because you can't." He shook his head. "I don't know that I want to be passionately in love with a woman who thinks I'm nice. And great husband and father material."

She was still stuck on the question. *Do I love him?* What was the feeling of contentment when he was there and dissatisfaction when he wasn't if not love? The rightness of being with him?

He sounded suddenly tired. "Suzanne, I'm not going away. I'll be right there next door. I hope we can be friends again. I've…really become attached to Jack and Sophia. I'd like to keep helping out with them."

Suzanne felt cold. "I miss you when you're not with us."

Immediately, she knew she'd said the wrong thing again. *With me.* That's what she should have said.

He shook his head. "I'll be around. Let's just…do some thinking. Okay?"

"Yes." Her voice was a thin thread. "Okay."

He looked as if he were about to say something more, then dipped his head, turned and left. She knew the moment he was gone, as the bell tinkled and then went silent.

She sat mute, frozen.

If she didn't love him, why did she hurt so much?

HE WAS THERE, WAVING when they left for an errand, helping carry in groceries, getting Sophia to bring over the tape of her first time anchoring the school newscast so he could see it, taking Jack out with his bike on Sunday. The kids didn't seem to notice he hadn't come to dinner in the last week.

Suzanne spent it struggling with self-doubt that might have crippled her, if she hadn't had the kids depending on her.

Am I in love with him?

How could such a simple question be so hard to answer?

When she lay in bed at night, yearning, she thought she knew. Now that they weren't even sneaking kisses, he was all she could think about. She would close her eyes, remember how he'd touched her, the scrape of his teeth on her lip, the vibration of his chest beneath her hands. Had she been crazy, to let weeks pass after their first kiss without them making love? Now, she would never know what his weight on her would feel like, whether he would be silent or talkative, unfailingly gentle or urgent.

Whether she wanted him wasn't what he'd asked, she reminded herself. In theory, at least, it wasn't the same thing, although she'd never known one without the other.

Did she not know him well enough, not trust him enough to let herself love him? Maybe she just didn't recognize what she felt, given how little frame of reference she had.

Or was she really not in love at all? Had she just turned to him because she wanted someone to lean on?

She knew that was what Tom thought she'd done, and she tried to honestly decide for herself. It was true she'd been grateful for all he'd done—for the things she never could have managed, at least not as well as he did them. For having someone to talk to, someone to take responsibility for the kids, someone to hold her. For someone who made her feel like a woman.

Even having to ask the questions she did made Suzanne not like herself. She remembered the day almost a year ago when she'd decided to hire a private investigator, her bottomless feeling of despair. She'd known she had to become someone she respected. Apparently, she'd believed that just finding Carrie and Gary was enough.

But she hadn't even found them herself; she'd had to pay someone else to accomplish what she couldn't. Yes, she'd quit her job and opened a business, an act of daring that made her a little bit proud. And then…then she'd applied to adopt, and no sooner taken in the kids than she'd been turning to Tom for help.

It hit her then that she wasn't used to making big decisions on her own, that, in fact, a sense of helplessness had permeated her life. Her parents had died, and she'd had no choice whatsoever in her fate or the fate of her sister and brother. She would live with her aunt and uncle. Lucien and Linette had been taken away, while she'd stood there with her mother's words ringing in her head.

You're the big sister, Suzanne. Take care of your little brother and sister.

I can't, Mama! I can't.

She'd found a boyfriend, too young, who'd told her what to do. The helplessness had burrowed deeper into hiding within her, because she'd felt safe with him. But as he'd eroded her self-confidence, it had also spread, like a cancer. If he hadn't hit her, she didn't know if she'd have ever found the strength to tell him to go.

She'd lived alone only three years out of her entire life, and had had so few choices to make. She'd been grateful to already have a job and a house. Josh had been glad enough to trade his share of the equity for all their other investments. In the first two years, all Suzanne had done was walk through the routine of her days.

Until the day the phone had rung and a young woman's voice had said, "Suzanne? Suzanne Chauvin?" She'd known immediately who'd been calling, even though Linette hadn't yet spoken her first word when she'd been taken away.

She thought, after that day, that she'd made bold decisions, started to become the woman she'd never yet had the courage to be. But that encompassed less than a year of her life, and most of the time she'd other people to call—Carrie, Mark, eventually Rebecca and Gary. And finally, of course, Tom. Were you bold, she wondered, if you talked through every nuance of every decision with five other people?

A week passed; then another one. And she started to get mad. She *had* made decisions; had quit a safe job with benefits, borrowed a whole lot of money and opened her own business; had found her brother and sister, even if she'd ended up needing help. She could be a good parent without Tom.

She would be.

"I will be," she said aloud, to her empty shop.

Nonetheless, she would have been very, very happy not to face any parenting challenges right then. Which was all but daring one to arise.

Thursday of that week, Sophia was in such a good mood

after the school bus dropped them off, Suzanne didn't notice for some time how quiet Jack was.

"Another new girl came today," Sophia announced as soon as she plopped down in back. "Mr. Schroder put her next to me."

"Is she nice?"

"Yeah. She's taller than me. I was thinking." She became busy with the zipper of her book bag. "Well, if maybe she could spend the night this weekend."

Suzanne almost cheered, but instinct told her not to make too big a deal out of a moment that most girls had when they were much, much younger.

"Sure. Either night is okay with me. Except remember I have to open by ten Saturday morning."

"Yeah, I thought Saturday night. So we could stay up late, and not have to get up. You know."

"What's her name?"

"Heather." She took books out of her bag seemingly at random. "So I can ask her?"

Suzanne smiled. "Yes, you can ask her. We can order pizza and rent a couple of movies."

Normally Jack would have asked if they could rent something *he* wanted to see. But instead he was quiet, head bent.

"Course, she may not want to come." Sophia shrugged, as if it didn't matter. "Or maybe her mom won't let her. But I thought I'd ask."

"That's nice of you. Being new is always scary, isn't it?"

Sophia nodded, finally looking down at the books and stuffing two back into her bag. "I have so-o much math homework!"

"How was *your* day?" Suzanne asked Jack.

He shrugged without looking up. One foot bounced rhythmically against the chair.

When it seemed as if he wouldn't answer, he said, "This kid in my class. Zane?"

Suzanne nodded. Jack had been dropping Zane's name with increasing frequency. She'd been keeping her fingers crossed.

"It's his birthday. He's having a sleepover Friday night. He asked a bunch of the guys." Her heart sank at the pause. "And me, too."

"That's great!" she exclaimed, puzzled by his lack of animation. Friends would mean so much to him.

Jack looked up, his face despairing. "Everybody would make fun of me if…you know."

Oh, no.

"You've been doing better lately." He had. He'd only wet the bed twice in the past week.

"I said I didn't think I could go." His shoulders drooped.

"I'll bet by a few months from now, you won't have to worry about it at all." How upbeat she sounded. But Jack was seven, and a few months from now might as well be years away.

"It's okay. It just woulda been fun is all," he mumbled. "I wish we could go home."

Suzanne glanced at the clock. It was three forty-five. Tempting though it was to slap that Open sign to Closed, she resisted. If Knit One, Drop In was going to be successful, she had to be reliable. If even one knitter dashed by to pick up a needle to replace a broken one or a last skein of yarn and found her closed, she'd have lost a customer for good.

She hugged him. "It won't be long. I'll tell you what? Why don't you and Sophia go pick out something yummy at the bakery? You can bring me a cookie, too."

"Cool!" His sister shot to her feet. "Come on, Jack."

Suzanne got money from her purse and watched them go out the door, Sophia with exuberance, Jack trailing dispiritedly.

Surely he'd make friends even if he didn't go to one sleepover. There had to be other kids who didn't. At seven and eight, some boys probably still got homesick, for example. If she made sure he had the chance to play Little League this spring…

She was cheerful when they got back, sitting while he read to her with painful slowness, glad she'd stayed open when two women who'd never been in before showed up at four-thirty and bought sixty-five dollars worth of yarn and patterns.

It was on the short drive home that inspiration struck her.

"Hey! I have an idea. What if you go to Zane's party, only you come home right before bedtime?"

"You mean—" hope quickened his voice "—you pick me up? But…how come?"

"This," Suzanne declared firmly, "is the time for a white lie. I won't let you spend the night, because we have to go somewhere early the next morning."

"Where?"

"Um…" She glanced to the side. "Sophia?"

"Aunt Carrie and Uncle Mark are taking us snow-boarding."

"Not bad. Except then he'd have to tell everyone how snowboarding was."

"Yeah. And I never been."

"Okay," his sister conceded. "We're just going to their house 'cause Suzanne has to go somewhere."

"That's good," Suzanne said. "No one will care where I'm going."

He bounced in the back seat, his voice ebullient. "So I can go to Zane's party?"

She smiled into the rearview mirror as she turned onto their street. "Yes, you may."

He was still cheering when he leaped out of the car in their driveway. Suzanne smiled at Sophia, who still hadn't unbuckled her belt.

"So, do you think making up a story is so bad this time?"

"No-o," the ten-year-old conceded. "I guess it's okay. Course, now he has to buy a present."

A small price to pay for his joy, in Suzanne's book.

Today, she didn't even look toward Tom's house. With Jack's cheers ringing in her ears, she was Supermom.

But she wished, all the same, that he'd happened to be outside to see the grin lighting Jack's face, and would come outside to hear the good news. Or invite them to dinner, or call tonight and say, "You want to meet in two minutes on your front porch?"

She went on in the door without looking, because she could do this alone.

CHAPTER SIXTEEN

KNOWING HE WAS THE BIGGEST fool on earth, Tom stood just inside his front window on Friday night and watched his next-door neighbors come home. Only Sophia and Suzanne got out of the car.

A few weeks ago, he could have wandered out and said, "Did you lose someone?"

Tonight, he could only wonder. Had Jack made a buddy? He hoped so. Last Sunday, the boy had been down. When Tom had asked about Dylan, he'd shrugged. "He laughed when I had to read aloud and I said *ass* instead of *ash.*"

Amazing how much anger you could feel toward a second grader. There was some sting in Tom's voice when he'd said, "Because he's perfect?"

"He reads better than me," Jack had said, as if it were a matter of fact that everyone did.

"But you might be better in math."

"You don't hafta do math out loud."

Which said it all.

"You think I'm ever gonna learn to ride by myself?" he'd asked later, sadly, after they'd wobbled their way up and down the street until Tom's shoulders had hurt.

"Of course you will. It's hard when you only get to practice once a week."

It had already occurred to Tom that the moment when Jack sailed off on his own would be bittersweet. He'd liked being needed.

The urge tonight to call Suzanne was strong. He'd said they would be friends. Friends called. Had easy conversations about their week.

He wanted to tell her that his best friend was shipping out to Afghanistan. He hadn't said—couldn't say—what his unit's role would be, but Tom guessed they'd be patrolling the Pakistani border or dealing with recalcitrant warlords.

Keeping it casual when he said, "You take care," hadn't been easy. There wasn't anybody but Suzanne he could tell about his mixed feelings: the guilt that he wouldn't be there to back up his buddy, the relief that he was out of it, the wondering if he served any real purpose anymore.

For a while there, he'd thought he had. Suzanne, Jack and Sophia had all seemed to need him, and not just for bike-riding lessons.

Lurking inside his dark living room, watching Sophia do a pirouette on the wet lawn before she and Suzanne disappeared into their house, he faced the fact that they were doing just fine without him.

And he'd never felt lonelier, despite all his solitary years.

Why it hit him so hard that night, he couldn't have said. All he knew was he sat in his chair in the dark living room without bothering to turn on a television he wouldn't watch anyway, and thought, *You stupid SOB. You had it all, and you threw it away.*

It was too little, too late, but he rested his elbows on his knees, bent his head and tried to figure out what had been going on in his head. He was a man who was happy planting bulbs and waiting months for them to send their first green shoots above the soil. He'd spent days sanding Sophia's dresser, watching the grain emerge, never once wanting to hurry, call it good enough and slap on stain.

Then, the first time in his life he'd really fallen in love, and he'd had no patience at all. Knowing Suzanne was wary of men, knowing why, had he really expected her to fling herself into his arms that day and cry, "Yes! Yes! I love you."

Were those few words that important anyway, compared to what he could have?

Frowning, bothered by where he was going with this, Tom realized that, almost from the minute he'd kissed Suzanne, he'd felt…edgy.

He'd spent weeks proving to Suzanne what a good guy he was, how different from her ex, then he'd resented being called *nice.* Instead of flexing his muscles to impress the girl, he'd played indispensable family man. Then he'd hated the idea that she wanted him because he would be a reliable breadwinner and responsible, affectionate father. Every step of the way, he'd tried to avoid scaring her. He'd been careful not to come on too strong, to keep their kisses gentle, careful never to imply that he would rather spend time alone with her. Then, when she saw him as advertised, he'd panicked.

He sat up straight and thought with dawning surprise, *Panic. Yeah, that was it.* He'd been scared. Scared she didn't love him. Scared that what was happening between them wasn't as good as it felt. He didn't *believe* in anything that good.

Aloud, to his empty house, Tom said, "I was looking for an out."

He was a coward, he thought in shock. In love with her, and sure that someday, no matter what, she wouldn't love him. So he'd make her tell him now that she didn't, when he thought he could still walk away.

And walk he had, which was why he'd been reduced to stealing glimpses of the family that could have been his.

So you're scared. And this, he cocked his head, as if to listen to the silence, *yeah, this is so much better than what you remember when you were a kid.*

Big question: did he have the guts to risk *really* getting hurt?

SUZANNE HAD HELPED SOPHIA PUT her favorite photo of her mother in the white ceramic frame she'd chosen, but they never had sat down to go through all the pictures. It seemed they were always too busy. Dinner, homework, housecleaning, bill paying. Start all over.

After dinner Friday night, with Jack not home, Suzanne said, "I'd love to look at all your pictures if you want to show them to me."

Sophia, who had been trying to decide aloud which videos to rent tomorrow for the big sleepover, said, "Really? You mean, now?"

"Sure, now. But only if you want to."

"Okay."

Sophia went and got the shoe box from her closet and set it on the kitchen table. They sat down side-by-side, and she started pulling out pictures.

"They're not in order. See? This is my kindergarten picture." She frowned. "Or maybe first grade."

Delighted, Suzanne took it. Sophia had been a formidable-looking little girl even then, with a gap-toothed smile that didn't appear altogether happy. Somebody had no doubt urged her to smile, so she'd done it, but she hadn't wanted to. Her eyes had been as vivid then, her dark hair done inexpertly in two pigtails that stuck out.

"You were so cute."

"It was hard to talk. That made me mad."

Of course it had. Poor Sophia, always combative, even as a little girl.

There were other grade-school pictures, both of her and of Jack. Most of the snapshots that included their mother had been taken when the kids were smaller, before the multiple sclerosis had stolen her ability to hold up her own head.

It was true that Jack looked more like her than Sophia did. She had a timid gaze, as if she didn't expect very much out of life. That made Suzanne unbearably sad, because she hadn't gotten much. Worse, she'd had to see how little she could give to her children.

Even further back, a few included their father. There was one, snapped on a beach outing, that Suzanne held for a long time. He had Sophia, perhaps three, on his shoulders. With his head tipped back, he was laughing up at her and her down at him. Her fingers, still plump, gripped handfuls of his hair. His eyes blazed as blue as hers, and his hair was as dark. More importantly, he radiated a defiance, a daredevil quality, that his daughter had gotten in spades.

Could he have swung her onto his shoulders and met her laugh with one of his own if he hadn't loved her at all?

"Sometimes I wish I remembered him," Sophia said, "but then I'm glad I don't. 'Cause he didn't want us anyway."

"Do you know, I'm trying to be furious, because he hurt you. But mostly, I feel awfully sorry for him."

Sophia tilted her face up. "Really?"

"Think of everything he's missed in your lives. Everything he will miss. Doesn't that seem a little sad to you?"

"I don't know if we're that great."

Suzanne's heart came close to breaking. Fiercely, she said, "Not that great? You two are fabulous. You're wonderful, funny, smart, loving kids. You're going to be the next Lindsay Lohan, remember? How's that not great?"

Her shoulders straightened. "Yeah, if I get real rich and famous, he'll be sorry, won't he?"

Suzanne gave her a squeeze and a kiss that hit the vicinity of her ear. "I think that someday he'll be sorry no matter what you end up doing."

"Oh." Sophia gave a watery sniff. "Jack asked me if he thought Mom would mind if he called you *Mom,* too."

Now her eyes burned. "What did you say?"

"I said I thought it would be okay. Because…well, you pretty much are mom now, aren't you?"

"Yes. I am. But I don't actually mind whatever you want to call me."

"Dummy."

She laughed and gave her daughter a gentle shake. "Okay, not anything."

Sophia giggled. "How about *Mom Two?*"

Suzanne wrinkled her nose.

"*Mom S.?* 'Cause that's what teachers do in class, you know. We have two Chads this year, so one is Chad B. and one is Chad O."

"Not, bad, but a little awkward."

"I'll think of something," Sophia said with a decisive nod. Then she turned her clear, all-seeing eyes on Suzanne. "How come you're not smooching Tom anymore?"

"I thought you hadn't noticed."

"Course I noticed. I'm not stupid."

"I never thought you were." She hesitated. "We're both supposed to be thinking. Deciding whether we really love each other."

Sophia's mouth dropped open. "You're kidding."

"No. Why would I?"

"'Cause… He has this moony look every time he sees you, and you always start smiling the minute you see him. Even if I don't see him, I know he's there 'cause it's like a light switch."

"Really?" She sounded pathetic, asking for reassurance from a ten-year-old.

"You didn't *know?*"

"I knew I was happy when Tom was with us."

"Well, duh. Why were you happy?"

"Because…" Not because he was nice. She knew lots of nice people. She thought she'd even dated a few of them. Ben Whatever His Name Was, the contractor who'd flirted with her every time he'd come into the escrow office until he'd finally asked her out. He'd told her about his big family, a divorce he hadn't wanted and how much he missed his kids, about the house he wanted to build. And she'd felt…zip. She hadn't blinked on, as if someone had flipped a light switch.

"Because…" she tried again. Not because Tom would be a great father, although she could never love anyone who wouldn't be. But she could be a single parent, and a good one. She really believed that, or she never would have applied to adopt, never would have had the courage to bring Sophia and Jack home. And they were doing just fine, weren't they, whether Tom was here or not.

And, no, she hadn't been happy just because she was attracted to him. Because she'd glowed the day at the grocery store as much as she did when he took her in his arms.

"I guess," she said, feeling like an idiot, "because I was falling in love with him."

"Well, duh," Sophia said again. As if it were settled, she began to put her photos back in the shoe box. "I should put these in the album, shouldn't I?"

"It's fun to do."

"Can I see *your* mom and dad now?"

When Suzanne got out her photo album, Sophia flipped through exclaiming how Gary looked *exactly* like their father, and Suzanne exactly like their mom. "Wow," she kept saying.

Then they watched a movie together, Sophia leaning against Suzanne on the sofa and giggling and snatching handfuls of the popcorn they'd made even after Suzanne told her it was going to make her sick.

Just like that, Suzanne remembered her dream.

Her, sitting on the sofa. A little girl who leaned against her trustingly. Knitting lessons. Giggles.

She had thought she needed to let the dream go for a more difficult yet satisfying reality.

How funny, she thought with wonder, that she'd ended up with both.

This was all she'd ever wanted. Except now…now she wanted more. Tom wandering into the living room, shaking his head over the chick movie they were watching, teasing them, maybe going out to the garage to work on a project. And she would be content with Sophia's company, knowing that later she'd have Tom's, too. In bed, he would take her in his arms, and they would join with elemental joy and love.

Why, she wondered, aching, hadn't she seen what a ten-year-old had so easily she had to say, *Well, duh?*

Had the pause been too long now, once and forever, or could she still say, "I love you"?

SUNDAY, JACK KNOCKED on Tom's door to ask if they could have a bike-riding lesson. He chattered the whole time they opened the garage door and wheeled the bike out.

"I went to a birthday party Friday night. It was a sleep-over," he confided, "only I didn't stay. Suzanne came and got me right when Zane's mom had everyone roll out their sleeping bags."

"That was smart."

"Only, guess what? I didn't wet my bed after I got home. So I guess I coulda stayed." He marveled at the idea. "A couple of the other guys had to go home, too, though. So maybe *they* wet the bed, too."

"Or maybe they're scared to be away from their moms and dads all night."

"Yeah! Maybe."

From the moment Jack slung his leg over the bike and began to pedal, Tom had a feeling this was going to be the day.

"You're doing great!" he encouraged. "That's it, that's it. Can you feel how you're balancing?"

"Yeah!" Jack yelled.

Running behind, Tom eased his hand up. Jack kept going.

"I'm going to let go, but I'll be right behind you."

The boy let out a huff of determination. "Okay."

Tom let go altogether and straightened. Jack pedaled on, straight and true.

"I'm doing it!" he crowed. "Look at me!"

"That's great. Okay, we're to the end of the block. Turn gently. Turn… No, not so sharp." He winced as Jack crashed down.

But he untangled himself and sprang to his feet. "I did it! I did it!"

"Yeah, you did." Tom couldn't stop grinning as they gave each other high fives. "But we've got to work on those turns."

"Can we show Suzanne?"

"We sure can. Why don't you ride back?"

Jack righted the bike and climbed back on. Tom held

back and let him wobble for a moment, pedal harder and take off down the street. He even managed to stop at his own driveway and put his feet down before he could fall. Then he dropped the bike and tore up to the house.

Suzanne and Sophia both came out to see. In jeans and a sweatshirt, her hair covered with a bandanna, Suzanne had a smudge of dust on her cheek that Tom ached to wipe off.

"Okay," Tom murmured to the boy. "Aim toward the far side of the street." He pointed. "Then turn the handlebars real slowly. Make a gentle, wide turn. You can do it."

Jack sucked in a breath. "Watch," he ordered everybody.

Tom stayed behind.

Jack not only pedaled to the end of the block, he turned like an expert and coasted back with a huge grin on his face. "I'm doing it! I'm doing it!"

Sophia rolled her eyes, but said, "Cool," to her brother.

Suzanne enveloped Jack in a gigantic hug. "You're amazing." Then she turned her radiant smile on Tom. "And you're an amazing teacher. Thank you so much."

"Yeah. Thanks!" Jack agreed. "Can I keep riding?"

"Just so you know to look really carefully before you start out," she cautioned. "And get to the side of the street if a car comes by."

"I know all that. Tom told me." He hopped on, looked with exaggerated care each way, then took off.

Watching him, Suzanne said, "Wow. I guess if you get it, you get it."

"And never forget it," Tom agreed.

"That's true. I haven't been on a bike in…oh, years, but I could ride one without giving it a second thought."

"Can Tom come to dinner tonight?" Sophia asked.

He opened his mouth to politely decline, but Suzanne looked at him, her expression open and friendly. "Will you? I'm making spaghetti. We'd love to have you."

God. He saw suddenly that, if she wouldn't accept his apologies, he was going to have to move. He couldn't stay here on the fringes of their lives. The day Suzanne brought home another man, it would rip his heart out.

"Thanks." His voice was hoarse, and he cleared his throat. "That would be great."

"Wonderful. Say, five-thirty? I'd better get back in. I've got Sophia helping with housework today." But first she cheered when Jack rode by, still grinning.

Five-thirty. He went back in and thought, *What in hell am I going to do until then?*

He ended up going grocery shopping, but was sorry he'd chosen Fred Meyer when every aisle made him think about Suzanne. He stopped by the used furniture store up on Highway 99 and found a great bookcase for Jack's room, only three shelves high but wide and deep. It needed refinishing, but it was solid. Maybe maple. He bought it, hoping Suzanne wouldn't think he was overstepping.

He changed clothes before he went over to their house at five-thirty on the nose. Sophia answered the door.

"Momess said to come back to the kitchen."

He raised his brows.

"I'm trying it out. She's, like, *Mom* with the initial *S* for Suzanne. You know?"

"Ah. Mom S. Gotcha."

"What do you think?"

"Well, it has a ring to it."

"I can't think of anything else."

"Hmm." He ran a hand over his chin. "What's *Mom* in French. *Maman?* Chauvin is French, you know."

"That might be cool. *Maman.*" She tried it out. "Maybe."

The phone rang, and she wheeled, calling, "I'll get it! It's probably for me."

His brows were up again when he walked into the kitchen. "It's probably for her?"

Laughing, Suzanne turned from the stove. "We've had big changes this week. Both kids now have best friends. The way they both go for the phone reminds me of short-track speed skating at the Olympics. They thunder down the hall, and whoever cuts the corner sharpest gets to the phone first. I'm afraid to answer it. I might go down."

His laugh felt good. "Anything I can do?"

Draining spaghetti at the sink, she said, "Um... Will you check the garlic bread in the oven?"

Both kids chattered at dinner, with every other word Zane this or Heather that. Heather's mom had said it was okay if Sophia spent the night next weekend. Jack was going home with Zane tomorrow after school to play. Heather thought it would be cool to learn to knit. Zane had Rollerblades. Could Jack please, please get some?

Suzanne presided with her usual grace and warmth, refereeing when they squabbled, handing out praise and quiet reminders that they not interrupt. All the time she made sure Tom felt included. By the third time she said, "I'll bet Tom could tell you...", he felt wise and important.

When they finished eating, Suzanne said, "Why don't

we have dessert later? Would you like a cup of coffee?" she asked him.

"Later is good." Sophia jumped up. "Come on, Jack. Let's go play that game you got."

"That game? Oh. Yeah. We can go play it," he agreed, and they hurriedly carried their dishes to the sink and left the kitchen.

Tom stared after them. "What's that about?"

Also carrying dishes, Suzanne turned, cheeks pink. "Well, actually, you've been had. I made them promise to go away after dinner and not come back until I called them."

"Really." His heart thudded. "Because?"

"I wanted to talk to you."

"I've been wanting to talk to you, too."

She set down the dishes next to the sink. "Let's forget the mess and go sit in the living room. I can clean up later."

In the living room she sat primly on the edge of the sofa, her fingers laced as if to keep her hands still. Her cheeks were brighter red now, but she met his gaze squarely when he sat beside her.

"I guess I'll just jump right in. Maybe you won't want to stay for dessert then, but…"

His stomach knotted.

"Okay." She drew in a shaky breath. "You may think it's too late for me to say this. But I want you to know what I figured out. The thing is, I always smiled and nodded when people said, 'You'll remarry,' and I had this vague idea that I might someday, but I didn't believe it. More than that, I'd made up my mind without ever actually putting it into words. I wouldn't fall in love again or marry."

"Because you couldn't trust a man?"

"No." Her mouth twisted in what might have been meant to be a smile. "Because I didn't trust myself. My ability to…well, please someone. Make him happy."

He couldn't hold back. "You make me happier than anyone in my life ever has. You have a gift for happiness."

"Thank you for saying that. But if I do, it's newly acquired. No matter how hard I tried, I couldn't do anything right where Josh was concerned, not that last few years. And, after all, he was my only experience. I didn't even have a chance as a child to see my parents delighted when I, oh, got an A on a test or…heck, learned to ride a bike. So you see, my confidence has never been what you'd call solid. And I'd never lived alone until he left. It was so peaceful, so nice only to have to please myself. I guess, somewhere in there, I made up my mind that I'd adopt so I could be a mom, but I wouldn't let myself be so horribly vulnerable ever again. And, hey, look what kind of judgment I had." She tried to smile again.

He laid his hand over hers, feeling the quiver of tension running through them. "And I pushed you to lay your heart on the line."

Her big eyes were soft and full of regret, making his chest cramp with fear that she was really saying, *So I'm sorry, but love…it's just not in the cards for me.*

"I just hadn't let myself think about how I felt. Except…I was happy. Then Sophia said something the other day that made me realize what an idiot I am. She said she didn't even have to see you arrive to know you were here, because I lit up as if someone had hit a switch. Me—" this smile was as wry as the others "—I didn't know I did that."

Throat thick, Tom said, "I've done my share of thinking. What I figured out is that I was scared. After my sister died, my parents…I think maybe in a way they died, too. If they ever loved each other, they quit. Our house got real quiet. And cold. It was as if they couldn't bear each other, and maybe not me either. We'd sit at the dinner table with only a few necessary words, then Dad would go out to his club and Mom to her bedroom. Every night. I don't want to live that way again." Suzanne's hands opened, and one squeezed his. Tom blundered on. "I saw other families, other marriages, but I always wondered what they were like when they were home where no one could see them. I guess I thought if my own parents couldn't love me, not enough to try to have a life, nobody would." He shrugged, voice raw. "I wanted to get it over with. Hear you say, no I can't love you. So I pushed until you did."

"But…I never said I can't."

"No. I know that. So now I'm asking if you'll give me another chance. I don't need the words, Suzanne. I think we can be happy."

"Oh, Tom." Suddenly, tears were streaming down her face, tilted up to his. "But that's what I've been trying to say. I do love you. I did all the time. I just didn't recognize how I felt because I was afraid to."

She loved him?

Unable to speak, he lifted trembling hands and framed her face, wiping at the tears with this thumbs. "Don't cry," he finally whispered.

She turned her face and kissed his palm. "I missed you so much."

"I've been empty without you. Imagining life without you…" He made a ragged sound. "Will you marry me?" It came to him that once again he was pushing, and he shook his head. "There I go again. We don't have to hurry. Just…give me a chance."

"Oh, Tom!" she said again, looking up with her cheeks blazing. "If we don't hurry and get married, how will we ever make love?"

Even as triumph and desire roared through his veins, he found himself laughing. "We could figure something out. But…yeah, it would be the most convenient."

Convenient. Not a word he'd have ever chosen to describe what a life with her would be like.

"Who's house will we live in?"

"Mine's bigger, but…it's just a house. Yours is a home."

"You can take care of the dandelions."

"You know what?" he said, rubbing his cheek against hers, no longer sure if the dampness came from her or him. "I'm going to have better things to do than weed and feed the lawn or wash the truck."

"Oh? Like?"

He whispered a few of them, then kissed her with all the passion and need and love he felt. The amazing thing was, she kissed him right back, just as fervently. And he began to believe.

Maybe, just maybe, things *could* be as good as they seemed. Maybe there really was a happily-ever-after.

Finally he lifted his head and lovingly smoothed her hair from her face. "Do you think we ought to put the kids out of their suspense?"

"You know," she whispered, "I would swear I heard a muffled giggle a minute ago."

"Well, then, to heck with them. They can wait." And he kissed her again.

* * * * *

New York Times *bestselling author Linda Lael Miller is back with a new romance featuring the heartwarming McKettrick family from Silhouette Special Edition.*

SIERRA'S HOMECOMING
by Linda Lael Miller

On sale December 2006,
wherever books are sold.

Turn the page for a sneak preview!

Soft, smoky music poured into the room.

The next thing she knew, Sierra was in Travis's arms, close against that chest she'd admired earlier, and they were slow dancing.

Why didn't she pull away?

"Relax," he said. His breath was warm in her hair.

She giggled, more nervous than amused. What was the matter with her? She was attracted to Travis, had been from the first, and he was clearly attracted to her. They were both adults. Why not enjoy a little slow dancing in a ranch-house kitchen?

Because slow dancing led to other things. She took a step back and felt the counter flush against her lower back.

Travis naturally came with her, since they were holding hands and he had one arm around her waist.

Simple physics.

Then he kissed her.

Physics again—this time, not so simple.

"Yikes," she said, when their mouths parted.

He grinned. "Nobody's ever said that after I kissed them."

She felt the heat and substance of his body pressed against hers. "It's going to happen, isn't it?" she heard herself whisper.

"Yep," Travis answered.

"But not tonight," Sierra said on a sigh.

"Probably not," Travis agreed.

"When, then?"

He chuckled, gave her a slow, nibbling kiss. "Tomorrow morning," he said. "After you drop Liam off at school."

"Isn't that…a little…soon?"

"Not soon enough," Travis answered, his voice husky. "Not nearly soon enough."